Also by George V. Higgins
Published by Ballantine Books:

THE FRIENDS OF EDDIE COYLE

THE DIGGER'S GAME

DREAMLAND

GEORGE V. HIGGINS

KENNEDY FOR THE DEFENSE

BALLANTINE BOOKS • NEW YORK

Library of Congress Catalog Card Number: 79-18484

ISBN 0-345-29315-0

This edition published in hardcover by Alfred A. Knopf, Inc.

Manufactured in the United States of America

First Ballantine Books Edition: March 1981

1

I HAVE A CLIENT named Teddy Franklin. Teddy Franklin is a car thief. He is thirty-two years old, and he is one of the best car thieves on the Eastern Seaboard. Cadillac Ted is so good that he is able to support himself as a car thief. He has been arrested repeatedly, which is how he made my acquaintance, but he has never done time. That is because I am so good. It is also because Teddy is so good.

Teddy is as cute as a shithouse rat. He is an expert. He never leaves any prints. He never does anything in the presence of unreliable people who might turn out to be witnesses for the prosecution. He does not become attached to any of the cars he steals, but unloads them within an hour or so of the instant that he steals them. If you have a car with a kill switch cutting out the ignition, and Teddy wants your car, he will have it started within thirty seconds of the time that he spots your car. If you have a car with a hidden burglar alarm, Teddy will have that alarm disabled before it has even gone off. If you have a crook lock, a steel bar immobilizing the steering wheel and brake, he will remove it inside of a minute—I do not know how Teddy does this, but Teddy assures me that he does do it, and I'm sure he does have some professional secrets. The only device that Teddy admits to be sufficient to defeat him is the invention which shuts off the gas and the ignition and seals the hood shut so that Teddy cannot get at the wires and jump them.

"I dunno," Teddy said, "I don't think I can beat that one. Short of taking a torch to it, I don't think I can do it. I tried a couple times, just for the hell of it.

Didn't even have an order for that particular car, but I saw the sticker that said it had one of those things, and sure enough, it worked. 'Course when the owner got back, he wasn't goin' nowhere in it neither, which is something, because if I need a torch to get into it, so does the guy who's got a right to get into it. I imagine the only way you could take one of those things is if you backed the wrecker up to it and towed the damned thing off to some place where you could work on it."

Teddy does not approve of the use of tow trucks to steal cars. He admits that it works, and is often the answer to prompt delivery of an order, but he does not like it.

"Look," Teddy said, "nobody pays any attention to you. You got an order for a Porsche, you get your CB and you go out in your car to one of the shopping malls and you drive around until you see one that you want. Now you don't want to fuck around all day in a shopping plaza, doing things to somebody else's car. Nobody else'll pay any attention to you, but shopping ain't like movies. You don't know when the son of a bitch is gonna get his new shirts or whatever he went there for, finish his fuckin' errands and come back and catch you. He does, he's probably not gonna like it. He won't be *pleased,* you know? He's liable to get rude with you. Some of these bastards're carrying now, and you never know what some nutty civilian's gonna do, he sees you catching his car and he's heeled.

"You sit in Howard Johnson's and you have a beer and you look out the window at the movie parking lot, you see something you want drive in, and the people get out and they lock it, you know pretty well for sure they will not come out for two hours. They're gonna eat the popcorn. They will drink the Coke. They will watch the previews. They will laugh their asses off at Peter Sellers. And you will have their car halfway to Hartford, Connecticut, before they finish their first candy bar.

"Same thing with, you see something you want and the guy's parking it on a street near a nice restaurant and gettin' out with his girlfriend and they go in. Now you know he's not gonna come tearing out the minute he finishes the salad bar. He's gonna sit there. She's gonna sit there. They will have some nice wine and look at each other and get themselves all horny over the Indian pudding and you got plenty of time to take their car. But you never know how long it's going to take for a guy to get a birthday present for his wife and a pair of Jockey shorts for himself and maybe an ice cream cone, so you got to be quick in a shopping mall.

"Now, in a case like that," Teddy said, "notwithstanding I like to work fast and alone, by myself, but if I really tried like hell to get you what you wanted, and you're getting restless, giving me some shit, I would use a tow truck. I would find what you wanted and then I would call up my friend in his truck and give him some directions, where to find your car and where to take it, and then I would get the fuck out of there, all right? And I would go some place and he would bring the car which you wanted to me, and I would work my magic on it. Whereas—" Teddy has been in court a lot, and likes to talk to people in language he thinks they will appreciate—"if you come out and the guy is putting the hook on your car, well, what're you gonna do to him, huh? He looks like he's official. He's got a regular tow truck. The chances are there's another car something like yours in the lot. How's the guy that owns yours know my guy's not telling the truth, he got a call to come bring in a Cadillac and he got the directions wrong and he just happened to hook up the wrong Cadillac? All right? Nothin's about to happen to him, even if you do catch him.

"My problem is," Teddy said, "this means I have to split my commission. My fee. I don't like doin' that. I also don't like, well, that I got another guy involved in things, that might get himself involved in something else and start to think about saying something he done for me, they start hintin' around they might put him in jail unless he decides, put me in jail. That don't appeal to me, you know? So I prefer to work alone."

Teddy specializes in Cadillacs. "Your Porsche, your Corvette," Teddy said, "your Jaguar, your Mercedes? I can get you them. But I'm not used to them, you know? And another thing is this: I am not greedy. I don't want to get myself in a position where I'm always runnin' around all the time like some guys I know, and they got careless and ended up in Walpole makin' license plates for cars they're never even gonna see, never mind sell. You know. I pace myself. I do three cars a week, max. Now and then I take a couple weeks completely off, and I get ahold of some broad and go down the Caribbean, you know? And completely just relax. I play a little golf, I go the track, I do a little gambling, the casinos, you know? Nothing heavy. Just nice and relaxing. And this is not because I am tired or I am gettin' old or anything like that. It is because something doesn't feel right, you know? And I don't do no cars when everything doesn't feel exactly and completely right. You know what I mean? I ain't never done no time, and I don't wanna do no time."

This, as Teddy intimates, is no small accomplishment or modest boast for a man who has been a professional car thief for almost seventeen years. Particularly when you consider that Teddy's occupation and specialty are almost as well known to the police as they are to me. "They know what I'm doin'," Teddy said. "I know they know what I'm doin'. You think I'm so fuckin' stupid, I don't know they know I'm grabbing Cads? Of course they do. They see me in a Cad, they come in their pants. Every time they stop me, the guy figures he's got me. That's why I always drive a Cad. And it's always a completely legal Cad. Drives them nuts. That's why my wife Dottie drives a Cad, always drives a Cad, a completely legal Cad. That's why I keep trading those completely legal Cads all the time, so one month you see me and I'm in a blue one and she's driving a white one, and the next month you see me and I've probably got a tan one and she's got a maroon Seville. Always completely legal. Drives them fuckin' *nuts*. I love it."

Teddy is correct, but he is not right. At least, I told him, not sensible. Goosing the cops is not a practice rich in wisdom for a professional car thief. Teddy did not like this aspersion on his cleverness. "You're outta your mind, Counselor," he said, his voice rising, "that's the best protection I could possibly have. Wear the bastards out, maybe some night they spot me in a hot one, they'll assume it's another one of mine."

"Yeah," I said, "and maybe they won't, too. Maybe you'll get them so pissed they'll stop you on a ten-speed bicycle if that's what you happen to be riding at the time, and it'll be smoking hot and you'll go to the clink. I just practice law, you know, Teddy. I don't claim to be able to perform miracles."

"Ahhh," Teddy said. "Forget it." Teddy is an expansive sort. He tried to retain me for a year, to handle his scrapes with the authorities, for a Cadillac.

"Oh, sure," I said. "Then we'll both need lawyers. You for stealing the thing, me for receiving it. No thanks. I'll take cash." Of course I'd take cash—Teddy never had a checking account in his life.

"This is completely legal," Teddy said, his hurt feelings noticeable in his voice. "Completely legal, title, everything."

"I bet you tell that to all the girls," I said.

"It is," Teddy said. "You think I'd hand you a hot one?"

"That's what the cops'd think," I said. "Here's Franklin's lawyer up to the courthouse to beat another Caddy rap for Franklin, and what's Franklin's lawyer driving? A Cadillac, of course. I don't think so, Teddy. Somehow, I don't think so. Besides, I don't want a Cadillac."

"Everybody wants a Cadillac," Teddy said.

"I don't," I said. "Cadillacs cause heart disease."

"Huh?" Teddy said.

"It's true," I said. "Every lawyer that I ever knew who wanted a Cadillac and finally got it, had a heart attack right afterward. No fuckin' Cadillacs, to borrow a phrase from you."

"How about a Thunderbird, then?" Teddy said. "Continental, maybe? Give you a nice Mark Five."

"Nothing doing," I said.

"Mark Five for you," Teddy said. "Nice little Versailles for the wife, maybe, or one of those Town Coupes, huh?"

"No," I said.

"*Jerry*," Teddy said, "you gotta understand my position, you know? You're beatin' me out of . . . , I got high legal expenses, the way these fuckin' cops keep arrestin' me. This overhead's killin' me. I got to get this thing on a regular basis here."

Teddy does have high legal expenses. But part of the reason for that is the broadcast notoriety he enjoys. Some kid pegged by the Malden cops as a joyriding troublemaker may encounter a certain amount of harassment if spotted driving a new Riviera in Medford next door. But he will be able to operate without much commotion in Worcester or Springfield, if he keeps his nose clean while he is doing it. Teddy has more trouble because every State cop in New England knows Cadillac Teddy on sight. There have been instances, which Teddy has recounted to me with relish, when some friend about his age, sporting a new Cadillac for the races at Rockingham Park in Salem, New Hampshire, has missed the bell for the Daily Double because he was detained by the police, who thought he was Teddy Franklin.

This means that Teddy's brushes with the law are scattered all over East Jesus. I have visited the Palmer District Court, the Stoughton District Court, the Quincy District Court, two lower courts in Vermont, one in New Hampshire, three in Maine and at least six in Rhode Island, filing my appearance slips as counsel of record for Edmund M. Franklin. That does cost him a lot of money, because while I am driving out the Massachusetts Turnpike to Palmer, I am not laboring in behalf of some other client. The grocer looks like a man who would not be sympathetic to my explanation that I can't pay for the vegetables this week because I earned no money for my time, spending it instead by driving to Palmer for free. I therefore bill Teddy Franklin for my travel time, just like any other plumber working door-to-door, and since he categorically refuses to substitute a lawyer living closer to the scene of his most recent infraction, I figure he wants me badly enough to pay me for my time. "Which is, after all," I told him, "all I have to sell."

One morning last August I returned to the office from the Dedham District Court. There I had requested and received a continuance of one month in the case of *Commonwealth v. Edmund M. Franklin.* The charge was driving without a valid operator's license in possession. The judge was as skeptical of the probable defense as I had been, when Teddy told me about the case. He told me about the case on the phone, because I was vacationing at Green Harbor with Mack and Saigon, and he was interrupting my time off.

"Goddamn you," I said. "What is it this time? Can't I sit around in the goddamned sun like any other respectable citizen and burn all the skin off my fucking back without having to listen to you? What the hell is it?"

"No license," he said.

"Nobody's got a license to steal cars, Teddy," I said. "You may think you do, but you don't. I've told you that ten thousand times."

"Driver's license," Teddy said.

"For Christ sake," I said. "You mean to tell me you've been stealing cars all these years and you don't have a driver's license?"

"I *had* a driver's license," Teddy said.

"And you let it expire, you asshole," I said. "Oh, for the luvva Mike, where the hell do I get these people."

"I didn't let it expire," Teddy said. "I lost it."

"And you kept on driving anyway," I said. "Jesus Christ. They lift your license, you're not supposed to drive anymore until you get it back. You're too smart for this, Teddybear. You're supposed to be smart. You're the guy that's always telling me how smart you are, and you're driving with no license? You don't need a lawyer. You need a fucking psychiatrist."

"If you can calm down a minute and listen to me," Teddy said, "I can tell you what happened."

"I might as well," I said, "you're going to do it anyway."

"They didn't take my license away from me," Teddy said. "When I said I lost it, I meant like, I couldn't find it, you know? Because I lost my wallet. Me and Dottie went down the Cape for the Fourth and we stayed with some friends of ours, this motel, and we had a few drinks and we went out this club one night and I lost my wallet. My license was in it. So was about eleven hundred bucks. I didn't see the eleven hundred again, and I didn't see the license, either.

"I got some more money from this guy I know down there, and I got a new wallet," Teddy said.

"You should've gotten a new license," I said.

"I did get a new license," Teddy said. "I went down the Registry and I got this temporary that was good thirty days until I could get a new permanent. Pink piece of paper."

"And you let it run out," I said.

"No," he said, "it was good until the end of next week and I was going over the Registry tomorrow morning, get the regular one, the one that's in the plastic thing there. But the guy stopped me on One-twenty-eight this morning, so I never had a chance, do that."

"Didn't you have the temporary with you?" I said.

"You're supposed to carry that, too, you know, if you don't have the other one in your hot little hands yet."

"Yes," Teddy said, "I carried it. And when the cop asked me for it, like a fool I gave it to him. Then he wrote me up for no license in possession."

"Did he give it back?" I said. "This is a pretty simple thing if he gave it back."

"No," Teddy said, "he did not give it back. He ate it."

"He ate it," I said.

"He ate it," Teddy said. "He tore it down the middle and tore it again and he put the pieces in his mouth, one by one, and chewed them up and swallowed them. Then he arrested me for no license."

"You want me to go into court and tell the judge that the cop ate your license," I said.

"That's what he did," Teddy said.

That was therefore what I told the judge. The judge is used to outlandish tales from people who have been charged with driving under the influence, scored so high on the Breathalyzer that one point more would mean coma, and stoutly maintain that they had had but two beers in five hours and did not finish the second one. He has endured tales of faulty speedometers from people arrested for doing more than one hundred and fifteen miles an hour on Route 128. He is a patient man. He listened.

"My client lives in Sharon, Your Honor," I said. "He was going to Boston on business . . ."

"What is Mister Franklin's business, Counselor?" said the judge, who had obviously the benefit of certain information supplied to him by the arresting officer, via one of the judge's court officers.

"He's a management representative for the Dolphin Pool Company," I said. "He . . ."

"Where are they located?" the judge said.

"Bakersfield, California," I said. "Mister Franklin . . ."

"That's a pretty long commute from Sharon every day," the judge said.

"He oversees the local franchise contractors in New England," I said. "Naturally, his job requires him to do a lot of driving, and . . ."

"For which he needs a valid driver's license in his possession, at least in this neck of the woods," the judge said. "As his counsel, you should've advised him of that."

"He claims he had one, Your Honor," I said.

"And Trooper Hudson here," the judge said, nodding toward an enormous man with very pale blond hair, standing like a Praetorian guard at the bench, "claims he didn't. What's his defense?"

I cleared my throat. "Mister Franklin," I said, "will testify that Trooper Hudson ate his license."

The trooper cleared his throat. The judge permitted his eyebrows to raise. "Trooper Hudson ate the license," he said.

"I did not," Trooper Hudson said, the back of his neck getting red. "That's ridiculous. That's the most ridiculous thing . . ."

"That'll do," the judge said. "Mister Kennedy, if you are willing to give me your solemn promise that your client is going to come into this courtroom and swear, under oath, that Trooper Hudson ate his license, knowing what the penalty is for perjury in the court—if you will make that promise, I will give you your continuance. But if that guy comes in here and says that actually he left the thing on his dresser, I am going to be very disappointed in you, and I will probably take it out on him. Now that's the deal. Do you want it?"

"Your Honor," I said, "I haven't even had a chance to see my client in my office yet. I just came up from the beach this morning, and . . ."

"That's the deal," the judge said. "You want it?"

"Yes," I said.

Having shot the morning, I saw no point in racing back to the beach. It wasn't much of a day anyway, gray, foggy and overcast. I went in to the office. Another mistake.

2

WHILE MY NAME IS KENNEDY, I am not related to the bastards. I don't even know the bastards. For all I know, they may be very nice people. For all I care, they can treat each other like wolves. What they do or don't do is no concern of mine; I only wish they would go at it a little less famously—*had* gone at it, a little less famously, a long time ago—because I happen to have the same name and I get sick and tired of explaining to people that I am a poor working stiff who ended up with the same name because the first guy who had it was the horniest man in Sligo, or some bogtrotting place, and none of the tads who descended from him had the common sense to change it to, say, Stein. I suppose if they had, people would be asking me all the time if I'm related to Gertrude. If it isn't one damned thing, it's another.

Anyway, I am a man with few illusions. At least about myself. I try not to have any about anybody else, either, and in my line of work this is easy. I am forty-one years old and I look it, every instant of it. My neighbor in the next office told me on my fortieth birthday that I didn't look a day over fifty-four. I told him to go fuck himself and he took me out for lunch at Jake Wirth's on Stuart Street where we quit splitting checks about eight years ago because we both have the same thing anyway—knackwurst, German potato salad, couple seidels of Jake's Special Dark—so Cooper pays this time and I pay the next time.

In the summer we talk about the Red Sox and in the winter we talk about politics and who's out committing sodomy on the governor's council in order to get himself a judgeship. In the spring we talk about how glad we are the goddamned New England winter is over and in the fall we compare the blisters we got raking leaves around our yards. Then Cooper goes back to his office and I go back to mine and we work our asses off trying to get enough money to escape from the supermarket without needing to call a bondsman. A few years ago I read in the newspaper about a guy who had a lot of business problems all of a sudden. He borrowed every dime he could and he was still going under. So here was this man, middle fifties, being marched out of a courthouse in handcuffs to do about ten years in the slammer, because he got desperate, tried to rob a bank in his own hometown to pay his wife's country club membership, and screwed up the robbery the same as he'd screwed up everything else in his life. And I thought, I know why he did that, and the hell of it is, the rest of us've got to support him now, as well as his family.

Anyway, that is the glamorous life, some of the glamorous life that I lead as Jeremiah F. Kennedy. The F. is for Francis. Before you ask: yes, there was an X, which was for Xavier, but I dropped that a long time ago because when you have two middle initials and they stand for Francis Xavier and you practice law in Boston, it is obvious to everyone you meet that you would be more than willing to commit unnatural acts upon a governor's councillor—or a sanitation engineer, for that matter—if it would get you just one little judgeship on the bench of any little district court that happened to be available. Altogether, my father gave me four names, any one of which would persuade a reasonable man that I had a perfect reason to have killed him, but he died before I got the chance.

I live with my wife, the former Joan McManus, in a four-bedroom house in Braintree Highlands, Massachusetts. I call her Mack, and she introduces herself as Mack Kennedy; if you think about it, the reason will probably come to you. If you ask Mack what kind of lawyer I am, she will tell you that I am the classiest sleazy criminal lawyer in Boston, even if I am standing right there. This is not flattering, perhaps, but she knows I will not argue with her. I go to my office to make a living, not to make a life. My life is at home.

When I got to the office that day, there were two people in the waiting area. I wished them a good afternoon without seeming to study them, hung my coat up, kept my foul mood on, and turned toward Gretchen with an inquiring expression on my face.

"That's Mister French and Miss Candelaria," she said. "Mister Kennedy."

The man stood up. He looked something like Trooper Hudson, but his hair was much longer and his body much smaller. He had a large blond mustache. He put out his hand. "Donald French, Mister Kennedy," he said. I could not identify the accent. "This is Jill Candelaria." I figured him for twenty-four, and her a year younger. I was wrong—he was twenty-five and she was twenty-six. But then he turned out to be wrong too, about a couple of details in addition to her age. "Jill's my girlfriend," French said.

"Pleased to meet you," I said. "Actually, I'm on vacation. Didn't even plan to be in today, but an emergency came up. I assume you don't have an appointment." I have been known to forget appointments. I am very careful about lambasting somebody for showing up without one, until I check to be sure that in fact he didn't have one. Besides, I need the business.

"No," French said. "Actually, it was kind of a spur of the moment thing, and I heard about you and Jill wanted to come up here anyway, so we came in."

"This is not a social call, then," I said.

"No," French said. "I think . . . I'm beginning to think maybe I ought to talk to a lawyer."

I looked at the girl. She did not approve of this

mission at all. Her face showed an expression of hostility that she was not entirely successful in concealing, though she had tried. She had bad skin, which she had broiled too long in the sun. Her face was pleasantly shaped, but it was mottled and charred under the black bangs and her eyes were swollen. "I told him it was ridiculous," she said. "But he wouldn't listen to me, of course."

"Yes," I said. "Well, I'll talk to you, but . . ."

"Mister Kennedy," Gretchen said, "before you do anything else, you simply have to go over the papers in the Gallivan matter. Those people will drive me crazy before I'm through. They're calling every day, and I'm sick of telling them you're working on it."

I apologized to French and the girl. "Small case," I said. "They're always the most troublesome. I'll see you in a moment."

Gretchen followed me into my office. She sat in the chair next to my desk and handed me a file folder full of mail. We have no Gallivan matter in the office. The Gallivan matter is our code for keeping people waiting, sometimes for time to figure out what the hell I am going to do before I talk to them, now and then to calculate how big a fee they can afford without shopping the case elsewhere, and occasionally so I can eavesdrop on their reception room conversation before seeing them. People know all about the attorney-client privilege, but they do not believe it. They hold things back, stupidly, when they are talking to their lawyers, instead of being overheard by their lawyers. This was an eavesdropping session. Out of their line of vision, Gretchen put her finger to her lips. I nodded.

3

WE WAITED, and they resumed their conversation.

"That isn't it," French said to Jill, tapping his fingers on the reception table, "I do understand where you're coming from, what you're saying to me. Basically, I guess, what it is, the problem is basically that you got something bothering you, and I dunno what it is. It's fucking me over. The whole summer."

"Frenchman," she said, "basically what it is, is: you make things too complicated. The summer, for instance. You're working, right? And you're getting paid for it. Paid for it, and laid for it. Quit bitchin' about it."

"You really oughta put something on that," he said. "Some Noxzema or something. And stay outta the goddamned sun for a while. Sooner, later, you're gonna do something serious to yourself."

"I hate people like you," she said. "I left California because of that. Because there were too many goddamned Aztecs like you running around. All my life, I had this crummy skin, and all my life I hadda look at people like you, that've got great skin, and then, on top of that, I hadda listen to you. Telling me what to do about my crummy skin. Whadda you know about bad skin? You don't know anything, is what you know."

"I'm telling you," French said, "your nose's gonna turn black and fall off, one of these days. There was a girl up at Stratton last winter, that I knew, that had your kind of skin, and she got too much sun on her face for about the ninth year in a row, and you know what happened to her? Skin cancer. Multiple mye-loma. Whatever they call it. That's terminal."

"They can call it anything they want," she said. "Some people're born with cleft palates. Others get glaucoma, and some people catch pneumonia.

"If it isn't one thing," she said, "it's probably going to be another. Christ, the way my father talks, you'd think a master's was a terminal disease, if you got one, and then decided you'd rather wait on tables. Happens, I want to spend my time in the sun. I don't want to wear tailored suits every day, and go wipe the snotty noses of the culturally deprived, that show 'way too much interest in what time you go home, and then wait in some alley to throw a switchblade up against your throat, and rape you for your trouble. I'd rather sleep late, smile nice, make sure the chowder's hot, get good tips, and live the way I want. Leave me alone."

"I was just worried about you," French said. "I didn't mean anything by it."

"Worrying about me's not in your job specifica-tions," she said. "This is summer help, remember? We agreed on that. It was only a week and a half ago, so you oughta be able to remember it. We're summer help, for these people, and summer help for each other, too. Speaking of which . . . ?"

"I can get a little, probably, for tonight," French said. "If Chris's got any left. Gotta warn you, though, it's not gonna be any better'n the stuff we had last night."

"When're we going to get something decent, like you promised?" she said. "Goddammit, this's taking too long. I never had this much trouble, hadda wait this long onna Coast."

"If I get the engines fixed today, which I will, this afternoon," French said. "I think he's planning to go out tonight. But he won't be back until tomorrow after-noon, the earliest."

"Shit," she said, "I got to learn to pick my spots

better. This winter, I think, I'll go to Steamboat Springs."

"Why?" he said.

"Principally because," she said, "I never been there. I've also never been to Katmandu, of course, but Steamboat has a certain appeal to it." She mused for a minute. "I went with a guy once, when I was down at Lauderdale, that spent every single winter out at Steamboat. He said it was the greatest place on earth, for powder. Then he, it turned out he was only about sixty percent right-handed, and he ended up as a male go-go dancer in the Hangar down in Maryland. I wondered why he always complained so much about the head I gave him. Shit."

"I wished I knew," French said, "how many places, that I heard about. Last year it was Telluride."

"Hey," she said, "look, you got the Rossignols, you find a place to lay your head, what the fuck, huh?"

"You still should get some blocking agent for your face," he said.

"And my chest, too," she said. "Maybe what I should do is jump in a tub of cold cream every morning, before I go outdoors. Gawd. I'm gonna pull off a strip."

"That's reasonably disgusting," he said.

"I know what it is," she said, "I figured out what it is about you. You get too involved in things."

"I never met anyone like you before," he said.

"Oh," she said, "that's enough talk about *me*. Let's talk about *you*. Do you say that to all the girls? What're *you* doing these days?"

"The principal problem, I think," French said, "is that I've been spending too much time, thinking."

"And that's what's wrong?" she said.

"Jill," he said, "I always know what's wrong, if it's an engine that's involved. Right off, I know, and I can fix it. It's when there's people that come into it, that I begin to get worried."

"I didn't realize you were fixing people, Frenchman," she said. "I thought you were working on that little old

Cormorant down there, the one that's only got a little
more chrome on it, 'n a Lincoln Continental."

"I am," he said, "but that's what I'm working on.
When I'm working right, I don't have to think about it.
In fact, it goes better if I don't think about it. This
morning, when I started? I saw that oil line around
the top of the bilge, I knew what was wrong. Which is
not surprising. What is surprising, is, I knew it was the
port engine that was doing it. Now that oil line is the
same all around the bilge. But I *knew* it was the port
engine. So I took the heads off it, and checked the
gaskets, and that's what it was. Now, that is not thinking. That is knowing. Now all I got to do is fix it. So
I've been fixing it, and I've been thinking at the same
time. Bothers the hell out of me. I was thinking about
my sister, I was thinking about . . ."

"What about your sister?" Jill said.

"She's really bitched her life up," French said. "I
know that, and she knows that. But maybe, she knows
why. I sure don't. She was married to this nice guy,
and I came home, it was when I got discharged and I
wanted to surprise everybody. Well, I sure did. She
was in the shower with her brother-in-law. Nobody
else was home."

"The fuck'd you do?" Jill said. "Did you tell on
her?"

"No," he said. "I never said anything about it before, to anybody, until this very minute. Not even to
her. Things like that, I don't tell anybody, usually.
I've got to change that. I was reading this book . . ."

"That's another thing, I think," she said. "You spend
too much time reading books, too."

"Listen," he said, "in the Nam, if you could read a
book, you counted yourself lucky. Most of the guys
were so full of skag they could barely walk, let alone
read. Jesus, what a change. You get the hell out of
college, because it's driving you nuts, and the minute
you find there is something that can *really* drive you
nuts, you get so damned scared you go right back to
doing what was driving you nuts in college. And being

damned grateful for it, too. I did a third as much at college as I did at Da Nang, I would've made dean's list every fifteen minutes.

"Anyway," he said, "think about this: first you got the situation where you're fixing the engines, right? And if you think, you're gonna fuck it up, if you think about that. And that means you got to think about something else, which is the second thing. The situation. My sister. You. What the hell'm I dealin' with? This could be dangerous. I don't know what to think."

"Think anything you want," Jill said, "it's easier, remember, anyway. You don't know shit. A guy, somebody you don't know, can't get you in trouble, for not knowin' him."

"Look," French said, "for workin' on *Catapult,* considering what Chris's promising us, that could get you in a whole lot of trouble. And, for not working on *Catapult,* that could *not* get you a whole lot of money, let alone the other stuff. If the guy that's paying, whoever the guy that's paying is, he is paying me real good money. I'm used to getting twelve an hour, but he pays me twenny, and it's always there, the bank check in the envelope in the radio compartment, when I check the boat the next day."

"Who puts it there?" she said. "Chris?"

"Couldn't be," French said. "Chris and I're usually together, the nights after I worked onna boat, and I generally have to take Chris home and pour him into bed. No, Chris isn't doing it. It's somebody else."

"Have you asked Chris?" she said.

"Nope," he said, "and I'm not gonna, either. Chris wanted me to know, Chris would tell me. Chris doesn't tell me, there's some reason, Chris doesn't want me to know. I haven't known Chris that long, but I trust him."

"I'll bet," she said. "You know something? Seeing that boat, I bet Chris does own it."

"Okay," French said, "but then, you look at the boat, right? *One* fire extinguisher. Oughta be at least four. Life jackets for six, but all stuffed in a locker so far forward nobody could possibly get at them in a hurry. One anchor, and it's not heavy enough. But *two* ship-to-shore, and CB besides. Which probably means: this is a guy that doesn't expect to get into trouble, which is the kind that always does. But if it happens, he's either stupid, which he obviously is not, or else he's got some reason to think there'll be somebody around, get him out of it. And when the boat's back in the morning, Chris never left all night, and I know. It ain't Chris. I think."

"He the shore side of the Navy?" she said.

"Could be," French said. "Boat's only got one chart, the Small Craft folding one, which has not been opened. But it also has radar, which means: guy always goes to the same place, or else he always follows somebody to the same place, and he knows the way, so the only thing he worries about is fog.

"No sleeping bags," French said. "No toilet gear in the cuddy cabin—just a couple rolls of tissue. No towels. No foul-weather gear. No portable, standard-broadcast band radio, for listening to the ballgame. No water-ski equipment, which *Catapult* would be a natural for. No charcoal grill, no fishing rods, no scuba stuff. So: he spends almost no time onna boat, he uses it only for business, it's got two Olds four-four-twos, does about fifty, sixty miles an hour when they're both synched at the red line, and every week I have to work on it, even though I left it beautiful the last week, because the plugs're all ashed out. The logs say she runs between eight and twelve hours a week. He's going full power, the minute he drops the docklines."

"Well," Jill said, "you know what he's doing, who-ever he is. That doesn't make it a crime, to fix his boat."

"Sure," French said. "But keep in mind, I worked on a lot of engines in Vietnam. I've worked on boats at Marina del Ray, in Cypress Gardens, Miami, Nassau, Port Everglades, the Keys, Nantucket, Martha's Vineyard and Newport, before I came to this rathole.

That kind of experience, I got to know, the only thing this guy is doing with this boat is this: he's booting her out beyond the two-hundred-mile limit, once a week, at night, and coming right back in. That could be hard to explain. I have to know that somethin's going on."

"And, as a matter of fact," she said, "you do."

"Sure," he said. "That's what makes me worry about the boat situation. When I get sick of doing that, I start thinking about you."

"Some free advice," she said. "Stop. I told you: I never give more'n a six-week commitment, and I never break one of those, once I make it. You got four and a half weeks to go, to treat me nice. You do it, I'll consider renewing. I oughta go see that guy."

"I'll see you tonight," he said.

"Probably," she said. "Depends on what time the bus gets me there."

I did not want Jill to leave until I told her to. I nodded at Gretchen. She mouthed the word "druggies." I mouthed the word "money." She grinned briefly and said loudly as she reached the door to my office, "Mister French, Miss Candelaria, Mister Kennedy will see you now."

4

I WENT BACK to Green Harbor that evening in August hoping that the lobsters in the bag from Hook's, in the back seat, would suffer hideously before turning red in the water. It would be fair to say that I was not in a good frame of mind, and would cheerfully have inflicted misery upon any beast that would stand still long enough for me to get at it. The traffic on Route 3 did not improve my outlook. I got to Green Harbor shortly after six-thirty.

"Some fucking vacation," I said to Mack, after I kissed her.

"Bad day at the office, dear?" she simpered.

"Goddamned fucking clients," I said. "Teddy's got me out on the limb so far with that judge that one squirrel jumps on it and I hit the ground helpless. If that son of a bitch can't convince the judge the trooper ate his license, I'm liable to get disbarred. Did the bastard call?"

There are two ways to reach Cadillac Teddy. One is to get him arrested. Then if you are his lawyer, you will hear from him promptly. The other is to call La Salle Dorothy, which is the beauty parlor Dottie operates on the Providence Highway in Norwood. Dottie and Teddie will lead you to believe that Dottie owns La Salle Dorothy, as well as operates it, struggling constantly to keep it, and this may very well be true.

On the other hand, it may not be true. Teddy and Dottie enjoy rather comfortable quarters over there in Sharon. They have an indoor swimming pool with a great big Jacuzzi. They have an Advent TV in the living room. They have large color sets in their bedroom and kitchen. They have a fountain in their back yard, and it adds a rather nice touch to the setting for the tennis court, I must admit. They have Persian rugs which most Persians would covet. The flowers are especially striking in May—they have a wonderful gardener. Their kitchen is equipped better than most of the workrooms in the best restaurants of New York, I should imagine. But then André, their cook, used to work in one of those restaurants, and would naturally insist upon the best. Maybe you can swing all those goodies by stealing cars and tinting the hair of matrons blue, but somehow I tend to doubt it. Anyway, if Teddy doesn't call you, the only thing you can do is call Dottie, which is another way of saying that when Teddy gets damned good and ready to call you, he will.

"Teddy did not call," Mack said. "If that's the bastard that you have in mind."

"Son of a *bitch*," I said. "Why the hell did I go into this? Why didn't I do what my mother told me, and go into something simple, like brain surgery?"

She asked me what happened, and I told her, as briefly as I could, while getting into my jeans and attending to a cold Heineken. "And when I got back to the office from that adventure," I said, "I had a punk kid in there with his goddamned girlfriend, she hating me for him wanting to see me—which I did not solicit after all—and him all jumpy about seeing me because she didn't want him to see me."

"I don't get it," Mack said.

"Neither do I," I said. Most lawyers of my acquaintance insist that they never tell their wives anything about their cases. I tell Mack everything. We have been married since 1962, when I got out of law school and she got pregnant. She got pregnant on our honeymoon at the Bermudiana Hotel in Hamilton. We were both very relieved, because if she had not gotten pregnant, I would have been drafted and sent off to Vietnam to get my ass blown off. We were also very much in love, and we still are.

Saigon Kennedy, as we refer to our daughter, is fifteen now; at school—Fontbonne Academy in Milton —she is more formally known as Heather Kennedy (which has been another bitch of a thing, finding first names for the kids that aren't the same as the first names of the Real Kennedys, as we call them, because those Kennedys have enough kids to fill up Milton Academy by themselves) and the nuns send home glowing reports about her.

She dates nice clean kids that I like, even though I know they probably spend most of their time trying to get her pants off and probably succeed now and then, at least partially. I know I would try, if I were one of those nice clean kids. She is cheerful and she gets home when she's supposed to. She was very much in favor of Mack's decision to go back to work, nine years ago, even though it meant that Heather would have to contribute some of the hours of housework that Mack would be spending at the real-estate office. Heather cooks and Heather cleans and when I look at this beautiful young lady, tears come to my eyes, particularly if Mack happens to be in the same room looking almost as young, but with the additional attractiveness that comes into anyone's face, man or woman, who has shouldered responsibility for a few years, met a payroll or two, sheltered and nourished a family, and never intentionally been a big pain in the ass to anybody.

Mack wanted a big family, but Saigon's was a very difficult delivery. The doctor had a way with words. "Mister Kennedy," he said, his green surgical gown covered with smears and gobs of coagulating blood and the blood sticking to the gloves as he removed them in the maternity waiting room, "if I were you, and I wanted to spend some time with that lady, I would make damned sure she didn't get pregnant again, because we almost lost the pair of them." Which put the big family out of the question, and which turned out to be another disappointment that Mack never once mentioned again. She's kept her figure, which is good enough so that men still try to pick her up when we meet at the Parker House bar if shopping or business has brought her to Boston for the day, and the woman refuses to keep her hands off me.

There are times in my life when I have made a thundering asshole of myself. When I do, I start thinking about knocking over a small bank so that the Commonwealth can support me and my family the way it does every other shiftless son of a bitch who can't be bothered to deal with the mess that he's created and is too lazy to make so much as an attempt at it. Then I think perhaps that any man who had the brains at twenty-six to marry Joan McManus probably shouldn't go badgering God about "what have You done for me lately." My mother died before my father, and I'm afraid I didn't know what he meant when he mourned that he could not live without her (he didn't, either. He apparently developed a total case of incurable cancer in the three months between his quarterly medical examinations, which I am assured is not possible, and died of it two months to the day of her funeral, at age fifty-nine), but I know now. I know exactly what he meant. A stupid mistake is one thing—ingratitude is something else again, and I'll be damned if I'll put myself in a position where I have to cop a plea to St. Peter for having been ungrateful. Mack is my life. I tell her things about mine, which, I think, is hers. Or part of it.

"The kid thinks he's in the shit," I said. "He doesn't want to get in the shit. If you're getting in the shit, and you don't want to get in the shit, you should get a lawyer to get you out of the shit."

"I should think his girlfriend would want him to stay out of the shit," Mack said. "And if that takes a lawyer, then why doesn't she want him to have a lawyer?"

"I don't know," I said.

"Does she want him to get in the shit?" Mack said.

"I'm glad you asked that question," I said. "That's the thought that crossed my mind. She's not really his girlfriend, judging from what I heard. What she did was shack up with him for the summer." I told Mack about the conversation between Jill and French in the reception area.

"Jesus," Mack said, "she's a cold-blooded little bitch."

"I think that would be a fair statement," I said. "I also think it would be fair to say that he's not the brightest article I ever saw. She's too much for him—that's for sure. He's gaga over her. She's about as emotional as a blackjack dealer in Las Vegas.

"I called them into my office," I said. "Sat them down, the Coke or coffee routine, nobody wanted anything, and I said, 'All right, Mister French, what's on your mind?' He said he didn't know, but he was worried. 'Well, for God's sake,' I said, 'I can't do anything for your worries. I've got worries myself. Everybody's got worries.'

" 'Mister Kennedy,' he said, 'I think I may be mixed up in something that I didn't mean to get mixed up in.' "

By then, as I told Mack, the broad looked like she'd just eaten something that she thought was chicken, and found out it was snake. " 'Donald's being silly,' she said.

" 'There isn't anything silly about what's bothering me,' French said. He wasn't as bright as a nightlight, but he was obstinate, even if it did mean that he was risking her disapproval and pussy by being that way. 'I don't want to go to prison.'

" '*Mister* Kennedy,' she said, in this tone that would have withered the ferns in my office, if I had had ferns in my office, 'is the Frenchman in trouble?'

" 'How the hell should I know?' I said. 'So far all I've heard is that he works on boats. Far as I know, that's not against the law. He gets paid for working on boats. Also not against the law. Law doesn't say anything about getting a premium rate for tuning one guy's boat before you tune another guy's boat, so that's legal too, as far as I know. If he's not doing anything with the boat that's against the law, and as far as I know, he isn't, it doesn't matter if somebody else's doing something with the boat, that is against the law. That's their problem.'

" 'That's what I told him,' she said.

" 'Jill,' he said, 'you're not a lawyer. If I'm getting myself in the crap, I'd like to know about it, because if I am getting in it, I'm gonna be the one that's in it. I wanna talk to this guy, all right?' "

"What'd she do?" Mack said.

"It was what I did," I said. "Seemed like a good opening, so I said, 'Miss Candelaria, I know you're a friend of Mister French, but I really can't talk to him while you're present. If he tells his lawyer something while somebody else is listening, that person can quote the whole conversation. It's no insult to you, and I hope you don't take it as one, but since he wants to talk to me, and I can't advise him unless he talks to me, I'll have to ask you to excuse us.' "

"And how'd she take that?" Mack said.

"Like it was bad enough when I shoved the umbrella up her ass, but unforgivable when I opened it," I said. "Got up out of the chair, stomped out of the office, slammed the fucking door and didn't answer him when he said he'd wait for her at the parking lot, and drive her back to Hyannis."

"Nice," Mack said. "What'd he tell you then?"

"Nothing," I said. "Clown'd shot his wad when she was sitting there. All he did was rerun everything I'd already heard. There's a crime there, of course. If they're doing coke with this Chris, whoever he is . . ."

"You sure it's coke?" Mack said.

"Got to be," I said. "Nothing else pays well enough. If they're doing coke, possession just for personal use's heavy weather in the federal court. And it's no damned picnic in the State court, either. Of course he didn't tell me that they're doing coke, which shows you what an asshole he is, but that's what they were talking about. Nobody runs a speedboat for grass. You've gotta do volume for that."

"So what did you do?" Mack said.

"I didn't do anything," I said. "I told the kid it'd cost him a hundred bucks for the consultation, which is what I used to buy those lobsters in the bag out in the kitchen that I'm gonna go out and murder in a while, although I didn't use all of the hundred, and I couldn't see any crime, and if the shit hit the fan he should call me and we would talk about real money. That was it."

"That doesn't explain your disposition," Mack said.

"I haven't finished," I said. "It was still only about one-fifteen. I whacked on the wall. Welden whacked back. I met him in the hall. I said I'd take him to lunch at the Athens Olympia and then he could go back to work and I would come back and sign some letters and get the hell out of there before the traffic backed up. I'm gonna get out of there before every Protestant in the world sneaks out early and jams up the Expressway.

"Now," I said, "I am coming down from being royally pissed-off. I get back to the office and what is sitting there in skintight pants and a whole lot of jewelry, looking like a black slave trader and patting his goddamned white dog?"

"Waldo," Mack said.

"Waldo," I said. "Waldo greets me with his customary affection as his favorite honky. He introduces me to his companion, who for some reason I have not noticed. I realize this is like saying you went to Rome and didn't notice Saint Peter's, but I didn't. The only thing missing on this particular darky is colored lights."

"Did the companion have a dog?" Mack said.

"I don't think so," I said. "I may be wrong, what with the glare from his uniform, but I don't think so. I didn't see a dog. I saw a damned scared little white girl that looked to be about three years younger'n

Saigon in age, and about thirty years older in street experience, but I didn't see a dog."

"Jesus," Mack said.

"Jesus has not been giving adequate attention to the meek and helpless lately," I said. "Were it not for us vigilant members of the bar, they would have no protection at all. As it is, we are ever at the ready, and keep them out of the cooler so that they can keep on hooking for the likes of Waldo's friend, whom he introduced to me as Captain Midnight. It seems the kid's name is Jane, and she's fourteen, and she propositioned a cop because the captain wants a new Pimpmobile, hasn't got the money, blames it on her and his other two ladies, and has indicated that he plans to beat the shit out of her and them if their production does not improve."

"Why don't you open a zoo and deal with animals that're honorable enough to admit it?" Mack said.

"Because I don't know anything about the kind that wears fur on their skins instead of over their silk jumpsuits in glossy black," I said.

"What're you two talking about?" Saigon said, entering the bedroom like a blessing from the Holy Spirit.

"Vice," I said. "Why aren't you dishing them out at Phil's Burger Quik, Gumdrop?"

"First," she said, "because I don't start until eight. Second, because nobody's bought me a car yet."

"You want a Cadillac?" Mack said. "Daddy knows a man who can get you one cheap."

"Sure," I said, "and also arrested."

"Not Waldo," Mack said. "Cadillac Teddy."

"Who's Waldo?" Saigon said.

"A client," I said.

"A pimp," Mack said.

"Jesus," I said.

"Which is it?" Saigon said. "They don't sound to me like they go together. Gotta be one or the other."

"We're not bringing this kid up right," I said to Mack.

"I've been meaning to speak to you about that," Mack said.

"Look," Saigon said, "am I going to eat here? Or am I going to eat there? Because if I'm going to eat there, I may take a diet pill or something, so I don't eat there. Toenails and stuff in the meat. Toenails from *cows, Yuck.*"

"You're gonna eat here," I said. "I'm gonna commit lobstercide in a minute."

"Barbarian," Saigon said.

"Have it your way," I said.

"Is he a pimp?" Saigon said.

"Not many bishops need criminal lawyers," I said.

"That's not what I asked you," she said.

"She's got a question pending, Counselor," Mack said. "Your answer's unresponsive."

"He's a pimp," I said. "He's a vicious bastard who beat up a kid. He used a claw hammer to do it. She's got a little trouble with her left elbow. Her right forearm mended funny. But she can still fuck and do blow jobs. The fucking goes for twenty bucks. The blow jobs are fifteen. She kind of misses her room in Weston, the one with the Teddy bears and the Raggedy Ann dolls and the Snoopys and the Paddington bears. She's beginning to think maybe the strict parochial school nuns were better'n working for Captain Midnight. At least they didn't want new cars, and make her blow businessmen from Westwood to get them. They maybe wouldn't let her wear hotpants to school, but then again, they never made her wear hotpants outside the Caribe Lounge, and hit her with a monkey wrench when she complained about it. She didn't like her braces, and she didn't want them replaced, but they were better'n what she's had in her mouth since, so's Captain Midnight could get his new car, and the fellow in the Toronado could get his cookies before he went home. That answer your question?"

"Jesus," Saigon said.

I looked at Mack. "I asked for it," she said. "You going to make dinner?"

"I am gonna make dinner," I said. "God pity those lobsters."

The lobsters perished without audible distress, and we tore them apart on the picnic table in the screened-in porch. Mr. Kelly was watering his squash and tomato plants next door, doing a little weeding around the carrots and dealing carefully with his potato plants. Mr. Kelly wins many ribbons each year at the Marshfield Fair for his squashes, tomatoes and other vegetables, and we hold him in high affection not only for his many gifts of garden products but for his fine quality as a human being. Mr. Kelly's hose made a sound in the twilight which I found soothing, and with that, the beer and the lobster, I had calmed down a little by the time Saigon went to work. Mack drove her in my car while I cleaned up the mess, wishing I could fit the garbage from my office into the green plastic bag with the shells and the beer bottles, but resigned to the fact that I could not.

Mack returned in a similarly pensive mood. She came into the porch, kissed me and went into the kitchen for her glass of white wine. "Ballgame tonight?" she said.

"Nah," I said. "They're in Anaheim. Doesn't start till ten-thirty, and every time I listen to the first four innings I end up listening to the rest of it and that's the night they decide they're gonna play sixteen innings so I can't get up in the morning. When's Saigon through? Twelve-thirty?"

Mack came out on the porch and sat down in the chair next to mine. "Yup," she said. "Cripes, but she's a good kid, Jerry."

"She sure is," I said. "We've done a damned good job with her, if I do say so myself."

"She's so good it scares me sometimes," Mack said. "I look at her and I wonder if we really had anything to do with it. Evelyn Mason's just as conscientious a mother as I am"—Evelyn being one of the other agents in Mack's office—"and you've met Joe. There isn't a nicer, harder-working, more decent guy around. So they've got Billy on the honor roll at Thayer Academy, headed for Columbia next year, and Jean probably going to transfer to Milton Academy for high school, and then in between those two angels they've got that little terror Kenny. Fourteen years old, and if you could ever spot a future client coming down the pike, he's it. Evelyn's beside herself with the kid. He's rude. He's contemptuous of any rules they set up for him. He stays out all night. At least once a month they have to go down to Archbishop Williams and talk to the principal. 'What did we do?' Evelyn says. 'What the goddamned hell did we do with him that was different from what we did with the other two?'"

"Sent him to parochial school, for one thing," I said. "I don't know what that does to a kid, but it would sure-God make me mean."

"Oh, cut it out, Jerry," Mack said. She occasionally gets uneasy about my views on the Catholic religion. "We sent Heather to Fontbonne, you know."

"That's not really a parochial school," I said. "That's more a finishing school with a good curriculum where most of the students and teachers happen to be Catholics."

"The other night," Mack said, "Evelyn was saying before we came down here, Joe told Kenny he was grounded. I've forgotten what he'd done. Didn't cut the grass or something, and then gave Evelyn some sass when she reminded him. Told her to go fuck herself, I think it was. So Joe grounded him, and the kid went out the back door and threw rocks through three of the bedroom windows. He's a mean, nasty kid, and they don't have any idea why."

"Probably puberty," I said.

"I don't think so," Mack said. "I tried to tell Evelyn that, reassure her, but she said Billy went through it too, and human beings could live in the same house with him without having to sleep with one eye peeled in case he decided to come in and murder them in their beds some night. She is actually scared of Kenny. He's punched her in the stomach a couple of times. I guess the last time he did it, Joe was home."

"What did Joe do?" I said.

"He belted him," Mack said. "Evelyn said she was almost more afraid of what Joe was going to do to Kenny than she was of what Kenny might do to her. She said he was just out of control."

"Joe's a pretty big guy, too," I said.

"And Kenny's a little kid," she said. "For fourteen, he's downright undersized. Joe hit him right in the mouth and knocked him spinning. They had to take him to the emergency room to get his jaw back in place. Doctor said Kenny was lucky it wasn't broken."

"Joe's luckier," I said. "The doctor could file a child abuse report as it is."

"Oh my God," Mack said, "you think he would?"

"He might," I said. "That's a hot item right now, all those foster children getting killed, all those kids dying of neglect and ending up in trash barrels. Those DAs've got the wind up them on this. It's a sure headline— who the hell's in favor of whacking kids around? Even kids like Kenny."

"Joe could be in trouble," she said.

"Mostly from publicity," I said. "He's got a right and duty to protect Evelyn, and it wouldn't take much to get the case thrown out if it were brought, but the papers'd have a field day with it until then. 'Electronics Executive Indicted'? They'd love it."

It was dark by then, and Mr. Kelly had gone inside, leaving the sprinkler working on his lawn. Half a mile up the road an occasional car rumbled into the Beach House, transporting underage drinkers to the same place where I had done my underage drinking years ago. But when I was underage, the age was twenty-one and I was eighteen. That summer the age was eighteen, and a lot of kids had to scout around for somebody old enough to drive them there. A woman on a moped rode down our street and turned right on

Ocean Avenue, the putting of her little machine more laughable than disturbing.

"It's such a dangerous business, isn't it?" Mack said. "This stuff about having kids. You go into it with no experience whatsoever, and if you screw it up you have really screwed up something. What the hell do you do then? If you don't know how you screwed it up, how in God's name do you make it right?"

"I don't know," I said. "I think about that sometimes, in the office. Here are these adults in pretty serious trouble, and some of them haven't been adults for very long, either. Charged with really difficult offenses, serious crimes. Crimes that could send them away for a long time. You sit there listening to some big kid bragging that he's not afraid, he knows he can do time, and there isn't even any point in telling him how delicious he's gonna look when he gets to the joint where the boss cons are. He sits there sneering at you, and what do you say to him? That he's gonna get buggered six times his first night on the block? He won't believe you. And here is this kid that was most likely a cuddly adorable little baby once. Maybe even had parents who loved him and took the best care they could of him, charged with wounding a liquor store clerk in an armed robbery that didn't even get him a dime. He'll go in, because there isn't anything that I can do to keep him out, or anything that anybody else can do, either. All you can do is try to make a deal that'll get him less time and let him do it at Concord instead of Walpole. That's about it. Maybe if he comes out of Concord after a five-year indeterminate he won't be quite as hard a case as he'd be coming out of Walpole after fifteen to twenty. Maybe. Only maybe. Not for sure. It's scary. It's absolutely scary.

"That fucking pimp, Captain Midnight?" I said. "Well, he probably never had much of a chance. He doesn't know who his father is, and his mother lives in Detroit but he's not sure where. This guy is an animal, hitting a kid with a hammer like that, putting her out on the street, but you can get halfway to explaining him, maybe, because he was always treated like an animal. But he's twenty years old. Get that? Twenty years old, and he's a rompin' stompin' pimp. He's got his ladies out on the street and he's got the savvy to keep them out there. Now he's up on an A and B charge? So what, man? A and B, dangerous weapon? No sweat. He'll get out of it."

"Will he?" Mack said.

"Sure," I said. "What the hell do you think brought the victim with him to my office? She's gonna back out of her story. The cops interviewed her while the emergency room people were setting the broken bones and fitting the casts. She was scared of him then, and she thought they could protect her, so she told the truth. He accused her of holding out some of the money and she denied it and he beat the shit out of her. Then she got out of the hospital and she refused to go home and she found out the cops couldn't protect her after all. So she went back to her man, and back to the street, and now the trial's coming up and she's hooking her tight little white ass off down on Stuart Street, to earn my fee and spring her man because she loves him."

"You shouldn't take that money," Mack said. "That's, that's dirty money. That's blood money."

"It's living off the earnings of a prostitute, I suppose," I said. "I know where it came from and I know how it got there and I don't like it either. But you could say that about almost every fee I get—it's somebody's ill-gotten gains. Most of the people I represent are professional criminals. They don't have segregated trust funds they can draw on to pay me. Cadillac Teddy makes his living—some of his living, anyway—stealing cars. Teddy pays me. Teddy pays me with some of the money he gets from stealing cars. Captain Midnight gets his living off of prostitutes. He pays me out of that, which is how I get my living. Maurice Stans got acquitted in the first Watergate case, so the Committee to Re-elect the President picked up his legal fees. Something like four hundred thousand dollars. Money that came from people who intended to purchase in-

fluence with the administration when they paid it over.
When you sell a house to somebody, do you make sure
he's paying for it with clean money? Trace it back to
the family fortune and make sure none of it was earned
in the slave trade? No, you don't. You sell the guy the
house and take your commission, which is what you
should do. If he got the down payment by cheating on
his taxes, that's his worry, not yours."

"It's not the same thing," Mack said. "It's not the
same thing at all."

"No," I said, "it's not. Trouble is, the Constitution
says every man's entitled to counsel of his choice. He
chooses me, I have my living to consider. The Constitution doesn't say that I can't consider my living.
Doesn't say anything about it. Because not eating is
unpleasant, I generally take the case. That cash
won't keep us healthy and it won't make us happy
and it won't keep Heather from going haywire and
deciding she prefers a Captain Midnight and a life on
the street to her stereo set and her own room, two
people who love her and some very nice friends. But
if she stays on her current course, it'll send her to
college and keep her teeth straight and allow her to
wear good clothes. If Captain Midnight's little waif
had come to my private office for oral surgery the
last time he kicked her teeth in, she would've paid
for the repairs with money that she got from hustling
because there's no Blue Cross Blue Shield Master
Medical down in the Combat Zone; if she had done
that, and I were a doctor, should I have refused to
make her well?"

"God," Mack said, "that kid's poor parents. I hope
they don't know what she's doing."

"They know exactly what she's doing," I said.
"They visited her in the hospital and tried to get her
to come home with them. The mother was on a fur-
lough from a private hospital where they try to convince alcoholics that they shouldn't drink any more
booze, and she never had a problem with the sauce
until the kid bolted. The father looked like he'd been

beaten up himself, except nobody'd taken a hammer to him—what he'd gone through'd been enough. They have one other kid, a boy, who entered West Point last year and offered to go down to the Zone and kill his little sister if she didn't come home and start behaving herself. He's on academic probation now, because he went AWOL from the Point when he found out what'd happened."

"Oh, my God," Mack said.

"And you know what'll happen?" I said. "Captain Midnight will get off, because she won't testify against him, and she'll go back on the street that night. Within a month he'll beat her up again, and she'll take it because she loves him."

"Can I come over there and sit in your lap and get hugged?" Mack said. "I think I need a hug."

"I have several available," I said, "but I could do a better job in the bedroom, and we do have almost two hours before I have to go and get Saigon."

"As long as you don't fall asleep afterward," Mack said.

"Promise," I said.

"I'll be as careful as I can, all my life, God," Mack said, getting up. "But don't you ever forget that we also need to stay lucky."

When I picked up Saigon that night, she asked me if I could give Margie a ride home to Pembroke. I was not very eager to go ten miles or so in the direction opposite to our house, not at that hour, but neither was I about to leave a kid to hitchhike home at one in the morning. Margie did not say very much. She did manage not to cry very much. She kept her head bowed on the ride, so that her long black hair, which she released from the hairnet as soon as she left the restaurant, hung down on her maroon and yellow uniform and prevented us from seeing her face. When she got out of the car at the dark house, she said, "Thank you, Mister Kennedy," and that was all. We waited until she turned on the light in the hall.

Heather said, "Thanks, Dad." I said, "It's okay, kid." Heather said, "Yeah, I know. But thanks anyway." We went home and she went up to bed. I was glad of Mack's warmth in the summer evening, and the lingering smell of sex in our room. I also reminded God about the necessity of luck, and then I went to sleep.

5

I AM A CREATURE of routine. Several routines, in fact. Chaos, clutter and disorder abound wherever I venture, on the top of my messy desk, in the tangled legal problems that disrupt the already disrupted lives of my troubled clients, in the shambling inefficiency of a court system which is still doing business by Morse code, and wasting everybody's time as though it were still 1872 and we had nothing to worry about between the spring planting and the fall harvest. If I didn't have my routines, I would go nuts.

I do not like surprises, even pleasant ones. When I am surprised, it is because I did not have brains enough to expect that something like that might happen, and prepare myself for it. I get up in the morning at 7:15. I shower and shave. I put on the shaving lotion and I get dressed, except for my coat and tie. I go into the kitchen and plug in the coffee pot, which I prepared the night before. I go to the door and bring in the papers. If the delivery boy is late, or if the unreliable little bastard has been in too much of a hurry to bother putting the papers between the storm and inside doors on a wet day, so that what I get from the step is a big wet glob all stuck together, I become very annoyed. I expect to fetch the papers in readable condition, return to the kitchen, pour myself a cup of coffee, and sit down while men less fortunate than I jam up the roads in order to get to their time clocks before 9:00. If I leave the house at 8:40, I will get to the office around 9:10. If I leave the house around 7:45, I will get to the office around 8:55. But that means I need something to do between 7:30 and 8:45, and what I am accustomed to doing is reading the papers. If the papers are not available, I become very grouchy indeed. That means I will have to fight the traffic, stop and get the papers, and arrive at the office about ten minutes earlier than I would have if I had read the papers at home, still without having read them.

I do not, of course, follow that routine when I am at Green Harbor. Instead I follow another routine. I get up around nine and do not shave. I go out to the kitchen and plug in the coffee pot, which I have prepared the night before. I go to the door and get the papers. I come back to the kitchen, pour my coffee, and sit down to read. If it is a nice day, I sit on the porch. If it is a lousy day, I sit in the kitchen. At 10:30, I go into the bedroom and awaken Mack— Saigon sets her own routine in the summer, working some days from noon until 8:30 and other days from 8:00 until 12:30, sleeping late all days, going to the beach on good days when she is not working. Mack and I take a tennis lesson from 11 until noon, and then play until 1:00. We come back from the Bubble and have lunch. Then we change into bathing suits, pick up our beach chairs, fill the cooler with beer and iced tea and go over to the beach. If the Red Sox have an afternoon game, I take a small portable radio. Each of us brings something to read, but we seldom get to read it. That is because of Mike Curran.

Mike Curran is the mayor of the beach. Mike's big white house, across the street from Kelly's, has wooden stairs leading down over the seawall to the beach. Mike, who retired about ten years ago as president of his own printing business, gets into his Bermuda shorts right after lunch and descends the stairs. The doctors counseled him after his heart attack to walk about three miles a day. Mike, his barrel chest covered with white fur, does it faithfully, though I doubt he ever gets more than five hundred yards from his house. Mike does his walking from blanket to blanket, exchanging greetings and gossip, reporting fresh gossip he has just collected from Billy Field and Dick Maguire, receiving some fresh gossip from you, if available, commenting on the baseball season, the weather and whatever "asshole" has just attracted his attention as a candidate or incumbent of elective office. Mike is universally addressed as "Your Honor" except by me, because Mike calls me "Senator" and I hate it. Which is, of course, why Mike does it. Mike being a great favorite with the kids, he has gotten them into the habit of doing it as well, to the point at which even Saigon, when peevish or mischievous, calls me "Senator." But except for that heckling, those languid afternoons on the beach, surrounded by people we have known for ten years or more, are among the most pleasant of the year. I treasure them.

Two days after I insulted Trooper Hudson and rendered the judge of the Dedham District Court incredulous with my tale of a license that had been eaten, I was sitting on the beach watching the kids play volleyball and talking to the mayor. Mack had gone to sleep in the sun, and Saigon in her white bikini had just dropped out of the game, complaining of thirst. I suspected she was suffering from cramps, but it was nothing to worry about because Mack had long since taken her to her own gynecologist and Saigon had been assured that everything was in order. She had a pain-killing prescription that seemed to help, but she did not of course have it with her in her bikini. There is no room for anything but Saigon in that white bikini, and I noticed that the lads played somewhat less gallantly when she had left.

"You know, Senator," Mike said, "that child is very round in places."

"This is true, Mike," I said. "I've been thinking of retaining two or three Dobermans until she's safely married."

"Won't work," Mike said. "I never had that kind of trouble with Judy, though God knows she's a wonderful kid and pretty, too, and of course the boys were off threatening somebody else's daughters as soon as the sap began to flow anyway. But when Carol grew up all of a sudden I was thinking about posting guards. You ever make a novena?"

"Woodworking? I'm not good with my hands," I said, retreading the old joke.

"The boys will be," Mike said, "if they haven't been already. Ye gods, Jerry, remember what it was like when you were about sixteen and you saw a child like that? My God, it was wonderful. Is Mack asleep?"

I strongly suspected that she was not, but she has feigned sleep before in order to hear some of Mike's stories firsthand, and I was not about to spoil her fun this time. "Yup," I said.

"Yeah, well, good," Mike said. Mike will not use language that he considers "bad," or tell stories he deems to be off color, when there are ladies present.

"Jesus, Jerry," he said, "I'll never forget it. I was about eighteen at the time and I was just learning the business from old man Allen, that skinflint bastard, and I'd get myself all cleaned up in the only suit I had on Saturday nights and go over to see Kitty Blanchard. She's dead now, poor soul. Married Frank Tobin, that was on the city council many years, many years, Jerry, and then the booze got him and he lost his insurance business and everything. Last time I saw her was at Frank's wake, I went to pay my respects of course, and here was this poor fat old woman that looked like hell. I didn't even recognize her, although she knew me right off, of course. And she said, 'Mike, Mike, what am I gonna do now?'

"Well, I didn't know what she was gonna do, so I said to her, 'Well, Kitty, lemme call John Lacey down at the building maintenance office and see what he can do for you.' Because after all, as I said to John, we couldn't have Kitty Tobin penniless and applying for welfare now, could we? So John put her on, the poor thing didn't know how to do anything of course, and they had her mopping up the floors in one of them new office buildings they're always putting up along with the tax rate. So she was all right, although Frank sure didn't leave her much to get by on, the bastard, but at least she wasn't starving. You wouldn't have a bottle of beer in that cooler, would you?"

I opened the cooler and took out two Heinekens, cracking one for myself. Mike tilted his head back and swallowed a good half of his. "Ahh," he said, "that's good." He wiped the back of his mouth with his hairy arm.

"That was the problem with us bucks in those days, Jerry, my boy," Mike said, squatting on his great haunches and holding the beer before him like a witch doctor making a sacrifice. "There were too many of us that never gave enough thought to what would have to happen to our loved ones when we were gone. Now, you take Frank Tobin. Frank was a hell of a guy, always ready to buy a man a drink. Or have one for himself for that matter. Always had a good story and he was a good family man, too. Why, Frank for all his boozing was a daily communicant down to Holy Rosary and he took up the collection at two Masses every Sunday. Not just the ten o'clock, but also the High Mass at eleven-thirty. Monsignor Cahill said the High. You didn't remember the monsignor, did you, Jerry?"

I told Mike that I did not remember the monsignor. "Well," Mike said, "there was a fellow that was a spellbinder. We did the parish printing for him, of course, and I'd get to spend an hour with him in the rectory every so often and then he'd invite me to dinner.

"Now there was a man that was death on the booze in the pulpit. Flannery, that owned the saloon down on Columbus Avenue, of course that's all gone now, all black naturally, and they tore the old building down, even, that used to be there, when they were thinking about putting that Southwest Expressway there, I think it was, the one that Sargent killed when he was governor. But Flannery hated the monsignor. Hated his guts. Because Flannery was in Holy Rosary, and being open late on Saturday nights, of course, he didn't feel like getting up for the early Masses on Sundays and he would end up at the High where Monsignor Cahill would be kicking the divvil out of the saloon keepers and Flannery'd have to sit through it. They didn't have those afternoon circuses on Saturdays and Sundays like they've got these days, all that singing and jumpin' around. Like a Rotary meeting. 'Though I notice,' Flannery said, 'he don't object, the good father don't, to the earnings I give him in the damned envelopes every Sunday.'

"But the monsignor in the rectory was a different matter, of course, and Flannery didn't get invited there on account of him keeping the saloon and all. And besides, he didn't like the monsignor and Cahill knew it.

"But I was there many's the time, myself," Mike said, "and I've got to be honest with you, Jerry, that man set a fine table and he poured a good drink, too. 'Holy water,' he called it, and it was always Canadian Club or some of that good scotch when you could get it, Haig and Haig or something along that line.

"He was a good man, Jerry," Mike said. "And that's what I mean, about the things that we just took for granted, the way Frank Tobin did and he didn't make sure Kitty was gonna be all right and taken care of, if something was to happen to him. Here he was, in the insurance business, and he had no insurance to speak of for his own wife and family. Of course the family was pretty much grown, Frank being close to seventy when he died, the boys all well established with their own occupations as it were, and one of the girls with the Sisters of the Visitation, but the house didn't bring much in that neighborhood by then and Kitty had to live somewhere, didn't she? And of course the boys all had families of their own, that they were taking care of, so they did what they could for her, but it was a hard life, nevertheless.

"Now you see, Jerry, that's what's happened. It used to be, when Curley was in office, and, well, it was the same way down at Jack Lacey's office, when

I called him, that you took care of your own, you know? And we assumed that. If Monsignor Cahill was still alive there would be a place for Kitty Tobin, and if there wasn't, he would know somebody, and that was the way it was. But now with this welfare thing and all, and the terrible way the kids're fallin' away from the church and everything, why, we've just *fallen apart,* my friend. We expect the government to do everything for us now, and the coons and the spics're just takin' advantage of everything, the stuff we should be keepin' for ourselves and givin' to our own kind instead of payin' all of it in taxes so them lazy niggers can loaf around all day."

Saigon came trotting across the sand to where I sat. "Dad," she said, "you've got a call."

"Tell them I waded out to sea and didn't come back," I said. "I'm on vacation." I knew it wouldn't work. Gretchen doesn't give out the unlisted number. If I had a call, it was from somebody important enough to me to have gotten it from me.

"It's Mister Kidd," she said.

"Ah, shit," I said. I stood up. "I gotta go, Mike."

Mike straightened up with some difficulty. "It's all right, young fellow," he said, "I was finished."

Saigon took my chair, and I went back to the house.

I sat on the tan vinyl couch with a fresh beer in my hand and picked up the handset of the phone. "You should've let me call you back, Roger," I said, "keep you waiting like this. I was over at the beach." Roger's secretary thanked me for responding so quickly, and I had to repeat the whole spiel to Roger.

"Forget it," Roger said. "I know how you feel. I was down at Chatham myself for the week, and then this damned thing came up and I had to come back up for it. I think I need some help, Jerry."

"What's the trouble?" I said.

"I'd rather not tell you on the phone," Roger said.

"Oh, for heaven's sake, Roger," I said. "This's an unlisted phone, not that anybody'd want to hear what

I have to say anyway. And your phones must be secure. Spit it out."

"I really don't want to talk about it on the phone," Roger said.

"How soon?" I said.

"This morning would've been better," Roger said.

I sighed.

"I know, I know," Roger said, "it's my vacation too."

"Okay," I said. "I'll have to get cleaned up though, and it'll take me a while to get there."

"I'd appreciate that," Roger said. "I'll keep everybody here."

I wrote a note for Mack—she's used to these sudden departures, unfortunately—and got into the shower. I was covered with soap when the phone rang again. Hoping against hope that it would be Roger, canceling the conference, I climbed out and tracked water into the living room. The call was from Gretchen. Teddy Franklin had phoned in a state of rage. All she knew was that he was in the Dedham jail, and would wait for me there. I told her to get a message to him that she had called me at home and learned that I was on my way to an urgent conference in Boston, where she would reach me and give me the message she had just given me. Then I went back into the shower and rinsed off, wondering if perhaps Monsignor Cahill, up in heaven, was getting even with me for missing Mass, and if not, why my clients could not stay out of trouble during August.

6

IF YOU START out at the Parker House and walk southwest on Tremont Street, you will pass the Park Street Congregational Church on the right and then you will come to the Boston Common. Jaywalking across, you will be on the northwestern side of Tremont, and you will be able to dodge panhandlers, grifters, young lovers and pigeons to your heart's content, all the way down Lafayette Mall to the corner of Tremont and Boylston. If you want to get blown, you can go hang around the public johns. If you want a paper, a joint, a good watch cheap or something presented as food that you really should not eat, you can get it on the mall. You can also get some diseases that will cause every restaurateur in town to put an out-of-order sign on his men's room the minute you enter his establishment, but if that is the kind of action which you have in mind, it is all right with me. Particularly if you get arrested, and need a good lawyer.

You cannot see the New Courthouse, now about forty years old, to the northeast behind the State House, as you walk down the mall, listening to earnest young people destroying perfectly good music on clarinets and flutes, but I can. The Boston Municipal Court is in there. That is where I make the rent and Gretchen's salary. So is Suffolk Superior, where I make the suit money and the cash for a Grand Prix and Heather's tuition.

If you make it through the human obstacles you will encounter on the mall, you will come to the corner of Tremont and Boylston. Behind you there will be a subway kiosk. (You will note that I have given you good instructions, thus far, on how to reach my office. This is because you may get in the shit some day, and need a good lawyer quick. The instructions will become more precise still.) Cross Boylston, leaving the Masonic Building on your left and the condominium building across the street from it—that building was the Hotel Touraine when I started out—and take a right. Enter the first door on your left. This is 80 Boylston Street. The law offices of Jeremiah F. Kennedy are on the sixth floor of the old building. Use the elevator.

Don't touch anything in the elevator except the button. Touch the button with your elbow. Almost all of my clients use the elevator (except for Curly, who was afraid of height but not of burglar alarms, and was always getting caught on the first floor of a dwelling in the nighttime, charged with breaking and entering said dwelling in the nighttime with intent to commit larceny therein, with the result that Curly became quite familiar with the layout of the Massachusetts Correctional Institution at Concord, but not before paying me about $17,000 in fees. Curly used the stairs), and leave the elevator car promptly when it reaches the sixth floor, because the cars are new and programmed to waste no time—they'll clip your ass off, if you linger. As you emerge from the elevator, look for the sign with my name on it. Follow the arrow down past the law offices of Weldon Cooper—he doesn't practice the kind of law that you need practiced anyway, so I am not taking anything away from him—and come into my office at the end of the hall.

If there are clients waiting to see me (as there probably will be, because, like all lawyers, I have a Very Busy Practice), you will not notice the furniture. I am virtually certain of this. The majority of my clients may fully warrant Mack's view that my practice is sleazy, but one thing may not be taken away from them: they are as colorful as a Grand National Stock

Car Race, a fire in a Mexican whorehouse and a Massachusetts Democratic primary. All at once.

For the moment, should any be sitting there, ignore the small, creepy-looking man with the harelip (Dingbat, as he is known on the street; he's a shoplifter), the small white lady with her arm in a sling and her foot room reduced by her four shopping bags full of papers, and the strange-looking kid. The lady would be Frances Gibbons, who is nuts, but fairly well-to-do, coming in to report the newest electronic transmission to her brain by her estranged husband. The weird-looking kid could be any one of hundreds—I get a fair number of small-time druggies and pushers, because I do a good job for them at a reasonable rate and word gets around. If there should be any flashy-looking women on the premises, whom you suspect to be whores, you are entirely right, but you will be safe enough—all hookers seeking my legal services are strictly advised that they are neither to solicit nor to mug any other client or visitor to my office while said visitor or client is physically present in my office; on the street, you are on your own, same as everybody else.

If the riffraff, the flotsam and the jetsam of the human race happen not to be sitting in the reception area wearing expressions either of boredom or haughtiness, notice first the comfortable chairs, which are upholstered tastefully in orange plastic. It is grained, like alligator hide. They have chromium arms and little pieces of wood notched over the chrome. There are six of them, and they are the most godawful-looking things ever peddled in a discount lumber yard. I got them for nothing in money, but much in effort. I represented Dr. Edward Carey, an M.D. from Weymouth, one month after I opened the office and was in serious need to do something about the bill for the hideous furniture I was renting until I could buy something. That stuff was upholstered in green tweed, and it had been rented out before. A lot. The trouble was that the rental bill prevented me from buying anything.

Dr. Carey was a man of very poor judgment. Close to fifty, he had abandoned his wife to shack up with a beautician about thirty, twice-divorced, whom he had met at the Wonderland Dog Track one night. His wife got herself a divorce lawyer with three rows of teeth, who pretty much took care of Dr. Carey's wagering money in the divorce action. Dr. Carey then compounded his mistakes by marrying the beautician, who chewed gum and used bad language. Her name was Clemmie, and she knew a lot of people. She knew more people than most governors of populous states can claim to know. She knew several who had advice for Dr. Carey on how to repair his foundering financial situation. Dr. Carey took to writing prescriptions.

Dr. Carey wrote a lot of prescriptions. Many of them, if not close to all of them, were for people whom he had not diagnosed, or, indeed, even examined. He had never laid eyes on them in his life. He seldom knew their names. The names he wrote on the prescriptions were real, but they were names that happened to be listed in the South Suburban phone book. The people who got the prescriptions filled were not the same. The prescriptions were for such substances as Quaalude and methamphetamine. In Boston's Combat Zone just a hop, skip and high from my office, a "Doctor Carey" was worth a hundred dollars on the street, just before he got caught. He was getting twenty. That was good money—he was writing them faster than the dogs could run at Wonderland. The ones he bet on, at least. He could do five scrips in a minute. A hundred bucks a minute is good pay.

The trouble was the Drug Enforcement Administration had its minions out on the street, and Dr. Carey's customers were too addled to think about what they were saying to those shaggy-looking guys who somehow were much clearer in the head than a real Head should be. Pretty soon Dr. Carey had a whole bunch of State cops rummaging around in his Weymouth office,

waving search warrants at Dr. Carey's personal lawyer, Roger Kidd, who went to law school with me and
did real-estate law and estate planning and no other
law at all. Roger called me, and I got the doctor
bailed, using the services of Walter "Termite" Green,
who got his name for precisely the reason that you
would expect—he looks like one.

The doctor was not popular with the cops, Staties
or Feds. They had a hard-on for him, and in a trice
he was under indictment in the United States District
Court for trafficking in controlled substances. I took
the proceeds of his retirement plan for that one, but
since his first wife had pretty much cleaned it out in
the divorce, that didn't give me enough for a year of
political fund raisers. Then he got belted by the Suffolk
County grand jury for a number of small accommo-
dations he had made for people who came up to him
in a seedy lounge in Boston, and the Norfolk County
grand jury chimed in with a few allegations about
some of his hobbies in Weymouth. By the time Termite finished with him, the only thing he had left was
his office furniture and the indictments. I took the furniture, as the rest of the price for taking the indictments. Dr. Carey had lousy taste in furniture, but it
was no worse than his taste in women, friends or
trades suitable for moonlighting, and having his furniture meant I could get that goddamned rental stuff off
my hands. Besides, I figured that any furniture sturdy
enough to endure the abuse which must have been
given it by Dr. Carey's patients would probably be
able to withstand even the damage certain to be inflicted on it by my clients.

Dr. Carey got six years, all tolled, and did more
than three of them. The beautician divorced him while
he was in the jug and took his apartment furniture.
The last I heard, he was a minister in the Universal
Life Church, where the divinity degree costs ten
bucks, counseling inmates seeking Jesus in the max-
imum security unit at Folsom.

Having cast your practiced eye on the furniture,

take a glance at Gretchen. Gretchen looks like a lady
with a few miles on her. The reason for this, as we say
in the law, is not far to seek: that is precisely what
she is. She is now about thirty-seven, completely unconcerned about the problems that a woman of thirty-
seven can expect from a figure that must have had
the boys running around in the shrubbery like randy
warthogs when she was seventeen. Twenty years is a
long time for a woman who must have needed C cups
when she was seventeen, particularly if she has used
those years to acquire and shed two husbands and
at least three lovers that I know about, and has been
consequently distracted from the effects upon her appearance of a great many hamburgers, cheeseburgers, pizzas, root beers, draft beers and Beefeater
martinis on the rocks. Gretchen is also not a bad hand
with a slab of roast beef, as I can attest from personal observation of her enthusiasm for the dish at
her annual visit with me to Victoria Station, during
National Secretaries Week. Gretchen disdained the
bunch of roses that I bought from the vendor on the
Common to take note of the first of those goddamned
weeks that she brought to my attention; she told me
she could not eat roses. She can sure eat roast beef,
though. She can put away a prime rib like Jim Ed
Rice puts away a high fast ball. The baked potato
filled with sour cream disappears simultaneously. She
doesn't seem to pay much attention to that, or the
plate of salad with Russian dressing, or the rolls
and butter. It's just that when the waitress comes to
clear the dishes away, the salad and the rolls are gone,
and there is damned straight little remaining of the
potato, too, because Gretchen is fond of the skins.

Now I do not mean to imply that Gretchen is fat.
She has every right to be, I guess, but she is not. For
one thing, she is a big woman anyway, about five-
eight, with a large frame. She can carry a good
amount of meat around on her without seeming corpulent. For another thing, she has what appears to
be a good metabolism; what she would not burn off

anyway, getting her two sons ready for school, coming in to work for me, getting home in time to cook dinner for them, herself, and whatever male happens to be sharing quarters and her bed, she seems to use up just being around. It takes a lot of gas to run a big car, and it takes a lot of chow to run Gretchen. But not as much chow as Gretchen takes in; she is not fat, but she is of generous proportions, at least, and I have heard her described as overweight.

This has not destroyed her ability to attract men. "Of course," as she has said. "it might be better if it did, considering all the ones I get seem to have something wrong with them. I mean: besides wives and other girlfriends." I always disagree with Gretchen when she says that. Gretchen is difficult enough just being Gretchen. Gretchen horny would be more than I could stand.

Gretchen will greet you courteously, though, whether on the telephone or in person. She will probably not tell you to go shit in your hat the first time; only if she decides that you are pretty much satisfactory to her as a human being, and require some intermittent shaping-up. Weldon Cooper has been conducting a flirtation with Gretchen for years. He regularly receives profane advice from Gretchen, which he deserves.

If you visit the office, and you have an appointment, Gretchen will announce you at the door to my office. We have an intercom which neither of us ever uses. We communicate between her desk and mine by shouting. Neither of us has ever been able to perceive any utility to adding the motions of picking up the handsets and pushing buzzer buttons in order to convey by such effort the same words and information easily transmitted without raising the voice very high, or putting down whatever work one has in hand at the moment.

In my office you will see on the walls my diplomas from Boston College and the Boston College Law School. I think the display of diplomas, certificates of

admission to practice before the Supreme Judicial
Court of Massachusetts, Federal District Court, Federal
Circuit Court of Appeals and United States Supreme
Court is tacky. Mine are all exhibited, along
with my membership certificates in the ABA, Massachusetts
Bar Association, Boston Bar Association,
Norfolk County Bar Association, Massachusetts Academy
of Trial Attorneys, American Trial Lawyers
and American Criminal Defense Lawyers. The certificate
from the ABA is framed—all of them are—
and glassed, and every year I put another little gold
sticker on the glass, showing that I am still a member.
The certificates have blue ribbons, green ribbons and
red ribbons on them. There is a possibility that they
do what they are supposed to do, which is reassure
skeptical clients that in fact I am a lawyer, Gretchen,
furniture and all other visible evidence to the contrary.

If you could see my desk, you would see that it is
a pretty good one. I got it cheap from the estate of an
old Yankee who had practiced law on it in Braintree
and evidently did not put his feet on it. It has a
leather top which I have not seen for years, because
I am a sloppy worker and feel employed only when
surrounded by piles of letters, briefs and lawbooks.
There are some scratches on the sides of the desk;
I had a bitch of a time getting it up the freight elevator
and into the office, and I scraped it a few times.

I have four blue upholstered chairs that I bought
from Pray's, which went out of business, probably
for selling stuff like those blue chairs. I have an
Oriental rug which perhaps saw better days, but is
definitely not enjoying them now; I got that from
under the dead Yankee's desk.

There is a beaten-up library table under the window
with the iron grating that looks out on the air
shaft—the old Yankee preserved the desk by working
on the table, apparently—and the table, too, is stacked
with papers, many of which have been there for years.
I have a picture of a clipper ship on the wall facing

my desk, which I purchased from the estate. I think the old bastard framed a calendar illustration, but I've never cared enough to inspect it. It looks okay, and it only cost two dollars; the frame alone's worth more than that.

I have a radio on the small credenza next to my desk, so that I can hear a little music or a ballgame now and then, and an antique clock that probably didn't work when the Yankee had it. In the corner farthest from my desk is a small iron safe, to which the executor of the estate gave me the combination. I can't open it, but it looks official and I leave it there.

I have no pictures of Mack or Saigon, because I love them too much to let some of my clients get any idea of what they look like; I never discuss my family with my clients, where we live, how many of us there are, or anything else. I'm sure most have surmised that I am divorced, or else that I never married. Fine by me; sometimes I part company with those clients under acrimonious circumstances, and have to remove the Smith & Wesson .38 Chief's Special from the bottom drawer of the desk, strap it on and wear it for three months or so. I am, by the way, an unusually good shot, for a man who never hunted and was never in the service. A man would be a fool to tackle some of the stuff I do, unarmed, and an even bigger fool to do so without having spent a number of hours in a combat crouch at the South Weymouth Sportsman's Club range.

Roger Kidd knows all of this, and does not hold it against me. Unlike most who have had a few advantages, Roger is the same tolerant fellow he was when thrown in with me before he was in a position to make use of his own advantages, but preparing himself to do so. Roger's family has been well-to-do for generations, English Catholics who somehow retained favor with the Crown notwithstanding their refusal to renounce Rome. They accepted grants of colonial land, emigrated, laid low during the Revolution and offended no one thereafter. Some of the males went into the church, while others served with distinction as officers and directors of trust companies and savings banks in the suburbs west of Boston. Since they never challenged the Brahmins for the turf, they were accepted by the Brahmins as controlling their own turf, and they were able to form alliances. I don't believe Roger has ever offended anybody in his life, not even by accident.

Ensconced in precisely the sort of quiet Catholic firm for which he had prepared at Cranwell, Holy Cross and BC Law School, Roger two years into practice sought me out when Kincaid, Bailey & Kincaid found itself quite appalled by Dr. Edward Carey's mounting difficulties. His divorce had been unseemly enough so that they had farmed that out. Now he was in the grief with the authorities, and damned near broke, as well. Clearly, though his estate had been carefully planned by Kincaid, Bailey & Kincaid, only to be ruined by Carey, it was time for them to obtain new counsel to represent him. Roger sold me to them on the ground that I was so hungry that I had to be cheap, and cheap was the best that Carey could do.

Cheap, I think, was all that they hoped for. But they got a little bit more. When Carey ended up doing six, I was a hero. The betting had been a fat twenty, and drawing and quartering thereafter. Kincaids look upon the criminal side with the same distaste that I reserve for their discreet civil practice: I am glad that there is someone else around to handle such tiresome matters, because I certainly do not wish to handle them myself; the first time such a client heard Gretchen mutter *"Fuck"* after striking the wrong key, or Cooper whack the common wall to let me know that he was in, and to receive his answering whack, the poor devils would faint dead away. And the Kincaids, good burghers that they are, grew up convinced that anyone charged with a crime probably deserved even worse. All they wanted was to be rid of Carey; all I wanted was to get some clients before Saigon, Mack and I starved to death.

That happy symbiotic relationship continued. When Roger got a nasty little problem from an orthodontist who had been arrested for driving under the influence and driving to endanger, as well as drunkenness, in Dedham, Roger called me. He was confident that I could get the fellow off, but less so, as it turned out, when I told him that the doctor had drawn the attention of the police by ramming their cruiser with his Porsche. To put it bluntly, I clean up after Roger's clients, and thus after Roger, and I have received many a damned good fee from it. I am more than happy to continue doing so, because what I did for Dr. Carey not only solidified the bond between Roger's office and mine, so that I continued to receive the stuff that smelled to them like catshit, but brought me to the respectful acquaintance of a number of folk who had manipulated Dr. Carey, and numerous other personages, each of those manipulators being engaged in the sort of trade that leads to a steady business for a capable criminal lawyer.

You don't need any directions to Roger's office on Beacon Street. If you're in the sort of mess that would prompt you to come and see me, you can come directly to me, without wasting Roger's time visiting him and then getting directions to my office.

If you are in a mess, and you go to see Roger, obviously you already know how to find Roger, and he will tell you how to find me. He will tell you because if you are in the kind of difficulty that causes Roger to send people to see me, he will not be able to get you out of his office fast enough. He will give you very clear directions. He will point across the Common to the very building where I am located. He will have his secretary—who does not approve of me at all, but regards me as a factotum similar to the garbage man, useful for the performance of certain unsavory tasks, much as a Mass. General cardiologist would contemplate an Army doctor unaccountably turning up at a dinner party in Pride's Crossing—call my office to make sure I am in, and if I am not, to make a firm appointment for you when I will be in. Anything to get you out of that converted town house, where the heat of the August afternoon is blocked by the white floor-to-ceiling drapes and the grandfather clocks chime on each of the three floors of the firm.

If you wander into Roger's office with a disagreeable case of statutory rape pending against you, because you finally gave in to the babysitter who showed you everything but California for the third weekend in a row as you were driving her home after a long and liquid cocktail party, they will do something that will make the bum's rush seem leisurely. They will fumigate the joint before you can reach the Parkman Bandstand.

Kincaids do not associate with roughnecks any more than necessary; when you see me walking in, you know that they think you to be roustabout, and have matched us up like a computer dating service, so as to get rid of you. They call me in to get you out—it's as simple as that. Because if Mrs. Wombat ever arrived to review her trusts and found you sitting there in odoriferous disgrace, she would recoil in horror from the mere scent of your turpitude, and take her lucrative business elsewhere. She wouldn't like me much, either.

Roger's secretary's name is Grace, and she has some sort of congenital facial paralysis which prevents her from smiling. Her lips are thinner than onionskin and she must let her red hair down before she goes to bed at night—alone, of course; no man with a cock of girth greater than an ice pick could ever get it into her, if the cellar door's no wider than her mouth is, and besides which, she almost certainly has teeth in there as well—because she could not possibly shut her eyes with her face pulled back like that into the bun. I first met Grace three hundred years ago, when Roger went to work for Kincaid and I was starting out at Culp & Hurley. I didn't like her very much, on sight, and when Roger got a couple in the boot one night at my house (Roger does not do that anymore, since he made partner), and told me candidly what old Grace thought of me, I revised my opinion. I revised it downward.

Since then I have needled her at every opportunity, figuring that no desiccated bitch who calls me vulgar on the strength of one encounter can be very much shocked by a solicitous inquiry as to whether she has recovered from her piles, and would indeed be disappointed if I did not ask her if that non-existent deposit, on her pure silk blouse from Bonwit's, was snot. I don't like Grace, and Grace don't like me. When Roger has pleaded with me to go a little easier on her, I have taken note of our long friendship and given him an irrefutable explanation of why I cannot promise that. "No," I say. "That woman is a lousy cunt, and anything I can do to piss her off is little enough. My duty to the human race."

I walked up the circular stairway, sweating like a $7,500 horse entered in a $10,000 claiming race, and finishing about where such a horse would finish in such company, to find Grace at her semicircular desk in her smart new suit, tapping her pencil on the leather blotter and looking annoyed. I don't know whether she could smell me or something else had wrecked her digestion, but I did not get the impression that I was the highlight of her day.

"Hello, Grace," I said.

Grace glared at me. "Yess?" she said. Grace can make four syllables out of "yes."

I glared at Grace. "I haven't propositioned you yet," I said. "I'm not liable to, either. I'd rather stick it into one of those electric pencil sharpeners they're making now."

"I'd rather you did, too," Grace said, sweetly.

"You and the pencil sharpener and I'd enjoy it a lot more, I'm sure," I said. "Buzz Roger for me."

"Mister Kidd has a client with him," Grace said.

"No shit," I said. "Did I ask you if he was in there reading the *Wall Street Journal?* Forget the names and numbers of the starting players. Buzz Roger."

"Mister Kidd is *busy,"* she said, with satisfaction.

"Mister Kidd called Mister Kennedy and interrupted his vacation to drag him up here and help Mister Kidd," I said. "As you perfectly well know, since you were the one that placed the call. Why don't you eat a freight car full of prunes and improve your disposition?"

"I don't have to take this from you," she said. I love it when I get to Grace. I don't think anybody else ever does.

"No," I said, "you don't. You choose to, because when I ask you to buzz Roger for me, you give me a whole bunch of crap. It's not my goddamned fault that you're not getting laid and had the whole thing turn to calcium. All I want from you is for you to buzz Roger. Work your frustrations out on some other man. If you know one."

I really don't know what Grace was about to say. Her face was sunset red and blood vessels were pounding in her temples when Roger came out of his office the way Ellis Kinder used to come out of the Red Sox bullpen. I guess Grace and I had been chatting a little more loudly than I'd noticed, because Roger looked like a Cardinal caught in a whorehouse.

"What the hell is going on out here?" he said. Through the open, paneled door to his office, I could see a gentleman of about fifty, who had spent a lot of money carefully on himself, and the left foot, Gucci-shod, of another man otherwise outside of my vision.

"Mister Kennedy was being very unpleasant, Mister Kidd," Grace said.

"Oh, my God," Roger said. "Come on in, Jerry." Roger allowed his shoulders to slump and walked back into his office. I waited until his body blocked the vision of the fellow with a lot of money, and gave Grace the finger. She said, "Mister *Kidd.*" Roger said, "Hold my calls, Grace." I went into his office.

Richard Teller wore a suit from H. Freeman & Sons, rather fine shoes, a becoming tan and his years very well. There was just the edge of a smirk on his face. Needing all the business I can get, I was glad to see that my blazer and slacks from Jordan Marsh confirmed his suspicions. That was good. It was good because it caused him to deduce that I was at home in the trenches, where they have no cut-glass decanters as fine as the one full of port in Roger's office—it has been full ever since the day he filled it; Roger doesn't pour anything stronger than coffee in his office. It was also good because it made him think that I would be cheap. Richard Teller was several years late for cheap, but I would explain that misfortune to him when we got to it.

Roger introduced me to Richard Teller. Then he made it clear that I should turn around toward the chair where reposed the body that had the Gucci loafer on the left foot. "And this is Emerson Teller," Roger said.

Daddy's suit may have been a customized Freeman, but Emerson's was strictly custom, all the way, made to his measure in the continental style. The waist of the coat was nipped in, and the handkerchief-weight gray-pinstriped silk draped faultlessly when he stood up. I got a glimpse of the Piaget wristwatch with the lapis-lazuli dial and the encircling diamonds on the bezel. The pale blue shirt was silk and there was an Yves St. Laurent trademark on his necktie. It would not have surprised me if he smelled of Opium or Patou's Joy, but his only scent was something that I could not identify. While we shook hands, I noticed his Vuitton shoulder bag on the Oriental carpet next to his chair. I objected to none of this.

I took the chair that Roger pushed between those occupied by Richard and his son, folded my hands in my lap, and put on an inquiring expression. Roger began. He said he had already described our long friendship to Richard and Emerson Teller, and had told them some of the "uh, sensitive matters" I had handled for Kincaid. I did not say anything. I do not get to roll around in money very often, but I recognize that aroma very well, too, and it was strong in my nostrils. I sneaked a look at Richard, who was clearly the treasurer of this operation. The smirk was still there.

Roger decided to introduce a note of levity, since I did not seem likely to contribute anything immediately. "Richard, Emerson, as you have, ah, *heard,* Jerry doesn't get along swimmingly with my secretary."

That sounded like an opening, but not for me. I was doing fairly well, saying nothing, so I kept my inquiring look, glanced at Emerson and glanced at Richard. Richard was having trouble with the smirk by then. It was breaking out on him like teen-age acne, and he was commensurately successful at controlling it. Richard spoke while I was finishing my visual sweep. I swung back to him. "You dislike Grace?" he said.

"Not at all," I said. "I hate her guts. She's rude, snide, uncooperative and deliberately obstructionist. Roger calls me up and she blocks my calls back. Grace is a tiresome old cunt and if I didn't know it was a felony, I would blow her up."

Richard's eyebrows went up. He nodded, once. He looked at Roger. He nodded again. "He'll do," he said.

Roger explained: "Richard doesn't like Grace either."

"Grace doesn't like Richard very much, for that matter," Richard said. "Welcome aboard." He extended his hand.

I was doing too well to change my act. "Aboard what?" I said.

Roger again explained. "Emerson needs a lawyer. A criminal lawyer." So far, Richard, Roger and I had utterly ignored Emerson. I thought it time to repair that oversight. I looked at Emerson. Emerson looked at me. Emerson lit a Dunhill cigarette with a Du Pont lighter. He reached into his handbag and brought out a pair of aviator sunglasses with pink lenses. He put them on and looked at me through them and the Dunhill smoke. I looked at Roger and then I looked at Richard. I said, "Yeah?"

"We called you," Roger said, getting damned straight little help from Richard, and none at all from Emerson, "because we, I, think you're the best man available for the case."

I thought Roger had worked hard enough on this thing. After all, he is an old friend, and he had interrupted his vacation too. I needed him a few times, and he needed me now. "What's the case?" I said. "Willful and malicious arrogance? Felonious muteness? Tort for being born without a tongue? This guy's the client, you do the talking, Richard joins in on the chorus? What's the goddamned story? I was sitting on the beach and you called me and I come tearing up here like Sergeant York to save a guy that I don't even know, and the guy won't even talk to me?" I knew very well that Richard was in full smirk by then, but I did not look at him. I looked at Emerson, hiding behind his shades and his imported-cigarette smoke. "You got a problem, kid?" I said.

Emerson had clearly not been so displeased since his couturier shipped the wrong shade of rouge. "I didn't think it was anything serious," he said, "until you came into it."

Now I had a number of lines about that one, and I have a fast larynx. But Richard Teller is a lot richer than I am, and it may be partly because he's got a tongue on him like a lion-tamer's whip. I was still looking at Emerson when Richard started talking. I continued to look at Emerson while Richard talked. It did not take Richard very long. I use a broadaxe, but Richard is a surgeon. He does not even raise his voice.

"That was what bothered Roger and me, Em," he said. "Your serenity in this matter. That was why we imposed upon Mister Kennedy to interrupt his vacation and attend this conference on short notice. You didn't seem to think this little difficulty was particularly distressing. You did seem to think that it was a matter of interest to me and Roger, but none to yourself. Your error is in overlooking the fact that you are the one nominated for jail. Not Roger and not me. I would prefer that you not go to jail, and Roger is of the same mind. You might enjoy jail, but I would find your incarceration embarrassing. Even if you might welcome it, I would prefer that it not occur. Roger felt that perhaps Mister Kennedy might be able to keep you out of jail. Mister Kennedy, as you will recall Roger assuring us, will do anything that Roger asks, because he is an old and responsible friend."

"Who owes Roger one hell of a lot," I said.

"Who's indebted to Roger," Richard said. "Roger is cashing his Kennedy chits endorsed payable to me, and I am trying to negotiate them over to you. You can accept them or not, just as you choose. But you won't enjoy jail, Emerson. It does not approach the comfort that you take for granted."

"Oh, very *well*," Emerson said. "What do you *want*?"

"*I* don't want *any*thing," I said. "I had what I wanted. I was sitting on the beach, having a beer, talking to friends who don't have to be coaxed to talk to me, patting my wife on the ass every so often and thinking about taking a nap in the sun. On a long list of things I *didn't* want, close to the top was a call from Roger, the gist of which was *Mayday*. The problem with Roger's *Mayday* calls is that when Roger sends out an SOS, just like your father says, I have to respond. Roger would come if I called, and when Roger calls, I come, like it, lump it or stick it. But I don't want anything.

"What you want," I said, "is a different matter. I dunno you. I've survived pretty well, not knowing you. You've survived pretty well, not knowing me. Apparently you've got a little problem right now. I've known Roger for a long time. Richard I dunno at all. You, I'm not sure I wanna know. But Roger seems to think you've got a little problem. When Roger calls me with a *Mayday*, my experience indicates the subject has a little problem. If Roger's wrong, I'll leave and go back to the beach. If Roger's right, then you got to decide what you want. You want tangerine sections and pekoe tea served on your tray by room service, overlooking the pool, see a travel agent or call the concierge where you stayed the last time. You want a long lease on a cell in the slammer, do what you want. You wanna talk to me, talk to me. But understand you're spending Roger's credit, and he's billing it to Richard."

"Richard is my father," Emerson said.

"Kinda figured he was," I said. "That's not gonna get you out of jail. And being surly isn't, either, if it means you're too fine to talk to somebody that honored a lot of obligations because the obligors asked him to talk to you."

"And you think you can get this cleared up?" Emerson said.

"Get *what* cleared up, you little cocksucker," I said. "What're you charged with? Regicide? Treason? Double-parking? Following too close? Molesting a hairdresser or bothering a beautician? How the fuck do I know if I can get you off? Which is what you mean, in case you didn't know it. I'm a lawyer. I try cases. That's all I do. I don't fix oil burners and I don't do any dowsing if your well runs dry. Did you put Jack Ruby up to it? Where the hell is Jimmy Hoffa, anyway? You're wasting my goddamned time. You're not interviewing me—I'm interviewing you."

Richard cleared his throat. Roger did not need the warning. His face was white. He could not have spoken if he had desired to. Richard's voice was smooth and his expression was composed. I don't think Richard had had such a good time in a long time. "Emerson," Richard said, "is charged with . . . Emerson was arrested by a State Police officer who said that Emerson asked him to blow him, and offered to blow the trooper in return. I see no need to beat around the bush on this, so to speak, Mister Kennedy. Do you?"

Emerson now had an expression of great superiority on his face. If the equator is an imaginary line around the middle of the earth, then Emerson's difficulties were his way of getting back at Richard. For what, I did not know. I found out, though. I said, "No."

"Emerson," Richard said, "is twenty-eight years old."

"I doubt it," I said.

"So do I," Richard said. "But Emerson's mother has the birth certificate, and I seem vaguely to recall both her and him, so it may very well be true." I was beginning to get a glimmer of the reason for Emerson's affection for Richard. "He doesn't act like it, but life's a history of disappointed expectations." For the first time, I felt a certain sympathy for Emerson. I did not let it show.

"Emerson is not asking for the impossible," Richard said. "All Emerson wants is total commitment to his cause. The best you can. That's all. If he's convicted, he's convicted. If he's acquitted, he's acquitted. What will it cost?"

Emerson sat there like one of those old highway flare pots that were black and burned kerosene and sent up clouds of smoke when the crews lighted them at construction areas before they left work in the afternoon. The kind you stole, when you were in college, and used to drive the mosquitoes and yourself out of your back yard on summer evenings. I did not have a glimmer of sympathy for Richard now—I felt sorry for the poor kid. He was a case of arrested development, and he was getting revenge for a lot of things about which I knew no specifics, but I could imagine what they were. It must be hard to be a kid in that position.

"I dunno," I said.

"Will you take the case?" Richard said.

"Mister Teller," I said, "I don't know. And I won't know until I talk to the potential client. In *my* office. By *my*self. Without you or Roger or anybody else, good-hearted, well-intentioned and protective as you all may be. If I get this kid in the bucket, he'll be the one that goes. Not me, not Roger and not you. So why don't you let me talk to him, and let him talk to me?"

"And then you can tell me what it will cost," Richard said.

"No," I said.

"Well," Richard said, "of course, Roger always knows how to get in touch with me. The marine operator . . ."

"No," I said. "Roger's tail's not in the crack, and you look reasonably content to me. If I decide I'm willing to represent Emerson, I'll tell Emerson, and I'll tell Emerson what it will cost. If Emerson wants me to represent him, he'll tell me, and he'll get the money some place."

"Emerson doesn't have any money," Richard said. "He'll have to get it from me."

"Richard," I said, "I don't give a shit if he gets it out of the mad money he keeps in his panty girdle. If I represent Emerson, Emerson pays me. If I represent you, you pay me. If I represent Emerson, Emerson pays me. Any questions?"

Richard said, "No."

I said, "I do. Emerson, you wanna talk to me?"

Emerson said, "Yes."

I said, "Nine o'clock tomorrow morning. My office. Nobody else." I gave him the directions. "I'll be late. You be on time and wait for me. Your problem's screwing up my vacation. I don't care what it's doing to your life, and I dunno how long it's gonna take me to get to the office from my summer house. I don't do it any more often than I can help, and I've had better luck in past years. You gonna be there?"

"Yes," Emerson said.

"Good," I said. "If I think I can stand you, I may take your case. If I don't, I won't. Fair enough?"

"Yes," Emerson said.

"Roger," I said.

"Yes," Roger said.

"Buzz that cunt out there and ask her what she did with the message she got about two hours ago that I just remembered I never got from Gretchen."

Roger got the message from Grace. I went out of Roger's office like an Apollo moon shot. Teddy Franklin was still at the Dedham jail, and now they were threatening to arrest *him*. For the second time. What interested me was the identity of the person they had arrested earlier.

7

I HAVE KNOWN Paul Finney since 1970, I think it was, when he was the arresting officer on one of the most appalling motor vehicle cases I have ever handled. Paul was first on the scene of a wreck on the hill on East Street in Dedham. When he got there, it looked like a pretty inconsequential matter. Some drunk had whipped his Chevy wagon around the curve too fast and walloped an unoccupied Olds convertible parked at the curb. The Olds slammed forward against the tailgate of a Dodge wagon in front of it. The Chevy driver looked all right; though he was staggering around and mumbling, it was not so much from the effects of the crash as from the hooch he had swallowed down at the Eagles' hall before heading home. The woman who had parked the Olds looked pretty upset. "But otherwise," Paul told me, "it looked like a straight property damage case, driving under, driving to endanger, and DK." DK is drunk. "What I couldn't understand was why the woman couldn't talk, and who was doing all that moaning. It was John Giametti."

John Giametti was a rookie on the Dedham police force with Paul Finney. He was twenty-three years old, a veteran slightly wounded in Vietnam, recently married to a pretty girl who was very, very pregnant. He was also a decent kid, and therefore delayed his arrival at home, after finishing his shift, to assist a female motorist who had had a flat tire on East Street. He had pulled in in front of her car, opened the tailgate of his Dodge station wagon, and used his jack and tools to change the left rear tire on her car. He was bending over the open tailgate—it opened down—and stowing his jack when the drunk hit the Olds and scissored Giametti's legs against the edge of the tailgate. Both legs were amputated, just above the knee.

The drunk was also a misfortunate wreck. I've forgotten his last name, but Cosmo was an immigrant from Greece who had come to this country around 1930 and gone into the painting business. He worked hard all day, and he raised his family of five children creditably. He was good to his wife and unlike most painters and contractors, he kept his own property up. Until he hit the Olds, he had never had any contact with the police, not even so much as a speeding ticket. The only evil thing that Cosmo ever did was drink too much at the Eagles' hall before dutifully hurrying home to be in time for dinner, and that was how John Giametti, pausing on the way home to *his* dinner, lost his legs.

I was apprehensive when I went to the Dedham police station to look at the records, after Cosmo hired me. This was partly because Cosmo, after nearly forty years in America, still did not speak English very well, and had brought his wife, Thea, who spoke no English at all, to assist him at the interview. Her contribution consisted mostly of crying and shouting. After an hour of useless effort to find out what the hell had happened, I knew less than when I started. I concluded that if Cosmo had not blacked out before the accident, and had an actual recollection of what had occurred, his English would prevent him from reporting it. The only way I was going to be able to get the facts in the case was by looking at the police reports.

Now that is a dodgy business in any case. Unless the cop in question knows you, he is going to be very reluctant to let you see his reports until after he has testified. This is because a statistically significant number of defense lawyers have a nasty habit of accusing cops of testifying falsely, and using their own reports to sneer at the cops. This does not cheer the cops; in fact, they do not like it. They therefore do not show their reports to defense lawyers, no matter how the lawyers beg, because they have seen beggars turn into gargoyles often enough to persuade them that it is not a prudent idea to arm them.

Cops are especially nettlesome where there is a cop personally involved in the case, and oh, boy, was Giametti involved personally in this one. By the time they finished fitting him with prostheses, he was able to scramble television reception in houses three doors down, just by crossing his new metal legs. Cosmo had pretty good personal liability insurance, being as how he worked alone and had learned long ago to cover his ass, but Giametti's friends didn't know that, and besides, what Cosmo had for coverage was not yet what Giametti had for damages. They did not want Cosmo beating the criminal rap; they knew damned well that conviction on the criminal charges would do wonders for the interest of the insurance company in offering a fat settlement to Giametti.

Realizing all that, I hauled my ass to Dedham with some trepidation. I went into the station house with my tail between my legs. The only man there was Paul Finney. He was drinking coffee and typing with two fingers. I told him what I wanted. He looked at me the way the sheriff of a small western town would gaze at a snake-oil salesman applying for a peddler's permit.

"Now look," I said desperately, "all I know about this case so far is that the defendant's name is Cosmo and he's clearly a poor confused asshole who doesn't speak English very well. I dunno what happened. I don't know who it happened to. *I'm* a little vague on where it happened, actually. All I know is that a cop got hurt. I don't even know his name. I'm not trying to sandbag anybody, and I'm not trying to whipsaw anybody. All I want to do is find out what happened, and this muddled old guy and his screaming wife can't tell me."

"You could ask Giametti's doctors," Finney said.

"What the hell can I ask them?" I said. "I know he

was badly hurt, and I wish he hadn't been. But for all I know right now, Cosmo launched his car into the air and came down on top of the guy. Gimme a break, will ya? You can't be risking too much. The way I get it, the only car moving was the one Cosmo was aiming, which sort of makes the whole thing look pretty clear-cut, except I dunno what the whole thing is. It's obviously something, and I gather it wasn't a hell of a lot of pleasure for the people in the immediate vicinity, but that's about all I know."

"Really," Finney said.

"Look," I said, "I'm a nice guy, as far as you know, right? I never pissed on your boots and said it was rain. I never tried to blow smoke up your ass. I never told you Dewey beat Truman or the sun comes up in the west or the moon's made of blue cheese or anything. I never saw you before in my life. Take pity on a guy, will ya? I got this Greek house painter that does not speak English and thinks he does, and he's got a Greek wife that doesn't speak English at all and she howls like a banshee instead. The guy's almost sixty and he's charged with a whole mess of things including disabling a friend of yours—I assume he was a friend of yours . . ."

"He *is* a friend of mine," Finney said. "There isn't quite as much of him as there was before your client did a job on him. But he's still a friend of mine."

"All right," I said, "my mistake. I don't have to assume. I know he's badly hurt. I presume some insurance company's gonna have to kick in a helluva lot more money on an extra-limits policy'n they really got in mind when they write extra-limit policies."

"Extra limits," Finney said.

"From what I hear," I said, "and you're not gonna hold me to this because for all I know my client just assured me that the earth is flat and Columbus actually sailed off the edge of it, trying to reach the New World, but for all I can tell, he's holding a hundred–three hundred policy in his trembling hands, plus extra limits on top of that."

"You're not shitting me," Finney said.

"Officer," I said, "for all I know, I am shitting you. I haven't seen the fucking policy. I asked him where it was, and I got a stream of Greek which for a minute or so made me wonder if I was still in my office and I didn't wander into a restaurant by mistake. I don't speak any Greek, Officer. I maybe should, but I don't. I don't want to copy any report. You like, I won't even make notes of what I read on the report. I won't even memorize the report. Yes, I will. I will memorize the report. But I cannot use my memory of the report to make your life a hell on earth, and you know it. Which even if I could do it, I wouldn't. If you like I will write all of this down, and you can wave it at me like the American flag if I double-cross you, and that will get my client convicted and me disciplined by the Bar Association, all right? Just tell me what happened. Please."

Paul Finney showed me his reports and the photos. He let me read the statement of the witness, the lady who had the flat tire on the Olds. When I finished, he was getting off work. We went down to the bar at Mary Hartigan's and had a few beers. We talked about various prosecutors Paul Finney had known, with particular emphasis on the one handling Cosmo's case. Paul considered that gentleman a reasonable man. He believed the prosecutor would listen attentively to a sincere recommendation from the investigating officer about an appropriate punishment for Cosmo. Paul further observed that the investigating officer would be greatly assisted in displaying sincerity by satisfaction that Giametti had been treated as well as the circumstances of the defendant would permit.

"Look," Paul Finney said, "I'm not tryin' to be unreasonable, all right? The kid's young. He's just a kid."

"I know that," I said.

"He's just a kid," Finney said, "and he'll probably find something else he can do, even on two mechanical legs. And he's got a good woman. But he's gonna need a start."

"I know that," I said. "On the other hand . . ."

"On the other hand," Finney said, "I know what your guy is. He's a shitbum."

"I don't think so," I said. "I think . . ."

"Look," Finney said, "you didn't come down here to drink beer with me because you haven't got any beer at home and you think I'm the salt of the fuckin' earth, all right? And I didn't come down here to drink beer with you because I don't know any other place in the world I can get a glass of beer, and no other guys I can find that I'd like to drink it with. Right?"

"Right," I said.

"You came down here," Finney said, "because you want something. You didn't particularly want to spend tonight with me, and I didn't particularly want to spend tonight with you. That tell you something?"

"Probably," I said.

"I'm after something too," Finney said. "All right? I got my friend that'll have trouble making the starting team on the softball squad from now on. I don't know him particularly well. I don't know you at all. But I know him good enough, and I am trying to take care of him the same way you're tryin' take care of that dumb fuckin' Greek that can't speak no fuckin' English but can cut a man's legs out from under him because he got a skinful for himself down the Legion hall. All right?"

"Eagles," I said.

"Eagles," Finney said. "Doesn't matter. You're tryin' do the best you can for your guy, I'm tryin' do the best I can for mine. Same thing.

"Now," Finney said. "You wanna plead the son-bitch?"

"Of course I wanna plead the sonbitch," I said. "You really think I wanna hump that cigar-store Indian up onna stand and ask him what he thinks of Thermopylae? I got no idea what the bastard'll say. I got no idea what he said already, and I listened to him, what seemed like a whole weekend, yesterday afternoon, his damned fat wife screeching like an engine running out of oil the whole time. I wanna try this case like I wanna get ingrown toenails. I wanna dump this case, is what I wanna do. I wanna get rid the goddamned thing and the goddamned crazy client and particularly that woman that hollers all the time."

Finney put his arm around my shoulders. His breath smelled of beer. I was not surprised. "You wanna maybe talk to the insurance company?" he said.

"Yup," I said. "Both of them."

Finney took his arm off my shoulder. "Okay," he said. "You talk the insurance guys, and I'll talk the DA."

I did talk the insurance guy. I talked the insurance guy like the insurance guy never had been talked before. I talked the hell out of the insurance guy. I talked the extra-limits insurance guy, too. I talked him even harder than I talked the primary insurer. Then I talked Cosmo. I made him promise to leave Thea at home. He did. I talked Cosmo until I was hyperventilating. I'm not sure Cosmo understood one word that I uttered, but there was one thing that he did understand: he understood that I was deadly serious.

Giametti settled his case for $263,000. No lawyer, taking a third off the top. All for him. Cosmo pleaded guilty. A year suspended, probation for two years, and stay out of the Eagles' hall, fines totaling $250, and no driving for six months. He bitched about it. I told him to go fuck himself and presented him with my bill for $1,150. He paid me $850 on installments, defaulted on the rest, and I quit hounding him after three mean letters came back, marked "Unknown At This Address." In Cosmo's handwriting, which was quite distinctive.

Paul Finney was on the desk when I arrived in Dedham to inquire about various problems recently involving Teddy Franklin. Paul said, "Hiya, Jerry." I said, "Afternoon, Lieutenant." He said, "Here on business, Counselor?" I said, "Yup." He said, "Good." I said, "Where's the business, Paul?" He jerked his head back toward the cellblock. "In there," he said. He whistled and the patrolman in the corner, with his feet on the desk and his eyes on the skin magazine, looked up, "Ralphie . . ." Paul said.

"Not so fast, if you don't mind, Lieutenant," I said. "Can I ask you who's back there, and how come? My information seems to be a little garbled."

"Siddown, Ralphie," Paul said. "Come in and take a seat, Jerry."

I opened the gate at the counter and sat down on the wooden chair next to Paul's desk.

"Where do you get these people, Jerry?" Paul said.

"Flea markets and rummage sales," I said. "How the hell do I know where I get them? Where does Father Flanagan get the tenants for Boys Town? How come he doesn't think there's such a thing as a bad boy? Who knows what evil lurks in the heart of man?"

"The Shadow knows," Paul said. "Look, all right? I dunno shit about this caper. Trooper brings the broad in. Talk about wildcats. I've seen skunks that got run over, didn't make the stink she made. No sooner'n I hear him tell me 'Lock her up,' her husband shows up. I thought I had a piece a work on my hands with her. The two of them together could fill Fenway Park all by themselves. Jesus, what a pair. She does the alto and he does the bass, and the two of them know language which offended even me."

"Paul," I said. "This is your old buddy, Jerry."

"Yeah," he said. "Well, the vocabulary was pretty rich, okay?"

"Yeah," I said. "Who's the broad?"

"Dorothy Franklin," he said.

"Well," I said, "that's a help."

"Better'n it was the bimbo down the pike about a mile and a half there?" Paul said.

"I didn't say anything," I said.

"I realize that," Paul said.

"What's the charge?" I said.

"Driving without registration in possession," Paul

said. "We give her the phone call and she calls her husband . . ."

"Paul," I said, "just out of curiosity: Who was the arresting officer?"

"Statie," Paul said. "Dunno him. Lemme check here. Guy brought her in because he couldn't handle her." He riffled through papers. "Hudson," he said. "Trooper Torbert Hudson."

"No registration," I said.

"Right," Paul said. "Lemme see here. 'Subject operating nineteen-seventy-eight Cadillac Sedan de Ville, color gray, Route One, stopped in routine check, no valid registration in possession.' "

"For this you lock her up," I said.

"Nope," Paul said. "We lock her up when Trooper Hudson brings her in and asks us to lock her up, on account she attacked him and we didn't have no trouble believing it on account his face looks like he just had a fight with a big bear and lost. All claw marks. Asked to sit down and she wouldn't, and then she called her goddamned husband, and he showed up, and I seen dogfights between bull mastiffs, went quieter'n what them two did. So we locked them both up. Which we're not supposed to do, but since they're husband and wife, what harm's it gonna do, they're both inna same cell? Some good, probably. They won't kill each other, and they can't kill anybody else, at least until the two of them can find a way to bend the bars apart. Which I am not betting against, given them two. You sure you wanna talk to them, go in there?"

"No," I said.

"Well," Paul said, "I am." He got up. He took a ring of keys out of the desk. "You are going in there, Jerry, and you are gonna calm those two wolves down to the point where I, as a peace officer, can release them into the general population without violating my oath of office."

"What's the bail?" I said.

"For her," Paul said, "it's a lousy hundred bucks. He ain't got none set yet, because we got him in the cell before he did what he wanted to do, which would've made it around a hundred thousand dollars. You won't need Termite for this one, if you can just sort of relax the fuckers. If you can't, Termite won't do you no good anyway, because I'll get the pair of them held without bail."

8

"IT'S VERY SIMPLE," I told Mack in the bedroom at Green Harbor as the eleven o'clock news ended, "Trooper Hudson ate Dottie's registration." I was eating chivier cottage cheese and drinking Heineken. I was also exhausted from driving all over the goddamned Commonwealth and irritable because I had had no dinner.

"He ate it," Mack said.

"That's what Dottie says," I said. "She claims she was coming up Route One on the way home from the beauty parlor and he pulled her over. He asked her for her license, which is the regular one in that laminated plastic, and she gave it to him. He asked her for her registration, which is one of those temporary ones on the flimsy yellow paper. He returned her license to her and he tore up the registration. Then he ate it."

"Uh huh," Mack said.

"Well," I said, "you want to be careful now. That was my reaction when Teddy told me that Trooper Hudson ate his license. Now we've got the same guy, arresting Teddy's wife about a mile away from where he arrested Teddy, and since she's got a license that a goat'd have trouble getting down, he eats her registration and then busts her for unregistered car.

"I had trouble believing it when Teddy told me about Trooper Hudson's diet, but doesn't it seem strange that it's the same trooper, first arresting the husband and then arresting the wife, separately, in the same week, and *both* of them have the same explanation for the charges?

"I know Teddy pretty well by now. He does things that I wouldn't do in a million years. But Teddy knows his trade, and he knows cops pretty well. I could believe that perhaps Teddy left his license at home and made up some cock-and-bull story just to plague the cop. Because after all, if Teddy pleaded guilty he wouldn't go to jail for it, or even lose his license. He'd get about a twenty-five-dollar fine plus a surfine of twelve-fifty and be on his merry way. Teddy's cheap, and he loves to goose the cops, but it's still a trial, and a day or three in court, and a bill from me.

"And now Dottie comes along, and tells almost the same story. Dottie wouldn't say *boo* to a cop. I think Trooper Hudson maybe *does* eat paper. I also think Teddy's probably right when he says the guy's just out to harass him, although I don't believe I would have chosen the same forum or the same rhetoric that Teddy chose to express those views. But it is sort of against the rules for a cop who's got a hard-on for you to go around harassing your family. He can needle you a little now and then—that goes with the territory. But you don't go around making obscene calls to his wife in the middle of the night, and he's really not supposed to bring your wife into the thing either."

"Maybe he thinks Dottie's mixed up in Teddy's business," Mack said.

"Maybe he does, and maybe she is," I said. "But until he proves it, he shouldn't be messing with her. The biggest thing with those guys, guys like Teddy, is that you treat a man like a man. You show a little respect. You know what I'm doing, and I know what you're doing, and if you can catch me doing what I'm doing, you can put me away. Me. Not my wife and not my family, but me.

"I'm not sure Hudson understands that," I said. "Maybe he understood it and forgot it. Maybe he just got frustrated. But Teddy's really pissed, now. He was screaming bloody murder in that cell, and I'm not using that as a figure of speech."

"Would he do something like that?" she said.

"Let me put it this way," I said, "if he decided to get it done, he would know who to call on the matter. Teddy's been around a long time, and he's done a lot of shady business for people without anybody ever getting hurt. This is not because nobody can get hurt in his business—it is because he knows how people can get hurt, and who the people are who hurt them, and he is very careful about getting those people pissed-off. As they are about getting him pissed-off. Teddy likes things to be nice and quiet, and everybody makes a little money. Nobody makes any noise, and nobody creates any problems. This guy is creating problems for Teddy, and Teddy doesn't like it. He thinks they're cheap shots. I had an awful time calming the two of them down."

"Did you get them out?" Mack said.

"Oh, sure," I said. "No real difficulty. Finney let them out as soon as I got their promise to behave themselves. He gave Dottie the summons that Hudson'd left for her, and there aren't any charges against Teddy. They put him in protective custody.

"Hell, Finney even gave me a commercial. When Teddy started yelling at him about how they held him with no charges, Finney cut him off and said, 'Look, Mister Franklin. I dunno you. I don't even wanna know you. I know him,' meaning me, 'and I've known him for a long time. You really want me to arrest you for something, I can do it, and if you told me anybody else's name but his, I would've done it about three hours ago. But because Jerry's in it, I'm letting you walk. You got nothin' against me, Mister Franklin, and I got nothin' against you. Now just get out of here and go home and have a couple drinks and go to bed and leave me alone, will ya?' So all I got to worry about now is what the two of them'll do when they see Hudson in court the next time, and what Hudson'll do in the meantime to stir them up a little more. Is there anything else to eat in the refrigerator?"

"I don't think so," Mack said. "I was going to the

store today, but I fell asleep again right after you left the beach, and by the time I woke up, I'd lost interest in it. I took Saigon to work and had a couple burgers there and came home and crawled into bed. I don't know what's the matter with me. I'm pooped, and I'm not doing anything."

"You're relaxing, that's why," I said.

"Mmmm," she said, rolling over. "Rub my back."

"No," I said.

"No?" she said. "What do you mean: No? What kind of an answer is that? When I tell you to do something, I expect you to do it. Now, rub my goddamned back. It's itchy. I think I'm gonna peel. Rub it."

"No," I said.

She looked up at me. "Why not?" she said.

"Because I'm still hungry," I said. "Man cannot live by chivier cottage cheese alone, and you haven't got anything else in the house for me to eat. Oh, sure, you had your burgers while I was out defending the constitutional rights of the downtrodden and stopping Teddy Franklin from setting fire to the Dedham jail. That was all right. But what about me?"

"I assumed you were having dinner," she said, "just like you always do when you get away from the house for a minute. I figured you and Roger were down at the Red Coach eating roast beef, and I felt very sorry for myself while I was eating those burgers and fries, I can tell you."

"Fries too, huh?" I said. "Good. Glad to hear you had some fries. Wished I had some fries. Fries sound awful good to me, right about now. Nice, hot french fries, little salt, little ketchup, maybe? Ahh, those'd be good."

"Oh, shut up," Mack said. "Rub my back. It'll get your mind off your stomach. That's all you think about anyway."

"No, it isn't," I said. "Look, if I rub your back, will you come across?"

"I thought you wanted to eat," she said.

"Pervert," I said.

"I knew I shouldn't've said that," she said. "I think there's some bacon and eggs left, if you like."

"I don't like," I said. "I want some fries, and I want a couple cheeseburgers."

"*Oh*-kay," she said. She turned over again and sat up. "Look, I'll make a deal with you. Saigon's got a ride home with the kid who runs the fryer. I'll call her and tell her to bring home some cheeseburgers . . ."

"Medium rare," I said.

". . . medium rare," Mack said, "and some fries. Is there anything *else* you'd like, Master? A strawberry shake or a huckleberry pie?"

"No," I said. "I'll drink beer."

"But only if," she said, "you rub my back."

"Deal," I said.

I could hear her on the phone as I got out of my clothes and into my bathrobe. It was a warm night, but the houses at the beach are fairly close together, and I don't walk around nude down there unless the lights are off. She said, "The Lord and Master of all he surveys came home and surveyed the refrigerator, Kiddo, and came up empty. You know how he gets when he's feeling abused. No, four. I want one myself, and I've heard all about your diets before. Yes. Better get six fries. See you soon."

"They'll be cold by the time she gets here," I said, when Mack returned to the bedroom. "They'll be the last ones on the tray, the ones that nobody wanted that got all dried out under the heat lights, and the fries'll be all soggy."

"*Jesus*," Mack said, taking off her robe and getting into bed, "bitch, bitch, bitch—that's all you seem to do. Rub my fucking back."

I rubbed her fucking back. I rubbed her fucking front, too. Afterward, she lit a Parliament. Mack only smokes after certain activities, such as dinner and one or two other things. I don't know how she does that—either I smoke three packs a day, which will kill me, and which is why I gave it up, or else I do not smoke at all. She patted my hand. "You ain't gettin' older," she said, "you're gettin' better." I said I was getting better than most men I knew, judging from what they said, at least, and they were boasting. I said I thought concupiscence was a wonderful thing, another matter on which I have not changed my mind.

"Sorry you had a lousy day," she said.

"I didn't, really," I said. "A lousy day is when you can't do anything right. I didn't do anything wrong today, mostly because I didn't do much of anything except hold hands. When you come right down to it, Teddy's just a big kid, and Dottie's not much more mature. I'm Teddy's daddy. When he gets in trouble, he can do it with confidence, because Daddy will come and get him out. God knows what I am with the other kid."

"Is he the one Roger wanted you to talk to?" she said.

"Roger wanted me to talk to Richard, actually," I said. "Richard is the kid's actual daddy, but neither one of them's too crazy about the arrangement. Richard's not all that keen on having a kid crowding thirty, because Richard's one of those flat-tummied, suntanned types that made a lot of money and had a lot of women and learned to smile a lot, so that he thinks God loves him. Which God probably does, being safely out of range when Richard's little problems surface."

"You don't like Richard," she said.

"No," I said, "I don't. I don't like people who were lucky and decided it was talent."

"What'd he get lucky at?" she said.

"I have no idea," I said. "I will, but I don't now. But I do know he got lucky. He's got a lot of bucks, but he hasn't always had them, and he's not properly grateful for them, now that he's got them. I don't think Richard really cares about anybody except Richard. He sure doesn't think much of the kid."

"What's the kid's problem?" she said.

"The first one was Richard," I said. "What the others are, except for one, I do not know."

"What's the one?" she said.

"Ecce homo," I said. "The kid's as queer as green horses. He's got all the mannerisms, the little fragilities, the merest touch of daintiness, the slightest flutter of the fingers as he lights his cigarette, the seductive lilt to his voice and the interesting poutiness of the expression. At least when Richard's around. He didn't have a dress on when I saw him, but after I heard a couple speeches from his old man, it wouldn't't've surprised me if he popped one out of his handbag and jumped into it. Matter of fact, I think if I was Richard's kid, I would do something to get him going, too. I dunno as I'd go quite as far as Emerson apparently did, but I would certainly do something."

"I know what I'm going to do," Mack said, stubbing out the butt. "I'm going to sleep."

"What about your burger and fries?" I said.

"Look," she said, "I know you and I know Heather. That food will not go to waste. When you get finished, come back to bed, and be quiet about it. I won't wake you in the morning."

"You won't have to," I said. "I've got to see Emerson in my office at nine."

"Oh, shit," Mack said, rolling over. "I might have guessed. Some day you are going to have to take a course on how to take a vacation."

"I hope I do," I said.

"Jerry," she said, "what did Mike Curran do to Kitty Blanchard?"

It took me a while to recollect what Mayor Curran had been talking about on the beach. "Oh," I said, "he had John Lacey get her a job mopping floors when her husband died."

"No," Mack said, "when they were kids and he got his best suit on to visit her. What'd he do then?"

"I really don't know," I said. "I suspect Mike doesn't, either. Probably nothing."

9

SAIGON BROUGHT HOME a box of chow and an unusually pensive mood. She is an extroverted kid and
she does not brood or sulk. When miffed, as she was
when I refused to let her stay out all night to attend
the junior prom at Boston College High School, she
expresses her feelings clearly. You may not enjoy
hearing what is on her mind, but you will not be in
doubt about what it is.

I know how to deal with cheeseburgers and french
fries, especially when I am hungry. I was somewhat
mystified as to how to deal with Saigon, who sat
frowning in her uniform and ingesting fry after fry as
though pondering an unusually difficult problem in
metaphysics. I figured she would speak when she was
ready.

She did. "Dad," she said, "I'm worried."

Now that is not a promising opening for a teen-aged
daughter embarking on a conversation with her father.
The next sentence, obviously, is that "a friend" missed
her period. I tried to maintain a façade of calm.
"About what?" I said, pausing in the mastication of
my second cheeseburger.

"Margie," she said.

That did not get me out of the woods. I continued
to stuff food in my face. " 'S matter with Margie?" I
said.

"Oh, shit," Heather said. "I don't know. She's all
screwed up. She doesn't know what the hell is going
down. Nothing works right for that kid. Nothing ever

has. She never had an even break. I just feel sorry for her, is all. I wish I could do something for her."

"Well," I said, feeling greatly relieved, "is it anything in particular, or just things in general?"

"Both, I guess," Heather said. "Right now it's her boyfriend. Joe wants her to go away with him. Just, *leave.* Get in his pick-up truck and leave. And, Dad, confidentially, Joe is an asshole. A real *ass*hole. He dropped out of school and he thinks he's gonna make his living fixing motorcycles and snowmobiles. Are you *kidding?* The only times I've seen him that he wasn't drunk, he was stoned."

"How old is he?" I said.

"About twelve," she said. "Actually about twenty-three, twenty-four."

"How old is Margie?" I said.

"She'll be eighteen in March," Heather said. "How come you always want to know how *old* everybody is, Dad?"

"Getting older myself, I suppose," I said. "I dunno. I've been around a while and I guess I think I know more now'n I did before I'd been around for a while. Not that being around makes you infallible, but it does rub some of the edges off and at least give you the opportunity to get some more sense."

"Yeah," she said. "Well, it didn't do Joe any good. He's eight or nine years older'n I am, and I think he's an asshole."

"I didn't say everybody took the opportunity," I said. "I just said it was there for the taking."

"Joe didn't take the opportunity," she said. "Oh, I suppose he's all right, but as far as I can see, the only thing he ever took was Margie."

"Oh," I said.

"You know something, Dad?" she said. "There're times when I think I'm turning into an awful snob."

"You're all right, kid," I said. "Living in this joint, you'd hear about it if you weren't."

"I mean it," she said. "Maybe Joe's a perfectly nice guy. Maybe he really loves Margie. Maybe she would be better off, married to him. I look at him and decide he's an asshole. How the hell do I know? How do I know so much?"

"But you do know, don't you," I said.

"Yup," she said, nodding. "Joe's an asshole, all right. There's no question about it. He's a jerk and a short-hitter and a loser. He acts like some thirteen-year-old, and he's at least six or seven years older'n most of the kids he hangs around with. He's always got a bunch of sophomores over at the shop where he works, and they're drinking beer from this cooler he's got in there and pretending they're big shots, just because they've got grease on their tee-shirts and he lets them test-run the bikes in the woods out in back."

"I don't like the sound of that," I said, thinking of a nasty little case on the North Shore which I had taken up and then dropped a few years back. The defendant was a sometime welterweight club-fighter who had opened a boxing gym for young boys to visit after school, and then seduced about seven of them into working as prostitutes for middle-aged business-men who would pay the poor kids five dollars a blow job. I withdrew from Canvasback's case because the son of a bitch was a pathological liar and could not seem to get it through his head that it is not a good idea to blow smoke at your lawyer, sending him off on one wild-goose chase after another while he wastes his time and your money.

"You wouldn't like the looks of it, either," she said. "Joe's been in jail once, and . . ."

"For what?" I said.

"Oh," she said, "I don't know. He says it was armed robbery. Claims he held up a liquor store one night when he was out of his mind. He thinks it's something to brag about. But I don't think it was that. He was in less'n a year, though. He wasn't in long enough for that, you think?"

"I don't know how long he was in," I said. "But if he was young enough when they caught him, it could've been. They're pretty lenient with kids who get grabbed for the first time. Give them another chance, that sort of thing. It doesn't make me like him better, though. Especially if he started hanging around the young kids after he got out."

"You think he's queer, Dad?" she said. "He seems to like Margie quite a lot. Says he loves her in fact. She sleeps with him."

"Let me put it this way," I said. "I wouldn't be surprised if he turned out to be double-gaited. A lot of guys go into the joint straight and come out switch-hitting. She seems like a nice kid, and what little I saw of her, she's certainly pretty enough. Why the hell did she take up with a loser like that?"

"Because he asked her, I think," Heather said. "I think he was the only one who did ask her. She lives down here all year long, you know. She knows all the kids on the beach, but they're only here in the summer. Labor Day comes, and they leave, but she's still off in the woods there with her mother. She's lonesome. There aren't any really neat guys at the school she goes to, I guess, and besides, she's a senior this year. All the guys in her class're going out with fresh-men and sophomores. All the guys she went out with've graduated and gone away some place, except the turkeys like Joe that're too gross to go any place else and end up pumping gas down at the Shell sta-tion. What's she got to look forward to, huh? Her mother works nights . . ."

"What's she do?" I said.

"She's an okay lady," Heather said. "She's the host-ess in the dining room at the Skipper. But she has to work nights, of course, so that means when Margie gets off work . . ."

"She works during the school year?" I said. I don't approve of that. I don't approve of kids *not* working, but between September and June their work is at school. Heather and I had a couple of crisp exchanges on that subject when she turned fifteen and a woman in Milton advertised at the school for a babysitter. She wanted a kid to work four afternoons a week, feed dinner to three young children, and stay until eight-fifteen while the woman went off to work as a volunteer in some goddamned child welfare program, most likely spending her hours messing up some family in which the mother was doing a hell of a lot better job than she was, for her own kids. There would also have been a certain amount of weekend sitting, because the woman and her husband were sparkling socialites and apparently spent most of their free time getting photographed in evening clothes at various chic museums where some new collection of meaningless daubs was being dazzlingly unveiled. The money was good for a teen-ager—three dollars an hour, as I recall—and Heather was nearly insane with desire for a new pair of Olin skis, but I was adamant that she should not work while school was in session, and despite the fact that she nearly went wild, I refused to budge.

"Yeah, Dad," Heather said, with that resigned tone of voice she adopts when I am being hopelessly stupid, "and before you ask: her marks do stink. She might be able to get into a community college, but it wouldn't matter if she could get into Mount Holyoke because she hasn't got the money anyway. She has to work, just like her mother does."

"What about her father?" I said.

"He took off, a long time ago," Heather said. "She doesn't know where he is. I don't think she's even sure what he looks like."

"He still has an obligation to support her," I said.

"Oh, sure," Heather said. "Dad, he was a bum when he was around. He didn't work when he lived with Margie and her mother. Then her mother got married again, to Don, the foreman down at the marina, and I guess he's a nice enough guy but they didn't get along and after a while, they split up. Margie and her mother both work because they have to, and then Margie gets off work, and Joe picks her up around seven-thirty, and they go home and watch television at her house. Which of course means: they screw. And then the next day she gets up and goes to school and goes to work and goes home and screws Joe. Now and then he takes her to a movie, when he can spare the money from his beer buying, and on Saturday nights when she gets off work they get a pizza. That's it."

"Sounds pretty grim to me," I said.

"It is pretty grim," Heather said. "The trouble is, it's the best she can do. At least she thinks it is."

"What is she, pregnant?" I said.

"No," Heather said, "I don't think she is. She's on the pill, she told me. She may be lying. Margie lies a lot. No, it's just that I feel sorry for her. Some of the kids there, at the Burger, aren't any better off than she is. Like the little punks that hang around Joe's place. But they don't seem to mind it, you know? They're actually looking forward to being like Joe when they get older. They think he's just neat. Margie knows better. She knows it stinks. She knows I'm getting Olins this winter. She knows Terry's going to Dartmouth and he asked me to Winter Carnival with him this year."

"Now there's some news," I said. "I didn't know Terry asked you to visit him."

"Well," she said, "that's maybe because me and Mom talked it over and we decided we weren't going to tell you until some night when you had a really good day and the Red Sox won and we had some nice steaks and cold beer, and then I would ask you if I could go."

I began to laugh. "Whereas Margie's a different matter," I said.

"I shouldn't've told Margie, either," Heather said. "Sometimes I'm not very smart. I'm a junior and I've got a chance to go to Winter Carnival, and she's a senior and she doesn't have anything to look forward to at all. I was going on and on about the skis and how pretty soon they'll be having the summer sales, and maybe I'd have enough to get a nice new parka and some real tight stretch pants and stuff . . ."

"No boots?" I said.

"Well," Heather said, "see, that's something else I didn't get around to telling you, but for Christmas you're giving me new Munaris this year, okay?"

"No," I said.

"Oh, Dad," she said. *"Why?* You spend that much on my present anyway, and this's something I really want. Please?"

"No," I said. "You'll wheedle the promise out of me, and then you'll wheedle me into going over to the shop right after Labor Day to get the sexy pants and the jacket and the skis that you're paying for, and your mother'll come along and the two of you'll gang up on me and make me agree it doesn't make sense to wait until the sale ends and then buy the boots for full price. So I'll give in and buy your Christmas present early on the promise that you won't ask for any other big stuff at Christmas. And you won't, either. But when Christmas comes, you won't have any big present coming from us, and if your mother doesn't fold up like the Red Sox do, then I will, and I'll end up buying you another present anyway. Which will mean that you took me for the boots, and I don't like getting taken."

"That was the game plan," she said, pouting.

"Of course it was," I said. "I may be easy but I'm not stupid, you know. In addition to which, my pride's involved. I hate getting taken. I will go to almost any lengths to avoid being taken. In fact, in this instance, I will buy you the damned boots when the sale starts, because you are right about getting them at the sale price. And in addition to that, if you're willing to work all summer to get the rest of the finery, I'll get the boots as a plain old reward for being a good kid. But not as a Christmas present."

"Oh, Dad," she said, grinning, "that's really, really great. Thank you."

"Actually not a reward," I said. "A bonus, for hard work. You're an okay kid, Heather, schlepping the food home at midnight for your starving old man. We're lucky to have you." Then we hugged each other and did not conceal the moisture in our eyes, and she went off to bed to dream about seducing some wheat-haired running back with a lopsided grin and a Porsche, some downhill racer whom I would hate on sight simply because he would be so perfect. I sat there by myself in the kitchen making solemn promises to God that if He would just be good enough to leave that kid alone, I would never ask for anything else again, or complain about what I got without applying for it.

10

IN THE MORNING I twice cut myself while shaving, a habit I have when running on insufficient sleep. Mack every so often presents me with some miraculous new electric shaver which is guaranteed to leave my face as devoid of whiskers as is a baby's bottom, but after I get the razor I still have the transparent skin and the very dark beard, and after I use it I get five o'clcok shadow around two in the afternoon. The carnage is preferable to stubble, in my opinion, and I have learned to fend off Weldon Cooper's japes about the bits of toilet paper bloodstuck on my muzzle by making some unflattering remark about his paunch. Cooper runs five miles a day, and treats his body with respect, as he was trained to do in the FBI. But he can no more get rid of that paunch than I can of my beard. I applied first aid as best I could, swallowed as much bad instant coffee as I could stand, and hit the road for Boston with every other dumb son of a bitch who moved his family to the beach for the summer and thus signed up for double or triple the commuting, in the worst traffic of the year.

Emerson Teller was waiting in my office when I got there, twenty minutes late and pissed-off at the traffic. Emerson looked positively ravishing. He wore a pale yellow silk shirt, open to the bottom of the sternum to display his gold medallion on his hairless chest. He wore a blue silk blazer, tan slacks, and a different pair of Gucci loafers. He still had the handbag and the shades, though, and he had regained some of the super-ciliousness which had deserted him in Roger's office. I had liked him better without it, but believed that I knew how to hand him his lunch again. I told him I was sorry I was late. Actually, what I said was that I was sorry to be late, and explained it by saying, "Fucking goddamned traffic." I noted with satisfaction that Emerson was, as I had believed, one of the delicate nances who dislike coarse talk; it rattled him slightly.

This liberated me to deal with the second visitor. It was the motorboat mechanic again, this time without the girl. He stood up. "Mister Kennedy," he said, "I dunno if you remember me, but . . ."

"I remember you, Donald," I said. "You're Donald French. I just didn't expect you, is all. I expected this gentleman here, because we made an appointment yesterday, which I am already late for. I did not expect you. Whaddaya want?"

"Well," French said, glancing at the apparition in the pink shades, "I think, well, I'm *sure* now, I'm getting in trouble and I don't want to."

"So you want to talk to me," I said.

"Yeah," he said.

"Okay," I said. "But you're gonna have to wait until I finish talking to the guy I expected, all right? And you can't get impatient, because I did expect him, as I say, and he is going to pay me some money. Which is what I work for, Mister French. I work for money." This was as much for Emerson's benefit as it was for French. "Quite a bit of money. I ain't cheap. You got it?"

"I got some," he said, rather timidly.

"Fine," I said. "You be thinking about what you want to say while I talk to this gentleman, and if you can't think up what, and how come, before he comes out, you can just excuse yourself the same way you came in, and it'll be okay, all right? The first conference is free; one hundred bucks is the same as free. After that it's just like a taxicab, and the meter runs. You've had your first conference. The instant you step into my private office, the flag drops."

"I might need some time," he began.

"I need a lot of time," I said. "I need more time'n I've got, because time is what I sell, and if I had more, I could sell more. But I can't get any more time, so I have to charge top rates for what I do have." I turned toward Emerson. "You wanna come in, sir?"

Gretchen said, "Good morning, Mister Kennedy." She said it very demurely. "I'm not sure I can afford it, but could I have a minute of your valuable time?"

"Gretchen," I said, "my sweet, my love. Of course you may, my dear." She followed me into the office and shut the door. "Where," she said, "did you get that pansy?"

"Outta Roger's window box," I said.

"Jesus Christ," she said, "does he wear lace panties?"

"If I'm lucky," I said, "I won't find out. If he's lucky, the wolves down in the slammer won't find out, either. But they will be interested, and I am not."

"Is he going away?" she said.

"I dunno," I said. "His old man wanted me to interview him in Roger's office yesterday, with the old man and Roger sitting there, and I wasn't gonna do that, which is why he's here today. So I can talk to him without the old man feeding him all his best lines."

"Who's the old man?" she said.

"His name's Richard Teller," I said. "He's obviously one of Roger's caviar clients, but how come and for what I don't know. Overbearing son of a bitch, though. If the kid's the fairy queen, and he is, the old man is not without culpability in the matter, as we say in the law. I dunno if I would take up sucking cocks to get even with a prick like that, but I would certainly have done something."

"Well," Gretchen said firmly, "if Emerson's done something for which Emerson is gonna do some time, I think he better pick up a *huge* jar of Vaseline on his way to the pokey, along with the new toothbrush and a little light bedtime reading."

"This is true," I said. "Now, what'd the juvenile delinquent have to say?"

"Not a hell of a lot," she said. "He came in here the same way he did the other day, except without the bimbo this time, and asked if he could see you. And I said you were coming in, but I didn't know for sure when you'd be through, and I didn't know if you'd be able to see him. And he looked very worried and scuffed up the carpet some and—you know something? That kid *stinks*."

"I know it," I said. "I got a whiff of him the other day and I thought for a minute he was doing something forbidden by the Geneva Conventions. Happens when you live in a truck, I suppose. No facilities for personal hygiene."

"I don't know," she said. "He dusted my crops for me while he was talking to me. His breath stinks, his feet stink, his hair's all greasy and what's in between the feet and the hair stinks pretty good itself. And there's more of it. I think before you represent him, you should make him take a bath. Ship him down the carwash and run him through twice without a car. He needs a good scrubbing, with real hot water, and maybe the hot wax, too."

"Well," I said, "grill him about cash and keep him sitting where he's sitting, and you sit where you sit, until I get through with the horticultural exposition. Then just pop in and we'll talk about the Gallivan case a minute or so before I let the compost heap in."

"Done," she said.

Emerson Teller arranged himself in the chair like Madame de Pompadour arraying the folds of her ball gown for a tea dance in the Hall of Mirrors at Versailles. If there is a Hall of Mirrors at Versailles. Emerson had but one noticeable fault, which was that he was faultless. "You're rather hard on people, Mister Kennedy," Emerson said.

"I say what's on my mind," I said, "and I expect them to do the same thing. That kid was in here before. He took up a lot of time, which he did not pay me enough for, and he did not tell me anything. Which means he wasted my time, after showing up unbidden on my doorstep like a homeless waif in a basket and blanket on the church steps on a snowy Christmas morning. I stood for that. I'm a soft touch. I'll try to help the guy who just assumes I haven't got anything to do but sit around here until he shows up off the crack of the bat, but I tell him that he only gets one bite of the apple, as I told that kid, and he has already had his bite. Now he waits, and if I see him, he pays. In advance."

"You've made your point, Mister Kennedy," Emerson said, not quite sneering. "You made it yesterday in Roger's office. It doesn't need doing again."

"I'm not sure about that, my friend," I said. "This is your second meeting, too, and I haven't seen any currency on the blotter so far."

"I didn't think yesterday counted," Emerson said. "You refused to talk to me."

"For which refusal you should be profoundly grateful," I said, "since whatever else you've got, you lack the balls to tell your old man where to head in."

That fetched him. It was a mean thing to do, but Emerson was a bit too resilient in his defensive feistiness for my taste. I followed up on it. "Let's we understand something, Emerson," I said. "I don't need you. You need me. If you don't need me, you need somebody like me. Roger knows that and Richard knows that, but neither one of them really needs me, himself. If they did, I would be talking to them. Since they don't, I am talking to you. If you think you don't, beat it. If you think you do, spare me the haughtiness and let's get down to business."

"I was framed by a police officer," he said.

"Right," I said. "And I was sculpted into my present graceful shape by a maniacal genius of a topiary gardener. Now, I did not haul my ass up here this morning to hear you tell me how you got framed and you're innocent and so help you God, you are the victim of a malevolent society. I came up here so you can tell me what happened. You tell me what happened. I will tell you whether you were framed, or whether there is some way I think maybe you got a shot at getting off, or whether you should hang down your head and cry and tell the judge that you ain't gonna do it again and you don't know what possessed you, you did it this time. I will also tell you what any one of those things is liable to cost you, and you will give me some money, and I will proceed. Or else you won't, and I won't. Clear?"

"How much do you know about the gay community?" he said.

"About as much as I know about the Home for Orphan Owls," I said. "Nothing, which is more than ample to satisfy my curiosity. Are you charged with being a member of the gay community?"

"Yes," he said.

"I hope you brought the complaint with you," I said. "I want to see the part where it says you maliciously and willfully, and with malice aforethought, joined the gay community. I particularly want to see what statute they cite for the offense, so I can look it up. Because I never heard of that offense, and I am inclined to doubt that it is on the books. If that is what you're charged with, gimme ten dollars and fifty cents and I will draft a motion to dismiss on the ground that the complaint fails to state an offense under existing law, and you can take it into court yourself and save everybody a whole bunch of shit and you a whole bunch of money."

"I am a victim of persecution of the gay minority," Emerson said.

"I am the tooth fairy, begging your pardon, sir," I said. "Now, begging your further pardon, *what is the fucking charge?*"

"I think they told me it was lasciviousness," he said, looking hurt.

"Right," I said. "Two-seventy-two, thirty-five."

"Huh?" he said.

"*Massachusetts General Laws,*" I said, "chapter

two-seventy-two, section thirty-five. Lascivious acts."

"Yes," he said. "Now, the Supreme Court has held . . ."

"Emerson," I said, "please. We need a fair division of labor here. You do the clienting, and I'll do the lawyering. I don't need a lawyer, okay? If you don't need a lawyer, that makes two people out of two, sitting in a law office, which I think is probably a quorum, talking about something that neither one of them needs a lawyer for. And that doesn't make any sense. At least not for the lawyer in the room, which happens to be me, and I do my best to be sensible. Okay? You tell me what happened. I will tell you what the law is, if it seems useful to me and useful to you. Otherwise I will not. I will now ask you again: what happened?"

"In the gay community," Emerson said, "we have . . ."

"More problems than a man fighting a swarm of bees while he's falling out of a tree onto a high-tension wire," I said. "Emerson, my lad, I grow impatient with you. I know the cops don't like you guys. I know you guys don't like the girls, except some of you guys *are* girls, and girls is all that them guys like." Emerson started to stand up. "That's fine by me," I said, "if you wanna leave."

Sure it was fine. I just love seeing fat fees shimmy out the door to go elsewhere. Next to an impacted bowel, it's the best thing in the world, as far as I'm concerned, and I knew Roger'd be pleased, too. On the other hand, I've been at this business a while, and it's been my experience that when one fat fee walks out, three thin fees walk in. Or as Cooper puts it, if you don't have a fork handy when they serve you, sharpen the edge of your spoon and scoop up the food with that, because it's better'n going hungry. "But if you do leave, don't come back. And treat your next lawyer better'n you've treated me, after dragging me away from my family and my vacation for the second day in a row."

Emerson sat down. He pouted a little. "You don't seem empathetic," he said.

"I'm not," I said. "You can get empathy down at the fuckin' juice bar. Or is that a poor choice of words? Doesn't matter. You are not here for empathy. You are here because somebody or other wishes to hoist you on your own petard. You wanna get stroked, get some musk oil and a friend. You wanna get legal advice, start talking to your lawyer."

"I was driving up to Amherst to visit a friend of mine last Sunday," Emerson said.

"Ahh," I said, "now we're making progress. Candor, that's the ticket—candor. What the hell happened?" Emerson was candid. Emerson was *very* candid. When he got through, I whacked the wall, and Weldon Cooper whacked back. I told Emerson I would be in touch with him. I told French, on the way out, to wait because I would be back shortly. I got Cooper to agree to wait for lunch until I finished with French, because I needed to talk to him and was willing to pay for the privilege.

11

BY THE TIME I returned to my office, Donald French
had been waiting for more than two hours. Gretchen
said something about the Gallivan matter, and I told
Gretchen I would deal with that later. Gretchen said
she had to talk to me about it "right now." I know
better than to argue with Gretchen. She can get stri-
dent. I said to French, "You're gonna have to wait
some more." French said, "Mister Kennedy, I gotta
get back to work." I said, "That'll teach you to show
up without an appointment, especially when I'm on
vacation and I'm not even here." I went into my office.

Gretchen came into my office. She said, "Would you
mind telling me what the fuck is going on here?" I
said, "Not at all. In fact I would tell you right off. If I
knew. Which I don't. So I won't. All I can tell you is
that there is definitely some goddamned thing going on
here, but what the fuck it is I do not know."

"Something," Gretchen said, "is going on."

"It certainly is," I said. "Here I get a top-notch
queer that gets busted for soliciting a State cop to
blow him in a Howard Johnson's men's room. I go
next door, see the unfrocked FBI agent and get him
to defend the queer for half the fee, and what has he
got? Nothin'. He won't touch it. Don't like fairies. I'm
not sure I like Cooper. I *know* I don't like Emerson.

"What I wanted Cooper for was to get my guy off
because there's no way inna world that you can ruin
my guy, unless you ship him to the slammer. So I go
into the Cooper's office looking to get a lay-off on a
case I don't want, and split the fee, and get some
company for lunch, and I come out of Cooper's office

with company for lunch and the same case I went in with. You think there's something going on? I *know* there's something going on. But what the royal blue bejesus it is, I do not know. I take that back: I do know what is going on. What I do not know is who is doing it."

"What're you gonna do?" Gretchen said.

"I wanna see Mulvey," I said, "and I wanna see him this afternoon. After lunch." Mulvey is the guy I use for investigations, and I will get to him in a minute or two.

"How about the turkey in the reception area?" she said.

"How *about* him?" I said. "There's another one I haven't got any answers for. You got any idea what he wants this time, and why he keeps showing up like the thief in the night?"

"Nope," she said. "I came in and he was standing there. I let myself in, and he came in with me. He followed me home. Can I keep him?"

"Yes," I said. "Keep him somewhere else."

"I don't want him," she said. "You gonna see him or what?"

"Yup," I said. "Send him in."

"My," she said, "we *are* getting hospitable. Shall I frisk him first?"

"Do you find him attractive?" I said.

"Fuck you," she said.

"Just trying to let you get your cookies," I said. "If you're not gonna get your cookies, there ain't no need to frisk him, because I will neatly dispose of that little problem by a few probing questions. And if the answers aren't right, you'll never see him again."

"My pillow will be wet with tears," she said.

"Send the bastard in," I said.

The bastard came in. Gretchen was right—he did stink. He smelled like something with hair on it that had died and been left out in the sun and the rain just long enough to get so ripe that no scavenger would be interested in him. The bastard sat down.

"Well," I said.

"Mister Kennedy," he said, "you gottta help me."

"That has a familiar ring to it," I said.

"I know that," he said. "But things . . . I know things, I *seen* things I didn't know when I was in here before. I'm getting into trouble. I'm doing something and I dunno what it is. Mister Kennedy, I don't wanna get in trouble."

"Where's the broad?" I said.

"You mean Jill?" he said.

I was tempted to say that I meant Lizzie Borden, but choked that one back. The kid did have something of a deficiency. As Cooper would say, his porch light was out. It would not do much good to heckle him. He didn't have the wit to handle it. I said, "Yeah."

"She hadda work," he said. "See, I wasn't sure I was gonna be able to see you. I didn't know how long it was gonna take, and everything."

"No," I said. "As a matter of fact, if the other guy didn't have a problem, you wouldn't've. Because I wasn't coming in. Let me ask you something, all right? If you're willing to fork over five twenties to talk to me, why aren't you willing to drop a few dimes in a phone and make a long-distance call to see if I'm gonna be here?"

"Well," he said, "I was worried."

"Okay," I said. "You got money with you?"

"Yeah," he said, writhing around in the chair and fishing in his pocket. He brought up a fistful of currency which looked as though it had been buried for a while. He began to uncrumple the bills. In the wad he had singles, fives, tens, and a few twenties, but he had a lot of them. He smoothed them out and piled them up, his frown showing his concentration, his lips moving as he counted. When he finished, he put the bills on my desk and looked at me like a puppy which has been neglected for about three days and would really appreciate a drink of water and a snack. "It's all there, Mister Kennedy," he said.

It was all there. From what I could tell, reading

his lips, there was something in the neighborhood of $6,800 there, all in used bills of small denominations. "How much is all there?" I said.

"Sixty-nine hundred dollars," he said.

"What's it for?" I said.

"I wanna be able to talk to you," he said. "Whenever I want. I want you, advise me, so I don't get in trouble. I don't wanna go to jail, Mister Kennedy. I got no interest in that at all, and I'm willing to pay to stay out of it."

"You're making me nervous," I said. It was true. People who talk like that after placing large sums of money on my desk generally have two things wrong: they are about to get caught for doing something that they did, which the government can prove they did, and they think that I can lease a prosecutor and purchase a judge or do whatever else is necessary to keep them on the street.

As it happens, I do not know any prosecutors for rent, nor any judges who are for sale. I am willing to concede that there may be some, but who they are I do not know. Furthermore, I do not solicit prosecutors or judges to accept gratuities for certain extraordinary services, nor do I know any lawyer who does. I know a couple or three lawyers who *claim* they do, habitually assuring new clients that they went to law school with whoever the prosecutor—usually a total stranger—happens to be, and that they can get to the judge. While they cannot deliver what they promise, it does not really matter, because the client who comes up with five grand for the prosecutor and five grand for the judge, all of which the lawyer pockets as a little bonus for his efforts, does not know it never left his lawyer's pocket. And probably never got reported on Form 1040, either.

A fool in deep trouble will believe anything a lawyer tells him, if it's uttered in sonorous tones and does not contradict anything the client knows. That leaves a lot of ground for the greedy lawyer—most fools in deep trouble don't know much of anything, which is of course how they got in deep trouble in the first place.

The trouble is that the Board of Bar Overseers knows quite a bit, as does the IRS. If the word gets round that Attorney So-and-so is buying off cases in wholesale lots—and it does get around because assholes who swallow such pitches also regurgitate them to everyone who will listen—it is not long before he finds himself looking down the barrel of a disciplinary proceeding. Maybe even a short spell in the penitentiary, if things get truly hairy. I don't feature that shit.

I therefore explained to Donald French: "You are making me nervous because you are putting almost seven grand on my desk so you can talk to me. You can write to Dear Abby for the price of postage, which is going up all the time but still doesn't come to that. You're not charged with anything as far as I can see; you haven't done anything. I don't know what you want me to do. Until I do, you put that money in your pocket, because it isn't mine." I was fortified in that by the fees I had already collared that day—I could've quit for half a year on what I'd made that day as it was. There is nothing like prosperity to firm up a man's conscience.

Donald French put the money in his pocket again. He began to talk about Christopher Lynch, and a man giving his name as Warren Gould who had shown up around the marina, asking questions. "He's looking for me," French said. "I know he's looking for me. Is there any chance you could be there when he finds me? I don't wanna talk to him alone." That was when I told French to take the money out of his pocket again. I never did see Mulvey that day—he was out. Mack was not pleased when I got home late that night. Nor was she elated when I told her I had to go to the Cape the next morning. She said she didn't give a shit about the money—what she wanted was the vacation she had planned on with her husband.

12

JAKE WIRTH'S, that afternoon, had been serving goulash, a favorite of Cooper's and mine. I am not sure that it is properly designated *goulash*—what it seems to be is a fine beef stew with tomatoes in it. But then *boeuf Bourguignon* has always struck me as beef stew with red wine in it. It does not really matter; I like Jake's goulash. We had it with dark beer and salads.

I brought Cooper up to speed, as he is fond of saying, on Donald French. This enabled me to pay for lunch and deduct it, and also debit French's retainer for the time spent eating the lunch, and the time Cooper spent eating lunch while conferring about French's case, because I paid Cooper $100 for consultation. That lunch cost Donald French about $225, including tip.

"All right," Cooper said, "you are clearly gonna have to go down there and take a look at things. Mulvey ain't gonna get you nothing, at this point. Probably not much later, either. I dunno why you use that clown. But you would have to if you didn't have to, because the guy wants you to, and that is his American money which you are sucking down into your gut."

"This is true," I said.

"When a man pays you some money to do something," Cooper said, belching softly, "and it is not against the law or anything serious in the canons of ethics, you've got to do it, am I right?"

"Absolutely," I said.

"Now there are several serious questions here," Cooper said. "I think I'll probably order up another pitcher of beer so we can consider them with the gravity they deserve."

"Absolutely," I said.

"The first thing," Cooper said, "is where the goddamned kid got all the money. You got any idea where he got all that money?"

"No," I said. "It's not funny, though. I inspected it closely and the serial numbers are all different. The paper looks good. Appears to be genuine American currency, legal tender for all debts, public and private. Probably came from the Bureau of Printing and Engraving, is my guess."

"Good," Cooper said with satisfaction. I don't know whether he referred to the currency or the pitcher of beer. "What I like about cash is that it doesn't bounce. What I don't like about cash is that I seldom have enough of it, and when I get enough of it, like I am doing today, it generally means that my guy probably got caught fair and square and I am going to have some trouble getting him out. Although I must say, between the two of us, we are having one hell of a damned fine day for ourselves."

"We are that," I said.

"Jesus Christ," Cooper said, "what a fucking racket. I go for months clipping the house money to keep the office landlord off my back, and I have to decide in the morning whether I got enough gas in the car to get me home that night and to the station in the morning, because if I have I can pick up the fucking cleaning and if I haven't, the cleaning's gonna have to wait because I got to get gas, and then I get a day like this which if I had a month of them I could buy a cattle plantation in the Argentine and spend the rest of my life playing Carmen Miranda records and having cocktails with SS officers who escaped in time. I'm either nigger rich or stone broke, and there ain't no in-between. In the next life I'm gonna be a motorman on a trolley, so I get a check every week and don't have to worry about anything.

"But since I didn't do that, this time around,"

Cooper said, "I gotta think some about where our client got all this money that he so kindly gave to you, and which you are kind and generous enough to share with me."

"My guess," I said, "and it is only that, is that Donald French did something that might very well get him into trouble, to get the money to pay me to keep him out of trouble. Which, as I told him when he was not in trouble, was not necessary because then he was not in trouble. I think he graduated from tuning motors to peddling a little stuff for the guy who pays him to tune the motors so he can go and get the stuff."

"This raises several further interesting questions," Cooper said.

"Chief among them whether he is liable to get caught," I said.

"Chief," Cooper said, "but last. The first question is who else knows about this little frolic and detour."

"The broad certainly does," I said.

"Did he tell you that?" Cooper said.

"Nope," I said. "I didn't ask him. If I'd've asked him, he would've lied anyway. But she's the dominant one in that little setup. If he wants to take a shit, he has to get permission first. And she didn't like him coming to see me, not at all."

"That's interesting," Cooper said. "I wonder why that is? I wouldn't think a lady'd want her boyfriend to get in the crap. I should think she'd be glad if he went to see a lawyer and got himself some well-informed advice."

"You would think that, wouldn't you," I said.

"You don't suppose the lady wants her boyfriend to get in trouble, do you?" Cooper said.

"The thought had crossed my mind," I said. "She reminded him in my office that she never signed up for more'n six weeks at a time. Maybe she'd like the government to break her lease for her."

"Or maybe she works for the government," Cooper said.

"You know, Cooper," I said, "that kid is getting a

bargain, taking you to lunch. I never thought of that."

"Well," he said, "it's worth a minute or two of reflection. There's very few agencies now, haven't got themselves a couple or three sparrows around."

"Sparrows?" I said.

"Cunts," he said. "Women who'll put out at GS-15 salaries to get guys to incriminate themselves. It's hookin' no matter what you call it, but it works. Shit, it's been working since Eve went into the fruit business and sold the first apple to Adam. Just that the CIA was about the only outfit that had 'em, until recently. I'd be very surprised if some of them drug investigators didn't have one or two of them on call now. Very surprised. Now, who else knows about it?"

"Well, obviously," I said, "the guy who sold him the stuff."

"And," Cooper said, "the guy that the seller got the stuff from, since that amount is more than a little, but a whole lot less than a lot and the major party wouldn't let the middleman hand it off unless he was satisfied the middleman had the new guy right. So that makes at least three other people, including the broad, who know that your client is no longer a law-abiding citizen, if he ever was one, and one of them could very well turn out to be a lady cop."

"You're not improving my morale," I said.

"Mine's been shot for years," Cooper said. "But still, let's think about it some more. Your guy hasn't been arrested. So that means they're either waiting for a grand jury to hook him, which they don't generally do when they're dealing with this type of fellow because this type of fellow is kind of footloose anyway, and has a tendency to scram unless he's being held in lieu of bail, or else he's not the guy they want but the guy they hadda get to get the guy they want, and they're gonna pay out a little more rope with him on the end of it to see if they can get something really big going down.

"Now," Cooper said, "that makes your guy safe enough for the time being, which in my estimation is not the kind of safety that would interest a careful man, because it don't last so good. The time being, I mean. And at the end of the time being, they are gonna make a decision about him. The law, I mean. If he takes them to his leader, they will probably grab everybody in sight on a conspiracy charge and then wait around to see if they need to cut a deal with your guy or one of the other guys to flesh it out a bit for them. Of course if they grab everybody with the plastic bags in hand, it's not gonna be necessary to be friendly with anybody, because they will all go away and not for any brief vacation, neither. But if they don't grab everybody, they are gonna be lookin' for a stoolie, I believe it's called, who will turn over and rat everybody else into the slammer."

"Which would be Donald French, in this instance," I said.

"He's the likeliest nominee," Cooper said. "He's probably the smallest boy in the group, which means they can give him a pass and get the big fellas, and that is what they generally prefer to do. The trouble is that the big fellas know this, and have ways of avoiding the problem, and that is not good news for your guy when they decide to use those ways."

"I'm beginning to feel sorry for this kid," I said.

"Don't," Cooper said. "You didn't tell him to go slam his cock with a mallet. He did it on his own. Fact, what you told him to do was absolutely nothing, because he wasn't *in* any trouble, and he went out and did the other thing, which is why he *is* in trouble now. Probably."

"To get money to pay me," I said. "I don't think I'm gonna tell Mack all the dreary details about this one."

She was still sleeping when I left for Hyannis in the morning.

13

IN MIDAFTERNOON of the next day, Harris made the first footsteps on the marina catwalk that I had heard all day. I was sitting on the catwalk while French was tinkering with *Catapult*. French looked up in the sun, sweat drooling down his mirrored sunglasses. Harris—at the time I thought his name was Gould— wore a pale green buttondown shirt with a pale yellow stripe, the collar open and the sleeves rolled up, the brown knit tie loosened so that the knot was at his breastbone. The shirt, full of belly, bulged over the brown suit pants and the gold belt buckle. Harris wore brown loafers, and a Corum goldpiece watch on a snakeskin strap. His Ray-Bans were mirrored glass, and his gray hair was cut short.

"How's it going?" Harris said.

"Ahh, you know," French said. "It's hot."

Harris looked at me. I said, "Hi." Evidently I persuaded him that I was just a casual loafer.

Harris surveyed the sky, as though the thought had not occurred to him. Appearing to find it reasonable, he said, "Yeah, but if you gotta have hot days, this is the place to be on them. 'Stead of inside, in an office someplace."

"Depends," the Frenchman said. "They air-condition offices, 'way I get it." He resumed work with the torque wrench on the left cylinder head of the port engine.

"You're pretty handy with that thing," Harris said, approvingly.

The Frenchman did not look up. "Yeah," he said. "When I was in college, which was long enough ago, all my wealthy friends had Corvettes, and I had all their wealth, 'cause I could fix them.

"Then one day," he grunted on the wrench, "the thought occurred to me, why am I going to all the trouble of taking their money, and then just going and handing it over to this place that's teaching me a whole lot of things I obviously don't need to know, and charging the ass off me to do it? So, I quit."

He stood up in the engine well. He wiped his forehead with his forearm. "Now, I know the answer: so I wouldn't have to spend hot days in the open, instead of an air-conditioned office. Only now it's too late."

"What're you doing?" Harris said, gesturing vaguely in the direction of the boat.

"I'm not really sure, you want the truth," French said. "I think what I'm doing is maintaining engines that get used too hard. This one here," he said, pointing to the port engine, "she started leaking a little oil, and it turned out to be a gasket. The starboard"—he pointed over his shoulder with his left thumb—"was misfiring, but I didn't get to that, yet. Probably a couple bad plugs. Down there," he said, pointing to a thin black line around the bilge at the level of the crankcases, "you can see the oil."

Harris looked as though he did not really understand. "What'll she do, when she's right?" he said.

"Ahh," French said, "tell you the truth, I really dunno. She's fast, though, with this iron in her. Probably, oh, fifty. In a sea like this. Millpond. You'd get banged around pretty good in anything very heavy, even three-to-five footers. But she'll move, all right. You floor these mothers, you'll have her up in the air in a minute. 'Course, you'll burn thirty gallons an hour, but if you got the money, it's all right with me."

"These cost a lot of money?" Harris said.

"I don't really know exactly what they cost," French said. "Fifteen, twenty, probably." He looked at the boat and curled his lip. "More'n they're worth: that's for sure."

"They're not good boats?" Harris said.

"They're not well built," French said. "They're awful light, and they're overpowered. What they are is copies of the Cigarettes, that they use for open-ocean racing. They look like Cigarettes, and with these mammoth mothers howling in the back, they go like Cigarettes, but they just shake themselves to pieces. What this is, is basically a lake boat. But it goes so goddamned fast you'd run out of lake in about fifteen minutes. Unless you happened to be on Lake Michigan, in which case you would need an ocean boat. This is actually junk. It's a cheap hotrod."

"Does the owner know this?" Harris said.

"He don't know it from me," French said.

"Don't you tell your customers things like this?" Harris said.

"In the first place," French said, "only if they ask me. People're strange about their boats. You don't go around insulting them. In the second place: this guy couldn't've, because I never met him."

"You work for people, and you don't even ask their names?" Harris said.

"No, I don't," French said. "I work for money."

Harris was immediately apologetic. He sat down on the catwalk and extended his hand toward French. "I'm sorry," he said, "my name is Gould. Warren Gould."

"Donald," French said, shaking hands. "Most people just call me *Don*. How ya doin'?"

"Okay," Harris said. "Sorry if I seem kind of nosy, but I was thinkin' about gettin' myself somethin' like this, and I thought you might probably know somethin' about them."

"Actually," French said, looking the boat over, "I don't know a helluva lot about the boat itself. The whole boat, I mean. The engines I know pretty good, but so would any Olds mechanic that you talked to. I never did any other real work on her."

"They work pretty well, do they?" Harris said.

"They're like any other engine," French said. "I

don't care if they're diesel or gas, old or new, big or little—you treat them right, they'll treat you right. You neglect them, you're gonna have trouble. You use 'em too hard, you're gonna have trouble. Engines're just like women."

Harris laughed. "Maybe it's the other way around," he said.

"Nope," French said, "in a way, they're worse. You mistreat a woman, she's liable, go and divorce you, cost you a lotta money. You don't treat your engine right, you're liable to find yourself with a helluva long way to paddle home, and a thunderstorm coming up, just to make things interesting."

"You take these things out yourself?" Harris said.

"Mister," French said, "about once every three or four weeks, when I just can't be sure the things're running all right, by testing them at the dock, I put on about three life jackets, check to make sure there's a copy of my will in a safe place, call the weather service and the airport every five minutes before I go out, and then, when I'm all through, I make a good Act of Contrition, commend my soul to the Holy Spirit, drive it once, very slowly, about a hundred yards out and a hundred yards back, and declare it operational."

"You don't like boats?" Harris said.

"I don't dislike boats," French said. "I don't hate sharks, either, but I don't mess with the fuckers any more'n I can help. I don't know from boats."

"Funny job for you to have, seems like," Harris said.

"I do know engines," French said. "Boats happen to have engines. I work on engines. I work on cars, I'd be in a hot garage all day, diving under the hoods of Cadillacs. I work on boats, at least I got the fresh air. Plus which, everybody that owns boats is rich, and when there's something wrong with their boats, completely crazy. So instead of getting union rates to do the next job in line, while the owner of the garage belts the hell out of the driver and keeps the difference, I get to do the next job that pays the best, because these guys can never wait. I had guys pay forty an hour, just to get me, jump their job ahead of two or three other guys. I know guys from Nam, aren't makin' that kind of money today, and they're killin' people in Angola. Maybe it's Cubans. I forget. This's much more comfortable."

"Are you good at it?" Harris said.

"Very good," French said.

"See, the reason I ask," Harris said, "my kids're nuts about water-skiing. But this friend of ours, that keeps his boat up at Winnipesaukee, he's always having trouble with it. Now, I can't afford anything in this class, obviously, but if I'm gonna get one, I'd like to keep it somewhere, I'm not gonna have his problem, that when it breaks, he can't get nobody, fix it. You follow me?"

"Yeah," French said.

"So, that's why I was asking," Harris said.

"Well," French said, "there's a few good boat yards. But, basically, unless you're talking where you're willing to spend a *lot* of money, you're not gonna get what you're after unless you go outboards. You get a couple big Mercs, match 'em properly to a good hull, you got yourself a rig that'll give you more'n enough power, what you need, couple, maybe three skiers, thirty-five, forty miles an hour, and you can hump them offa the transom yourself and take them somewhere, where they aren't swamped with business, they can take care of you. Follow me? You get something like this bucket, you are gonna get ruined before you're through. And you're not gonna have the use of your boat a lot of the time, either."

"Outboards," Harris said. "Some reason or other, I dunno, that doesn't appeal to me. How 'bout one of these, year or so old?"

"I wouldn't do it, I was you," French said. "The reason these things . . . you could save a lot of money offa the list price of one of these things, year or so old, but the reason you can is because the people that buy them, know what they are, and that they can't take the beating which they give them for very long. So instead of buying something good, that could take the beating, but would have to get fixed a lot, three, four years down the line, they think up some kind of business reason, they got to have a boat, buy one of these, beat the shit out of it for a season or two, sell it at a loss, take the loss offa their tax, buy another one, beat the shit out of that, and so on. After about three years, you're buying their boats for them, which there is nothing you can do anything about because you gotta pay taxes. But there is something you can do about riding around in those boats that they beat the shit out of, which is: stay out of them; they're dangerous. They still go fast, and they look like rockets when they're standing still, but they tend to come apart in the water, and all of sudden spring leaks in a seaway, and this can be upsetting to those near and dear to you."

Harris stood up. "Thanks a lot, Don," he said. "I ever decide to go nuts and buy one, I'll come in here and let you service her. Forty bucks an hour right?"

"To you," French said, "seeing as how you're such a nice guy and all, thirty-nine ninety-five." He went back to work on the engine.

I went up to the pay phone after Harris had left. I called Cooper. Cooper said, "If that's the guy I think it is and hope it isn't, that is not his name. Son of a bitch. I wonder when the hell he got up here."

14

CHRISTOPHER LYNCH, his beard neatly trimmed, shucked oysters and clams with professional speed at the bar of the Calumet Harbor Club Inn at Hyannis, flipping the top shells into the gray plastic rubbish bag set in the green plastic pail to his left, pouring red sauce into small pewter vessels, flourishing lemon wedges onto the iced pewter plates with the shellfish, humming "Me and Bobby McGee" as he worked.

Two corpulent realtors, Fred and Lurleen, co-owners of Cape Elite Real Estate, and veterans of a nine-year adulterous relationship greatly relieving to their respective spouses (who could not stand them), huddled in shorts and Lacoste polo shirts at the end of the bar, winded after eighteen holes of pitch-and-putt golf. I had told them I was interested in a piece of land on the Cape. They told me all the rest.

" 'Nother dose of them silver bullets, Chris baby," Lurleen said, waving her martini glass. "Christ, it was hot out there today. And give my man here a few dozen, them oysters."

"Clams," Fred said, poring over the line on the game (7:30 at Cleveland, Tiant, 7–5, Bibby, 4–6, line 6–8 Boston, *Herald American*).

"Oysters," Lurleen said. "You're gettin' along in years, Freddie, babe. Use all the help you can get."

Christopher Lynch served oysters to Fred, who ate without noticing what he was getting. "Whaddaya think, Chris," he said. "Line sucks, I think. Odds make no sense, 'way they been going."

"The way they've been goin'," Lynch said, bracing

himself on the edge of the bar, "nothing makes any sense."

Harris, looking hot and uncomfortable, entered the bar through the screen door, and took up a seat at the opposite end. He glanced at me without apparent interest.

"Eight homers a game," Lynch said to Lurleen, "that doesn't make sense. Look at the goddamned lineup they got, and your skin practically crawls. Look at the pitching they got, and you feel even worse. What the hell happened to Torrez, for Christ sake? Campbell? He is dead, I think. One way you're gonna get your brains beaten out, they start hittin' homers, and the other way, you get your brains beaten out, the other team throws a pitcher that's on, and he holds them to merely five or six runs while our guys're giving up nine. And, we lose."

"So whaddaya do?" Lurleen said.

"Ahem," Harris said.

"Right with you, sir," Lynch said cheerfully. "You do this," he said to Lurleen. "What you do is, you figure this outfit's gonna win two outta three from every club in their division except the Yankees and the Orioles. When they're playing anybody else, every time they take two, you bet them, lose the third."

"They won nine in a row," she said.

"They lost nine in a row, too," Lynch said. "Which, if you were following my system, as I was, you lost three bets in the win streak, and three in the losing streak, except the win streak has three Yankees and four Baltimores in it, which I laid off, and the loss streak had three Yankees in it, which I also laid off, so I lost three times. But I been winning since the middle of May, when I started this thing, and I'm up, about now, a hundred a bet, about four thousand dollars. This is not bad."

Lynch addressed Harris. "What'll it be, sir?"

"Beer," Harris said. "You got anythin' on draft?"

"Sure," Lynch said, "we got . . ."

"Mister," Lurleen said to Harris, "forget it. Beer

you can get any place. What we have got here is the finest martini thing a man ever made. Show him the penguin, Chris."

"I just want a beer," Harris said.

"Uh uh," Lurleen said. She shook her head vigorously. "Christopher, show him the penguin."

Lynch held up a silver-plated penguin, eighteen inches high.

"See that?" Lurleen said. "That there's the best martini thing ever made. Show him how it works, Chris."

"You take it here," Lynch said, grasping the bird at the middle, "and you take the head off, and you fill the mother up with ice and booze, and you put the head back on, and you shake her up some, and you pour the nectar out the snout, here. And there's a strainer in the beak, see?" He flipped the beak up.

"Puts hair on your chest, and desire in yer heart," Lurleen said. "That there penguin used to be inna bar of the Hotel Plaza in New York. It's a fuckin' heirloom's what it is. You don't get yourself a charge outta one of them things, you never had a martini in your whole goddamned life."

"If I have one," Harris said to Lynch, "*then* can I have a beer?"

"You can have a beer without havin' one," Lynch said, grinning. "You don't have to do what she says."

"Uh, actually," Harris said, "I think as a matter of fact that I do. Looks like, it might be safer."

" 'Nother thing," Lurleen said to Harris, "where you from?"

"You want some oysters or something?" Lynch said to Harris.

"Uh," Harris said to Lurleen, "yeah."

"Whaddaya mean, 'Yeah'?" she said.

"I'll have some oysters," Harris said.

"You better get a room," Lurleen said. "I got a girlfriend, you oughta meet."

"Actually," Harris said, "I've got to go back tonight."

"You can still have the oysters, though," Lynch said. "Give you some strength."

"Oh, yeah," Harris said. "I can have the oysters."

"Where're you going?" Lurleen said.

"Home," Harris said. "I'm going home. I was down here for the day, on business, and now I'm going home."

"What's your business?" Lynch said.

"Where's your home?" Lurleen said.

Lynch finished making the martinis, and began pouring them.

Harris spread his hands. "Look, you guys, all right? One at a time. The last time I got this many questions was the night I was coming through Northampton, and some guys got out of the Hampshire County House of Correction and I was half in the bag, and I run a goddamned roadblock. And they were easier on me'n you are.

"My business is I represent some investors, who are interested in some land down here, and I've been down here lookin' at it."

"Over Chatham?" Lynch said.

"I said all I'm going to say about it," Harris said. "I already said more'n I should say about it. These people're very jumpy about people finding out what kind of things they got in mind, and I shouldn't even've said that."

"The reason I ask," Lynch said, "I know a couple people with some prime shorefront land to sell, and you really oughta talk to them."

"My turn," Lurleen said. "How'sa martini, by the way?"

"Excellent," Harris said, tasting it. "Best I ever had. Of course, I never drink martinis, but this's really good."

"Still my turn," Lurleen said. "Where's your home?"

"Boston," Harris said.

"Boston actually, or Boston-somewhere-inna-suburbs?" she said.

"The suburbs," Harris said.

"Dunno why I asked," she said. "Still good enough. Gotta question for you, all right? Tiant-Bibby, six to eight, Sox: geddown, or lay off: which is it?"

"Jesus *Christ,*" Harris said, finishing the martini. "Can I please have a beer, now?"

"Sure," Lynch said, drawing a draft Heineken.

"Whaddaya say?" Lurleen said. "Geddown, or lay off?"

"Actually," Harris said, "I don't bet that much. I hate to admit it . . ."

"You're buyin' up land, and you say you don't bet?" Lurleen said. "You're not only a liar; you're an asshole."

". . . but I don't even follow the Red Sox. I don't *like* baseball."

"He *is* an asshole," Lurleen said to Lynch, with satisfaction. "He admitted it, and he's goddamned right, I say."

"Oh," Lynch said.

"Freddie," Lurleen said, "do what Christopher said. Only, make it a grand."

"What did he say," Fred said.

"I didn't say anything," Lynch said.

"A grand against," she said. "They're gonna get their ears beat off."

"Oh," Freddie said. "That's half of what we made, today."

"Yup," she said. She whacked him on the shoulder. "Now, go do it." Freddie staggered off to the pay phone. Lurleen finished her martini, crossed her arms on the bar, and went to sleep. She snored delicately.

"Jesus," Harris said to Lynch.

"I know," Lynch said, "but they're season members of the club, and they tip pretty good, and they otherwise leave a lot of money here. They're both crazy, of course, but that's the way it was sometimes, movin' west."

"The world," Harris said, "you know something? The world is full of crazy people. They are in the vast fuckin' majority. God only knows what we're going to do with all of them."

"Same thing we're doin' now," Lynch said. "Leave them take care of themselves. They generally do a lousy job of it, but it's better'n the job anybody else can do for them."

"This is true," Harris said.

Lynch leaned across the bar. "Come on, now," he said. "What're you actually doing here?"

"Just exactly what I said," Harris said. "My name is Warren Harris, and I represent some people who invest in real estate, and I came down here today, to talk to some people, and that is all you get."

"Oh," Lynch said. He stood up.

"I also looked at a boat," Harris said, "on account of as how, my daughters've somehow gotten the idea that I am Nelson A. Rockefeller, and they want to go water-skiing. Except for that, that is the whole thing."

"You oughta see a friend of mine," Lynch said.

"What's he sell?" Harris said. "Land, or boats?"

"Neither," Lynch said. "What he does, he fixes boats. Name of French."

"Never heard of him," Harris said.

"Donald French," Lynch said. "The Frenchman."

"Young guy?" Harris said. "Blond hair, kind of long, mustache? Pretty good mechanic?"

"That's the one," Lynch said.

"Met him," Harris said.

"He's all right," Lynch said.

"Seemed very nice," Harris said. "Gave me a lot of good advice. I liked him."

"There you go," Lynch said. "There's nothin' I can do for you, then. You got the best there is."

Harris belched. "As a matter of fact," he said, "there is. It's a long ride back to Sudbury. Can I get some dinner here?"

"You better take a room, too," Lynch said. "You look pretty well shot, to me. Call home and do it, and go home tomorrow."

Harris stood up, somewhat unsteady. "Where's the phone?" he said. "I'll do it."

If I had not been in the men's room after dinner that evening, emerging just as he reentered the bar with Jill Candelaria, I would have blown the whole detail. As it was, they went directly into the dining room and were seated next to the service bar. When they were out of sight I took my seat at the bar again and told Chris that I had changed my mind, and would have another beer for the road. I could hear them, but I could not see them. Chris served the beer and went back to the other end of the bar, where he was engrossed in the baseball game.

15

JILL SAID that the trouble was that she was not making any progress. "I'm not getting anywhere," she said.

Harris said, *"Shit."*

"Facts're facts," she said. "The fact is, I haven't got much. I think we moved too soon, moved in on French too soon. I could get it out of him, if it was in him, but it isn't. He's just the wrong guy. We made a mistake. He just doesn't know."

"You're sure," Harris said, "he's not just being cute with you."

"Absolutely sure," she said. "The Frenchman reminds me of a guy I knew in high school: he's just bright enough to know he's really stupid.

"People can sense that, Warren," she said. "If I can do it, the people in this operation can do it, and they reach the same conclusion, they *reached* the same conclusion, I did. Which is that a guy like that is dangerous. Because he knows when you're not telling him everything, and he knows *why* you're not telling him everything, and he resents it. It makes him mad. But he also knows, in a strange sort of way, that you're *right,* in not telling him everything, so he just sort of teeters back and forth between being mad at you and being obedient. It's like keeping a Doberman: they're efficient, but you're never quite sure what they're going to do next.

"What we should've done, I think," she said, "is, I should've made the move on Chris."

"He seems harmless enough," Harris said. "Nice,

personable chap. Sort of a bum, but fairly cagey, slow-moving, easy to get along with."

"That's exactly right," she said. "And that's why, he is the guy that we should've cuddled up to. Chris is smart. He's so smart, he doesn't act smart, and that is really smart. That guy can do the *Times* crossword puzzle in his head. You can trust him if you want to, but you better count the spoons."

"Has he got a girlfriend?" Harris said.

"Every night," she said. "A different one. Chris runs that bar like a ringmaster. Any animal, wanders in, he will train her, and by the time the week is up, she'll be jumping through the hoops with the best of them. Chris is sexy, and what makes him even sexier is that he knows it."

"You couldn't move in on him, then," Harris said, wistfully.

"Warren," she said, "Chris wouldn't give me house room. To him, I'm the Frenchman's lady, and that's another thing about Chris: he plays by the rules. Not all of the rules, but the ones he likes, he plays by. You're all right if you know the ones he subscribes to, and *only* if you know and obey 'em. That's one of them."

"Women as property, huh?" Harris said. "I didn't really expect to hear that from you."

"Lately, Warren," she said, "I notice expectations've been getting us in a whole mess of trouble. If it wasn't for expectations, I maybe might not be neutralized as far as Chris's concerned. Although, thinking about it, the way he goes through women, I probably couldn't've kept him entertained long enough to get anything out of him anyway. Of course assuming that there's not another buffer between Chris and the guy that owns the boat, and does the business."

"Shit," Harris said. He sighed. "This guy never drops the ball. He's handed off to me at least twelve times, since nineteen-sixty-eight, and he just never drops the ball. Of course, if he did, he'd be doing ten or so down in Atlanta, but that's beside the point. If he says that there's a deal going down, there is always a deal going down. Always."

"Maybe," Jill said, "you should call him up and have another little chat with him."

"I did," Harris said. "I got a rerun of the stuff I got before, and it cost me a cousin of his, by marriage, that I had every intention of dumping this weekend. Little shit—he's got a lousy hundredweight of grass in a false-bottom Plymouth going into the sovereign state of New Hampshire tomorrow night, and we were going to bag him so good he'd never have a tan again till nineteen-eighty-one."

"You win some," she said, "and you lose some. Ah, well."

"Ahh," Harris said, "doesn't matter, really. Mosquito. Nothing to worry about. I told him, I said, 'My friend, you deked me. You're not supposed to do that.' 'Well,' he says, 'his mother was worried about him, and she's my favorite aunt, so I thought I would just sort of ask, is all. You want favors from me, the least I can do is get a favor from you, now and then, it's something that's important to my family.' 'Well,' I said, 'okay. If he was prudent, he wouldn't take that trip he's got in mind. And yes, I do recognize the name, and that is all I'm going to say to you about it.' 'Oh,' he says.

"'And let me tell you something else, in case it's necessary,' I said, 'if he should take it in his head, ignore this excellent advice that I assume you're going to see he gets, those guys're going to be in place, and I will've never heard of him. You got it?' 'I got it,' he says.

"'Okay,' I said. 'Now that I'm through acting as bail bondsman for your crooked relatives, what've you got that might interest me?'

"'Well,' he says, 'my favorite client got arrested again, the poor old bastard. Felt the urge while he was standing on Tremont Street at high noon, whipped it out and peed in the gutter. If he didn't have about a half a million bucks in spare change, I wouldn't even bother with him, eighth or ninth time this year.

" 'Then there's my brother-in-law, down at the bank, who strongly believes his wife oughta get out of the public defenders and become the new Congressperson from the Eleventh District. Which laudable goal I can measurably advance by giving my beloved sister sixty percent of everything I make for the next twelve months. "Only don't mark it down as campaign contributions, because that's illegal," he says. "My friend, there is no way in the world that I'll do anything illegal in that line, because I never reach the question of *legal*. This kind of thing, I stop at *stupid*," I said. 'Other'n that, nothing much going on.'

" 'This,' I said, 'is not exactly the sort of thing I had in mind, for so splendid a deed as I just did for your favorite aunt.'

" 'Ahh,' he says, 'but you owed me one. You guys got Tiger Grable fifteen years, when the poor lad was merely tryin' to eke out a modest living in a trade which ought not be illegal anyway.' "

"Jesus *Christ*," Jill said, "the Tiger got fifteen?"

"Damned straight certain," Harris said. "Fifteen large ones. The government is under the impression that it has some kind of monopoly on methadone, and that old judge didn't like it one bit when they proved how much Tiger hijacked from the warehouse."

"Well, what the hell," Jill said. "It's not like it was Tiger's first visit to the bar of justice."

"That's essentially what I said," Harris said. "Did not impress the gentleman.

" 'I'm short on love for Tiger Grable,' he said, 'inasmuch as Tiger took violent exception one night to some competition he was getting from a valued client of mine, and wasted the guy when he had at least three hundred K worth of indictments pending against him from here to New Orleans. Thing of it is, I'm also short on getting Tiger mad. He may be down in Georgia there, getting rehabilitated, and learning useful trades, but he has friends at large, and a fertile mind for instigating things for them to do. You got me in the hole on that one, Warren, and you owed me one for nothing.'

"I went after him," Harris said. " 'Since I put you in the hole, you know, I can deepen it if I want, with a word in the right place.'

" 'You know, Warren,' he said, 'a long time ago, I thought of that possibility. You looked like a devious man to me, both useful and dangerous for the same reason. And I thought to myself that I should build a backfire. Which I did. If the FBI had any notion whatsoever, of ten percent of what you do, they would be galvanized into paroxysms of activity.'

" 'If the FBI got my files,' I said, 'the FBI would burn them. Don't you lawyers read the papers?'

" 'That we do,' he said. 'And this is why, what my untimely misfortune would cause is not a letter to the FBI, but a series of affidavits, to the *Washington Post*.' "

"Well, well, well," Jill said. "That lawyer is cute."

"Cuter'n Liz Taylor in *National Velvet*," Harris said, "the son of a bitch."

I left without either of them seeing me, and met French, late, at the Poseidon Lounge in Harwich.

16

Mack was still awake when I got home just before midnight. "Jesus Christ," she said, after she kissed me, "you look bushed. Are you okay?"

"I am bushed," I said, "and no, I'm not okay. For a goddamned vacation, I've had one fucking day of it. The kid paid me almost seven thousand dollars and I swear to God I earned every damned dime of it today."

"Want some more good news?" she said. "Teddy Franklin called. Wants you to call him at home no matter what time you get in."

"Christ," I said, "what is it now? That damned cop eat one of Teddy's Cadillacs this time?"

"He wouldn't tell me," she said. "Just that he's got to talk to you tonight, and you should call him at home."

"And I will," I said, "and he'll be out, and I'll wake up Dorothy and get her all pissed-off, and he'll get home about three in the morning and wake me up and get me all pissed-off, and when we get all through making life miserable for each other, we won't've accomplished a single solitary thing we couldn't've done better if we waited till the morning and tried it on a good night's sleep."

"You want a beer first?" she said.

"No," I said. "I had too much beer already. I'm all bloated. Yeah. I would like a beer."

"And sit down and unwind a minute or ten before you call him," she said.

"For whatever good that'll do," I said. I went in

and collapsed on the couch. I damned near slid off it. I hate vinyl couches. If the house hadn't come with it, and I could afford another one which would take the abuse this one has taken, I'd replace it. But this one has absorbed several years of our wet bathing suits, not to mention God only knows what kind of treatment it got from the previous owners, and I am not inclined to screw around with things that stand up.

"What's going on?" she said, bringing the beer.

"Christ," I said, "I don't know. I know more'n I did, which is not more'n Cooper led me to suspect, that that broad is an undercover nark, but I dunno what to make of it. More important, I dunno what to do about it. I got to talk to Cooper."

"Shit," Mack said. "Does that mean what I think it means?"

"If you think it means that I've gotta go to work tomorrow," I said, "that's exactly what it means."

"Oh, my God," she said. "Tell me this, how do you tell the difference between when you're on vacation and when you're working? Is vacation when you go to the office from Green Harbor, instead of Braintree or something? Why can't Bad Eye handle this?"

Let me explain to you about Bad Eye Mulvey, my trepid private eye. Edward J. Mulvey was a detective in the Boston Police Department for thirty years, retiring when he finally got discouraged, at age sixty, about his prospects of ever making lieutenant.

He is a small, pineapple-shaped man with a mournful expression that is not brightened by his horn-rimmed glasses and the wisps of white hair on his dome. He wears polyester clothing that he gets from Zayre and he always looks as though he had something wrong with his stomach. He has a lazy left eye, which he was born with—Bad Eye never pulled a gun in anger, or fought anyone in the line of duty or anywhere else.

He is a ferret. His specialty is finding things out. That is what he did in those three decades of backing up the fellows in the detective bureau who were investigating the hot stuff and needed some drone to run registration numbers. Somebody stupid enough to endure the tedium of checking records, interviewing neighbors, examining land titles, locating possible witnesses. Somebody smart enough to perceive the fact that nobody would ever trust him to dispose of a partially eaten lollipop (because he would certainly discard it inside a file of critical importance), but dumb enough to accept it without getting mad.

That is exactly what Bad Eye is. He fits the bill perfectly. He may be a donkey, fit for no more than donkey work, but he is a willing donkey, not a presumptuous jackass who tries to give you more than what you ordered up, and fails to give you what you needed. He is cheap. He charges $7.50 an hour, plus expenses—Bad Eye's expense sheets never include more than $1.55 for lunch, including tip—partly because he works out of his house and your secretary types up all his reports for you, and partly because Bad Eye has his pension and his wife has her pension from a lifetime of drudgery at Jordan Marsh, and that $7.50 an hour nicely covers what few extras Bad Eye and his wife desire.

You can always find Bad Eye by phone. If he says he'll need till Wednesday to get what some hotshot could produce for $20 an hour by the middle of Monday morning, you nevertheless have the consolation that on Wednesday Bad Eye will show up at your office with the stuff, and not call in from an expensive restaurant around dinner time on Monday to explain that he's hit a few snags and can't deliver until Thursday. What Bad Eye is, is reliable. He would be a total loss at detecting the actual killer in the murder of your spouse, with which you were wrongly charged, but if you want to know whether the chief prosecution witness really was in Worcester on the seventh of the month, and saw your client robbing a bank, Bad Eye will find out. And if that witness was not in Worcester, Bad Eye will find out where he was, and what he was doing there.

There are times when I think we should clone Bad Eye, bad eye and all, and put his products to work in every local, State and federal agency that deals with the public. They would inevitably paint all of the offices light gray, and everywhere you looked there would be one of those goddamned coffee machines that dispense hot water, colored gray with sawdust and sweetened with saccharine. But the fucking goddamned work would get done even if they were doing it in metallic blue and gray double-knit slacks and maroon double-knit blazers.

"No," I said to Mack, "I can't put Bad Eye on this. It involves thought, not drudgery. Bad Eye is good at finding out answers, but you have to state the question very precisely. He knows every cop in the State, and he will ask them anything I want, but I don't know what I want him to ask them. Cooper uses a guy named Spenser and says he's pretty good, but Spenser's one of those fresh bastards that thinks he's the sword of justice and goes running off to London every chance he gets, like he was trying out for his own television series. This is something I've got to do myself, I guess, at least until I find out what the hell it is I'm doing, so I can tell somebody else what to do. I can use Bad Eye on the fairy case, but I've got to talk to Cooper about this one.

"The reason that I need some help," I said, "is because French isn't likely to know what's going on, and probably never will. That kid doesn't know anything. Now here is a kid that I don't understand at all. I meet him in this clapped-out saloon where he's got this drunken woman draped all over him, and I dunno whether to shit or get offa the pot. He's a big kid, and he looks like the kind of guy that's quick with his hands if you get him pissed-off. He's living with this broad that I just saw in the company of another guy, which is one thing she's got wrong with her and would be enough for most guys even if they couldn't do what French can probably do if he gets all steamed up. So I got reservations about telling him that, because it's bad enough he's drumming up a drug charge for himself and I don't want him arranging for a murder-one case against him. Plus which, the other thing she's got wrong with her is that she's a nark and she's trying to put him in jail. Which is certainly information that he maybe oughta have. But if I give it to him, something nasty is liable to happen.

"So there I am," I said. "I gotta move to one side or the other, but I got the rock on my right and the hard place on my left, and I'm about as confident as a kid in the drugstore to buy his first pack of condoms. So I start off kind of easy. Gonna edge into it, you know? So I said to him, 'Donald, I dunno quite how to tell you this, but I saw Jill while I was in Lynch's place there.'"

" 'I know,' he says. 'She goes in there a lot. She gets off work at four-thirty, and she goes in there for a drink and dinner a lot.'

" 'Yeah,' I said, 'well, uh, fine. But she was with this guy. She had drinks and dinner with him.'

" 'Sure,' he says, completely unconcerned. 'See, I don't get off most nights until at least six, usually closer to seven. I know she's got a date, I'd just as soon finish up a couple jobs until it gets dark. And I also got a lot of stuff like carbs and things I gotta clean and rebuild, inna shop. I got more work'n I can handle anyway.'

" 'Oh,' I said.

" 'See,' he said, 'she's got a lotta debts and stuff she had from college, which she has gotta pay back and everything.'

"Now," I said, "I thought I understood what he was telling me. I mean, it *seemed* pretty clear what he was telling me, but there was nothing in his expression that'd let me think he was really saying what he certainly was saying. It was like some kid'd learned one sentence in Spanish without knowing what it meant, and was going around asking people to kick him in the nuts when what he really wanted was directions to the men's room. So I waffled, which seemed like a reasonable thing to do under the circumstances, and said, 'Debts?'

" 'Yeah,' he said. He was being patient with me, old relic that I am. 'She went to college and then she got her master's and her parents didn't have the money so she borrowed it. Tuition, board, room, books. Stuff like that.'

" 'Tuition,' I said.

" 'Yeah,' he said. 'She owes a lot of money, and she's gotta pay it back and she don't earn enough waitressing, so she goes out on dates with guys.'

"Mack," I said, "he said it like he was explaining to a kid that the sun doesn't really come up and it doesn't really set—it's the earth revolving that makes it seem that way. The woman's hooking, as far as he knows, and he takes it matter-of-fact, because she's got a lot of debts."

"Jeez," Mack said, "I should've thought of that when we were in the clutches of the bankers."

"Over my dead body," I said.

"Yeah," she said, "I guess one member of the family on the street's enough at any one time."

"Fuck you," I said. "Can you believe that? Kid's perfectly calm about his girlfriend turning a few tricks. Nothing wrong with that. She needs the money. Which would be incredible enough, of course, except he's wrong: he's the trick she's turning. He thinks she's a whore, but she's much worse'n that—she's a fuckin' informer.

"Now that is what I call a real bucket of chuckles," I said. "Here I am with a boob for a client. He's got a nark for a girlfriend, and she's got an agent for a boyfriend. My poor jerk's out in front, as far as those two're concerned, on a major drug business, and that'll be exactly where the major drug businessmen'll put him if the nark and the agent start getting too close to the big boys.

"Out of this little assembly," I said, "I have somehow got to escort my nitwit with such skill and daring that he doesn't get indicted and imprisoned in the process, and also without getting his head or mine blown off.

"Now," I said, "I'm a confident man, but I'm also a nervous one, and I have to admit I have got my work cut out for me. Particularly when I don't think I know more'n a tenth of what it is the work's about, and when I am in that situation I get nervous."

"I don't like you nervous," Mack said.

"I don't like me nervous, either," I said.

"Talk to Cooper, then," she said.

17

I WENT TO SEE COOPER, who was startled. "You didn't whack onna wall," he said.

"I haven't been in my office yet," I said.

"Wait a minute," Cooper said, "I'll get a pail of boiling water and some laundry soap, clean this joint up."

"Don't be a wise ass," I said. "This is serious business here. Another hour or so of this and I'm gonna order the wagons circled. We got hostiles bearing down on us, is what I think."

"Don't sit down," Cooper said.

"Ah, come on, Cooper," I said, sitting down. "A joke's a joke, but enough's enough. I know my client's a piggy little piece of shit, but he probably knows the same thing about you, and I certainly do, but I still talk to you."

"I didn't mean for sanitary reasons," Cooper said, getting up. "I've been trying to reach you all morning. Had Gretchen try the house, Mack tells her you're here. Gretchen hasn't seen you. I got a line on that son of a bitching cop. Come on."

We went to the John F. Kennedy Federal Building, where Cooper introduced me to Merrill Carpenter. Carpenter acknowledged my existence.

"Be honest with you, Merl," Cooper said, in Carpenter's government-green office, "I've been worried about this."

Cooper looked just the same as Merrill Carpenter looked, Cooper was thirty-nine. Carpenter was forty-eight. This plainly meant a great deal to each of them, neither fully appreciating, on the conscious level, how much it eased their relationship, and improved their mutual trust. Each of them had grayish-black hair, which had started thinning and then had gone into a holding pattern. It reassured Cooper to see that Carpenter, chief of the Boston office, had remained in his holding pattern, because it gave Cooper confidence of another ten years or so in his. Cooper did not wish to lose all of his hair.

Carpenter had his feet on the regional chief's desk, which was real walnut and had a two-foot overhang. He had a chromium water carafe on a chromium salver on his desk, and a large American flag in a floor-stand behind him. Next to the flag there was a picture of the President of the United States, autographed to no one in particular by the same machine that printed it. Under the picture was a government-issue credenza; on it was a two-foot model of a Cadillac El Dorado convertible made of gold plastic. It contained a transistor radio tuned to a beautiful-music station. Carpenter clasped his hands behind his head and nodded twice, in time to the recording of "You Are the Sunshine of My Life," by Enoch Light and the Light Brigade. "Anything that Harris was involved in," he said, "you got a right to be concerned. You weren't worried, I'd be worried. The guy . . . the guy has a tendency to do things. You got to watch him, and you got to watch him every minute."

"Which, of course, you can't," Cooper said.

"Which I can't," Carpenter said. He took a pack of Marlboros from his pocket and lighted one with the red Bic lighter on his desk.

"The only thing I can do is stay here and worry about what crazy men like Harris're doing, that's gonna get everybody in trouble before nightfall. Gets my mind off my own troubles. I got official things to worry about. What's he doing, anyway, brings you here?"

"Part of what brings me here," I said, "is that I'm gradually getting the idea that I don't really know for sure, what Gould is doing."

"Me too," Carpenter said. "All I really know is what he tells me that he's doing. Except his name's not Gould, of course. It's Harris."

I said nothing.

"I'm pretty sure he is doing that, although he may not be. But I'm getting kind of worried that he's also doing some other stuff, quite a lot of other stuff, that he's not telling me about. Now, I was worried enough before, when it was just the stuff he told me he was doing, that was making me jumpy. If there's something else as well, I'll be a basket case, before I'm through. Where the hell'd I get him anyway? Fordham Maroney?"

"Uh huh," Cooper said. "Fordham Maroney."

There were two Maroneys in the agency, each of them named Leo. Even I knew that. Loyola Maroney was widely admired for his ability to train new agents, and for his patience with older ones who had trouble at home, or too much booze away from it. Fordham Maroney was universally despised for his talent in driving promising young agents out, and for buffaloing older ones until they developed the kind of problems which required their transfer to Loyola Maroney's Chicago office, for rest and recuperation.

"I knew it," Carpenter said. "That rotten son of a bitch probably planned it years ago. First he ships me out of Boston, for sittin' on his hat or something, back around the turn of the century, two weeks after Debbie started first grade and I thought Marie was probably going to divorce me or something. Then, when I finally get back, by way of Baltimore, Chicago, Buffalo and Albany before San Francisco, there was this accident waiting to happen to me. Harris agent in place. Old Fordham planned it. Where'd he get the guy? He wasn't there when I left. Of course, come to think of it, neither was Bobby Orr, and he came and went while I was seeing America and serving my country."

"I think Fordham won him in a raffle or something, when they shut down BNDD," Cooper said.

BNDD stood for Bureau of Narcotics and Dangerous Drugs. "There was quite a few of them, that had long enough on the job, enough civil service, or protectors in high places, that were distributed around to other outfits that did *not* want them, but were given very little choice about taking them. Except the Bureau, of course. The Bureau still had a certain amount of clout in those days. Today, I doubt they'd get away with it. Maybe, though, they might. The kind of guy that Harris seems to be, at least. Although come to think of it, it could've been Harris got himself into some kind of snit with BNDD before the powers that be decided to scatter its loyal operatives to the four winds, and Fordham took custody of him. Because Fordham was around, down in Washington, bragging up and down he's bagged this great, aggressive, young and energetic agent out of Border, that's gonna revitalize the entire operation.

"Must've been . . . I didn't pay a hell of a lot of attention to it then, because I was packing to go out to Seattle, having been myself personally insufficiently aggressive, young and energetic to delight a few of those crazy people Richard Nixon recruited from various asylums to enforce the laws of the United States, and Fordham sure wasn't about to send me one of his hotshots. Might've made me look good.

"Although, come to think of it, I'm glad Maroney didn't," Cooper said. "For your sake. I looked Harris up a while ago. Quite a while ago, as a matter of fact, right before they retired me from this esteemed position. I heard somebody mention, one day, at lunch, I think it was, they had this mad bastard up in Boston that . . . the guy who was talking about him went through initial training and orientation with him, and he says, 'Warren Harris is a nut. We went out one night, right after they issued us the sidearms, down in Washington, and we're out having a few and he decides there's a hold-up going on in the alley. So we're all laughing at him, and tellin' him he's gone soft, although this was kind of a rough section we were in, and the next thing you know, he's gone into the crouch and he's got the piece out.

" 'Now,' the guy says, 'there was this abandoned car down there. Don't know what kind it was. Stolen and stripped, probably, and Harris's got the piece trained on it and he tells whoever's in it to come out, hands up, of course. And somebody moves in the car. At which point Harris lights off two of them, and then another one, and he hit the guy, too. All three times. He is a damned good shot, I'll say that for him.

" 'You know what it was? A wino. Crawled into the car to sleep. That was where he lived. Old newspapers for a bed, little Sterno stove, some to drink and some to cook with, few old musky bottles, pieces of stale bread, he's in there, dressed in rags, and all of a sudden some crazy bastard working for the government comes by and shoots him in the leg, three times, with a nine-millimeter automatic.'

"At this point," Cooper said, "I still didn't have the guy's name. I didn't know who he was, or where he came from, and Jesus God, it never occurred to me that he was still with the agency, let alone assigned to my region. I was laughing, as a matter of fact. 'What'd they do about it,' I said, 'charge him and broom him out administratively, I assume?'

" 'Oh, absolutely not,' the guy says. 'Warren Harris has two things going for him, that protect him in his hour of need, and which I wished I had myself, on one or two short days I can remember. He's got a cousin from Missouri who occupies a chair in the U.S. House of Representatives, and a seat on the Appropriations Committee, and he's got a family with about ten million bucks in petty cash, some of which found its way into the checkbook of the Committee to Elect Richard Nixon President of the United States in 1968. And in 1960, too, before that.

" 'No, they did nothing to Harris. They invented a fleeing felon, who had threatened these new federal agents with what appeared to be a sawed-off shotgun.

They claimed that Harris had been courageously pursuing him, but denied Harris's marksmanship, and commended the new agent for valor, I guess it was. He's still around, some place.'

"That got my attention," Cooper said. "I pulled his file, and it was a good full one, too. That first commendation was in there, just like the storyteller said. So was the report from Gordon Liddy, who evidently won the guy as one of his honchos in Operation Intercept, that marijuana blockade that practically got us into a new war with Mexico. You wanna hear something that'll turn your blood curdling? Liddy gave him a bad report. G. Gordon Liddy said that Warren Harris was too aggressive, lacked judgment and discretion, and was being reassigned to less sensitive duties."

"Oh, grand," Carpenter said. "I sure do want to thank you, Fordham, for sending him my way. Really appreciate it, I surely do. Haven't got time, right now, thank you properly, but I bet it won't be long before he does something that'll get me shipped out to Anchorage on the next plane, and I'll have lots of time to write my bread-and-butter notes from there."

"All right," Cooper said. "Now, when you get finished feeling sorry for yourself, what is it he's *supposed* to be doing, while he's out slipping his leash and demonstrating you to be incapable of maintaining discipline in the Boston office?"

"Well," Carpenter said, "while he's devoting much of his time blowing smoke up my ass, apparently, he's supposed to be running a little undercover enterprise that'll tell us who's set up a small but rapid ferry service between Cape Cod and some, probably, South American, fishing boats lying off Nantucket shoal."

"Tough job?" Carpenter said.

"Keeping in mind that I may have a guy with a piece of it," I said.

"Mezza-mezz," Carpenter said, fluttering his hands, ignoring me. "It's not easy, by any means. What we've got, so far, has to make you think that the stuff that's coming in is pretty damned good quality. And there's quite a lot of it. Mostly coke, some small amount of grass. The stuff we hear about, like I say, we hear is very fine, which probably means that it is pretty good, at least. So we're dealing with experienced folks, with some money to fool around with. But then, we usually are."

"So it ought not to be something that'd panic a reasonably capable guy who was put in charge of handling it," Cooper said.

"Not so's he'd do something really and truly stupid," Carpenter said. "I wouldn't hand it to a kid right out of school, but I didn't have any reservations about handing it to Harris when I did, about two months ago, and I had reservations about Harris even then."

"Like what?" I said.

"Counselor," Carpenter said, "it's feelings and reactions, things that just rub you the wrong way. Look, we've got a lot of things that just rub you the wrong way. There's a lot of things going down right now in Boston, and this's very far from being the most important of them.

"We've got a couple of very impressive colored gentlemen just returned from extended periods of rehabilitation in the federal hotel down there in Atlanta. We've got strong reports that neither of them is pleased by certain alterations made in business interests during the period of their confinement, and we have excellent reason to know that each of them is experienced in the use of firearms. PD Boston's going nuts, and some folks in the State Attorney General's office are quite apprehensive about the possibility of loud noises being made down in the jungle, where the heroin changes hands. Now this one is important. It needs very delicate handling. We are liable to have a nice little tong war on our hands, and the last time that these gentlemen were involved in one of those, a number of public employees were wounded in the course of quelling it, I believe the phrase is.

"That one's an important case, and so's the one that's cooking up in Springfield, where the problems

of free competition've inspired the businessmen to
start using twelve-year-olds as mules, and making up
shit in super-strength, to kill off wayward customers.

"Somebody ferrying coke and grass in speedboats is
not the kind of individual that we tend to leave alone,
but he does not get top priority, either. What I don't
want is a fellow like Harris doing something stupid
that'll require top priority for the case he's working on,
and fuck up all the other stuff that really oughta have
it.

"And that is why," Carpenter said, "keeping in mind
that I know all our top guys're otherwise engaged at
present, I said okay, when Tommy Finch told me
Harris is about the only guy he's got left. I wasn't
overjoyed, but I do know Tommy's team is spread
awful thin, and I also know that Tommy's deliberately
left his team spread thin, rather'n get Harris involved
in a nitro type of case. Tommy's never said it, and
I've never asked, because neither of us needs to. In a
way, I was doing Tommy a favor, getting Harris out of
his hair for a while, about having nothing to do while
everybody else's running around crazy. Besides, I don't
like having agents around with time on their hands.
Particularly Harris. So I went to Tommy, and he said
to me, 'Warren Harris. He's got a couple people that
he uses for this kind of thing, and they'll be naturals.' "

"Who are they?" Cooper said. "That could tell us
quite a bit, right there."

"Until yesterday," Carpenter said, "I didn't know.
Today, since I sweated the guy white last night, I can
tell you that he's got one in place, and another working
his way in. The one in place is Informant WB17, and
when I tried to get the name he went through all the
usual rigmarole about confidentiality until I finally
threatened him with bodily harm. And then all I got
was her first name, which, he said, 'New York'll recognize. And leave her alone. She's only been in for
about a week. She needs some time.' "

"Jill," Cooper said. "Jill Candelaria, and I think

you'd better go down and see Investigations now, if I guessed that correctly."

"You did," Carpenter said.

"His name's Pete Riordan," Cooper said, to me. "Get used to him before you make your mind up. This guy is the best there is. I don't know much about him except three things: he doesn't look like much; he tends to make the careful types extremely nervous; and he is the best he is."

18

MACK NOTICED RIGHT OFF, as she always does, that I was carrying the gun again. Mack does not like the gun. Mack believes that firearms are intended to kill people, and that if they are carried around long enough, they will. She is particularly firm in this view when the weapon in question is a .38 with a two-inch barrel, loaded with 194-grain hollow-points.

On that issue I have chosen not to argue with her. The notion of using a Smith & Wesson .38, with a two-inch barrel, as a goose gun is so obviously idiotic as to refute itself by the mere statement of it. The purpose of that carefully machined chunk of stainless steel with the walnut grips affixed is to enable the possessor to kill any human being reckless enough to approach within twenty or thirty feet. The gun does not give a good goddamn whether the human approaching is a bad guy, a good guy, or a mere trespasser. If the fellow who has the gun is inclined to slay the fellow coming into range, the gun will function efficiently to assist him in doing it.

The fellow with the gun is a different matter. He removes it from its hiding place, points it in the direction of the interloper, makes a quick decision on whether to fire single or double action, lights off the first round, observes the result, and either does or does not light off the next round. The gun kicks up when it is fired and makes one hell of a goddamned noise. This is because it has one hell of a goddamned short barrel. A significant chunk of lead goes flying out the front end of the gun at around 950 feet per second in the general direction of the interloper. Which is another thing about a two-inch barrel: it's convenient for stowing, but it's a noisy sucker and it does not exactly steer that lead with a great deal of precision.

If the lead strikes the interloper, he is certain to dislike the sensations which follow. Unless, of course, the lead has hit him in an organ which monitors the sensations. In this event he will not feel any sensations, ever again. Neither will he bother anybody else, no matter whether anybody else happens to be carrying a .38. After he gets a good peck of that stuff in a vital spot, he will be about as well-behaved a citizen as any other dead man. The principal problem that he will pose to the community is whether he can be gotten into the ground before the sun shines upon him for too long and he begins to stink.

A guy with a rifle can take a man out while seated comfortably a mile away from him in downtown East Jesus, give him what the morbid call a Dallas ride in an open car. A guy with a shotgun can pretty much complicate your social calendar from fifty yards away. A marksman with a pistol that has a six-inch barrel will have you perforated before you ever get a chance to think about that little popgun on your belt. But if some son of a bitch comes at you with a knife, another popgun, or a couple friends, and you spot him emerging from the blocks on the other side of School Street as the *WALK* sign flashes white, you can give him more to think about in ten seconds than he has ever had to think about before in a whole lifetime of purse-snatching. You may not hit the bastard in the cerebellum, but he will know that you are in the neighborhood, and your second round may very well do something nasty to his spleen. A shotgun is a preferable weapon, but it is awkward to carry in polite society, except in Rhodesia. The scope on a rifle invariably hangs up on the lining of your coat, and the .45 automatic plays hell with the cut of your jib, not to mention the lining of your pants. The .38 is a nice menacing little trinket that will right speedily come in-

to action in a time of need without severely compli-
cating your life and disconcerting everybody who sees
you while you are carrying it in expectation of a possible time of need.

Everyone except Mack, that is. She is too well acquainted with the ridges and the valleys of my deteri-
orating body, and can tell right off when I have
strapped the metal thing on my love handles.

"All right," she said, "the hell is it this time, Wyatt
Earp?"

"I don't need any shit from you, Miss Kitty,
ma'am," I said. "I had my quota from some other
folks today. I had my quota before noon, you want
the truth."

"More news that doesn't interest me," she said. "I
asked you a question."

"You wanna be careful," I said. "You keep asking
questions, I am liable to start giving answers."

"Start," she said.

I told her about Pete Riordan.

Pete Riordan, thirty-one, had been intemperate in
his judgment, his use of alcohol and cigarettes, his
consumption of food the night before, and his choice
of clothing suitable for a basement office in Boston:
he sat in a federal building in Boston, where the energy
problem was considered sufficient reason to turn the
air-conditioning thermostats up to around eighty de-
grees (this was in order that the GSA administrator
might directly impress the President of the United
States, and win appointment to the First Circuit Court
of Appeals). Pete Riordan sat unshaven, hungover,
bleary-eyed, bloated, and packed with phlegm that
made him gag, sweating steadily in a red-and-black
flannel shirt, corduroy pants and Adidas jogging shoes,
in a swivel chair that had had its left arm discarded
long ago, reading dull Xeroxed reports, talking on the
phone, and disregarding an all-news radio station
while a cylindrical Braun electric fan blew on his
crotch, and his spread legs on the top of the walnut
desk, its surface scratched and gouged, lost circulation.

"Pete Riordan," I told Mack, "is the meanest looking motherfucker I ever saw in my life. If you saw
him and asked me what he did, and I told you he
worked for the government, you would want to know
which government, and probably suspect it was some
oppressive regime terrorizing an economically stricken
Third World country while robbing its inhabitants of
their oil resources. He looks like a thug, is what Pete
Riordan does. He wears clothes, but they are the
kind of clothes that a man wears when he doesn't
give a shit and knows he does not give a shit.

"The chances are he doesn't really need to wear
clothes at all and is actually completely covered with
thick fur under them," I said, "and he could go out
of the shower in the morning and roll around in the
wet grass with all the other wolves in perfect comfort.
He's about six-three, six-four. He's got black hair
that's too long and looks like he goes to a big gorilla
for a barber and the gorilla doesn't use any shears
—he gnaws off the parts that're too long. He's had
his nose broken once or twice and obviously didn't
want to take the time to have it set right, so it's all
gnarled up and there's something wrong with his sep-
tum so he's always snuffling. I tell you something,
Mack: I would like to meet the paratroop battalion
that attacked him and managed to break his nose in
a couple places before he disabled the lot of them,
with his bare hands and what was lying around in the
form of furniture, because that guy has got to go two-
thirty, two-forty or so, and it doesn't look like fat to
me, either. He's got old cuts on his face and his hands
are about the size of my feet and they're all bent out
of shape too, because he's been using them for years
to hit people. Cooper told me the guy's got all kinds
of belts in karate and whatever the hell they give
you in judo. He was a Recon Marine in Vietnam,
and . . ."

"What's a Recon Marine?" Mack said. She handed
me my martini.

" . . . a Recon Marine is a highly developed piece

of machinery which is designed solely to make trouble for other nations, and to kill any of their citizens who try to interfere with that work. It is a machine which used to be a human being and is a little out of sorts and out of place now when it is instructed not to sneak around in hostile darkness anymore, seeking to kill people and blow up ammunition dumps. It can swim underwater and it can climb impassable mountains. It can sabotage a powerplant, ambush a troop convoy, demolish a radar installation or booby-trap a command headquarters. When Castro shut off the water at Guantanamo Bay, there were several dozen of those gentlemen on hand in the barracks and when it looked like the President was gonna order them to go turn the water back on, they spent a couple days filing their teeth and beating each other with pieces of chain until they got themselves into the proper frame of mind for the mission. Then Castro turned the water back on without causing a fight, which was certainly the most sensible thing to do, and those guys went down to the saloon so riled up that they started killing each other."

"He sounds like an animal," she said.

"I'm sure he'd give a pretty good account of himself if he got in a fight with an animal," I said. "Almost any animal, in fact. He looks like he could give a royal Bengal tiger a good scrap for himself, if the tiger was in a grouchy mood and wanted to mess around. I would say Pete Riordan would be even money in a fight with anything that weighed under a thousand pounds, and that would just be if he didn't have any weapons handy at the time.

"The thing of it is," I said, "this Pete Riordan also happens to have a master's degree from the Fletcher School of Law and Diplomacy, which he got after he graduated from Brown. And he's almost finished his doctorate in economics. So he may be an animal, Mack, but he's one damned smart animal.

"Now this fellow speaks to me," I said, "on a subject about which he knows a good deal. I know a little bit about a lot of things, but he knows a lot about a lot of things, and when he talks I am inclined to listen. And what he says to me is this: The guy Harris that says his name is Gould and is the agent on the case? This guy Harris is not a very nice man. He is not even a very smart man, and a man who is not nice, Riordan thinks, should at least be smart so he doesn't get any innocent bystanders injured when he is going around not being nice. For one thing, Mister Harris is corrupt, Riordan thinks, and it is just a matter of time before he gets caught doing something corrupt and then does something reckless trying to get out of it. Mister Harris has done reckless things before, and at least one of them involved a firearm. Therefore, Mister Riordan thinks, it is wise when tinkering with some enterprise in which Mister Harris is involved to equip yourself with some trustworthy means of personal protection.

"In addition to that," I said, "Mister Riordan's superior, Mister Carpenter, who also happens to be Mister Harris's superior, is of the opinion that this is probably the time that Mister Harris is going to blow himself out of the water. Mister Carpenter does not disagree in any manner with Mister Riordan's view that Mister Harris is a man of very limited intelligence. Mister Carpenter thinks that Mister Harris is diddling around in shark-infested waters and that sooner or later he will have to double-cross someone or other to save his own skin. In the past, Mister Harris has drawn his government-issue sidearm when he has become upset, and the thought has probably glimmered even in a mind so dim as his that one way to avoid difficulty in presenting your explanation for certain embarrassing situations is to make sure that there is nobody else around who is both alive and liable to dispute your explanation."

"The guy doesn't even know you," she said.

"He has seen me," I said. "He has seen me in the company of that kid, French, that he is trying to set up pretty good. The chances are that he will see me with French again sometime, because I have to see

French now and then, and Harris and his government-issue portable twat are snuggled up closer to French than that cheap underwear you bought me on sale at Jordan's last year that starts crawling up my ass every time I try to shift my position in the car."

"Why don't you throw that damned stuff away?" she said.

"Because whenever I remember that I want to throw it away," I said, "I am sitting in my car on the Southeast Expressway behind twelve million other cars, all of them stopped, in broad daylight in East Milton Square. That is no time for a grown man, a responsible member of the community, to get out of the car, remove his coat, trousers and underwear, and throw the shorts in the drainage ditch. That kind of behavior could cause talk, and it is not the kind of talk that I have in mind to cause, inasmuch as I would like to make a living practicing the law for the next few years or so instead of being committed to the State Hospital at Bridgewater for not less than a day and not more than the rest of my life, as a sexually dangerous person. That is why I don't throw them away.

"On the other hand, when I put them on in the morning," I said, "they are garments washed and folded and placed in the bureau drawer in amongst other garments of remarkably similar texture and appearance. Particularly in the dark, which is what I am in, in the winter when I get dressed before the goddamned sun comes up or you do and I don't therefore want to turn the light on and wake you up so that I have to listen to you all day when I get home that night, about how tired you are. And which dark I am also in, in the summer, because I wake up in a stupor every morning and I am not capable of human reflection until after at least my third cup of coffee. By which time I have the shorts on, and if it occurred to me that I ought to take them off before I leave the house and get stuck in East Milton Square with the other twelve million people, I would probably lack the energy to do it anyway. The only way I am going to get rid of those goddamned shorts that crawl up is if you throw them away when you sort the laundry, because I will never think of it at the right time to do it, and I will never have the right time to do it when I do think of it."

"Sorry I asked," she said.

"Anyway," I said, "that, in a very large nutshell, is why I am carrying the piece. According to this forthright gentleman, I seem to be messing around in something that could easily turn into a crossfire. That's why."

"Ah, Shane," she said, "Shane, Shane, come back, Shane. I hate you when you're like this. You fucking men, you're all alike. There isn't one of you that doesn't think there'll come a day when you'll have to renounce your peaceful ways and take the old forty-four in the old leather holster off of the peg on the bunkhouse wall, strap it on and tie the thong around your leg, ride into town and shoot Lee Marvin in a black hat." She hummed a little of the theme from *High Noon.*

"Oh, shut up," I said.

"I mean it," she said. "Every so often you get a little simple and decide you've got to march around with a gun in your hand, like one cock made of flesh isn't always enough for you and you need a metal one for a spare. What's bothering you, anyway? What is it about little boys that play cowboys and Indians and cops and robbers? Don't they ever grow up? You start fooling around with that gun and you're more'n likely to run up against somebody else who's fooling around with a gun only he'll fool around with his faster'n you will with yours, and because you're so damned determined to have two cocks, I'll end up with no cock at all to fool around with. And I'm too old to think that I'd have much success getting a replacement."

"You could scout up one or two of those young dandies that're always sniffing around Saigon," I said. "They look you over speculatively, to say the least."

"That's sweet of you," she said. "It's an outright lie, but it's supposed to make me feel better, and I appreciate it. Trouble is, Senator, I don't want another pretty face, or something that I have to train to go potty. I'm used to you. I admit you may not be much to look at, and you've got a fresh mouth and when you take me on vacation you leave right off and go back to the office while I sit on the beach every day with Mike Curran and two hundred other old walruses of one sex or the other, it's kind of hard to tell, and sometimes you chew your food with your mouth open, and you snore, and . . . that little Terry *is* kind of good-looking, isn't he? Has he been gazing at my rear end again?"

"Oh, for Christ sake," I said. "I didn't mean for you to do it right now. This is supposed to be *after* the cattleman's gunslinger plugs me. Not while I'm still oiling my spurs."

"Nah," she said, "it wouldn't work. When I wake up in the middle of the night I don't want to have to reach out and grope some kid with a hard, flat belly. I want my regular roommate, the one that comes home and drinks Heineken and lies there and farts every so often so I'll know everything's still working all right. I'm set in my ways. I don't want you to get hurt. Please don't get hurt, Jerry, okay?"

I assured her that I would not get hurt. She told me Saigon was depressed about Margie again, and asked me if I would fetch her home from Phil's Burger Quik and have a talk with the kid. "You won't need your gun," Mack said. I agreed. Mack told me that Teddy Franklin had called again. "It figures," I said. "It figures."

Like most professional jerks, or most of the jerks who entered the professions, I tend to slough my family obligations when my job takes too much time. Mack complains about this, spending too many vacations alone, eating too many dinners by herself, having to wait four hours until I get home at eleven, exhausted, so that she and I can celebrate some ten-grand commission she has earned on a deal she is proud to have put together, but Mack puts up with it.

Heather does not put up with it. Heather does not put up with my early departures and late arrivals any more than Heather puts up with summer turning into fall, and fall into winter. My conduct is not greatly different now from what it was when she was first conscious enough to notice it. Daddy is the guy who leaves the house before I have my breakfast. Daddy is the guy who comes home when Mummy is putting me to bed. Sometimes on the weekends Daddy does not have to work at his desk and we play. Heather wrote those sentences, or sentences very much like them, when she was in the second grade. Heather got a B plus on that little composition, and promptly forgot about it, but I remembered it vividly, and for maybe a month or two I even mended my ways some. But not for long enough, or to a degree large enough, to force Heather to see Daddy in a light which Daddy would have found more agreeable. Heather didn't even know that she saw him in terms which made him uncomfortable. I think she was around four years old when she decided I was not merely an occasional visitor, but an actual resident of the same house. She was pleased by that discovery. Heather, as I have said, is a very cheerful child, and always has been.

Heather, that night, was not cheerful, and I am afraid I was too preoccupied with what had happened to me to draw her out as I should have. Mack and I had sat on the porch listening to Mr. Kelly watering his vegetables, enjoying the quiet and the calm at the end of a long day (I was enjoying them, at least—she was probably craving some excitement). Then I went up to Phil's Burger Quik to collect Heather.

The lights on the signs were out, but the lights in the restaurant were on. I could see Heather inside, talking to somebody whom I did not know. I did not notice the violet, sparkled dune buggy parked ahead of me, one row up and three spaces down to the left. The kid was at the driver's side window of my Grand Prix and leaning on the sill blowing beer and cheap whiskey fumes into my face before I knew of his simultaneous existence on the earth. His eyes were half-lidded. He had not shaved in a couple days—there was light enough to see that, and his crooked teeth. He had rather full lips. He wore a cheap acetate imitation-silk shirt open four buttons down, and two gold chains at his throat. I couldn't say how tall he was, or guess his weight, although I could see that he had the beginnings of a pot belly.

He said, "Mister Big Lawyer." He startled me. I looked at him and saw a stranger. That was when I got the gust of breath. "You talking to me?" I said stupidly.

"Yeah, fucker," he said, "to you. I'm talkin' to you. I'm standing right here and I'm leanin' on your car and I'm talkin' to you. You, Mister Big Lawyer that thinks he can go around and tell everybody else how they're gonna live."

"What're you gonna talk to me about?" I said, having recovered some of my wits (enough at least to wish to God I had not left the .38 at home and had it in my right hand in the shadows of the car, pointed at his throat). When in doubt, keep them talking.

"My kid," he said, "I am gonna talk to you about my kid, see? My fuckin' kid."

"I don't believe I know your fuckin' kid," I said.

"You gonna give me some shit, Mister Big Lawyer?" he said. He had enough altitude to outclimb a 747. "Is that what you are gonna do?"

"My friend," I said, "I would like to if I could. Count on it. But I can't because I don't know who the hell you are, or why you're talking to me."

It was just then that God sent me a police cruiser, rolling slowly into Phil's parking lot, probably to escort Phil and the day's receipts to the night-deposit drawer at the bank.

The kid stood up. "You will, Mister Big Lawyer," he said, "you will." Then he swaggered off toward the dune buggy. I did not get the registration number as it roared out of the parking lot. The cops ignored it.

Heather came out as the lights were reduced inside the shop and got into the car.

"Jesus Christ," I said, "have I gone nuts or is it the world?"

"What's the matter, Dad?" she said.

"This rotten, slimy excuse for a human being just showed up at the car, gave me a whole hod of shit, and walked off," I said.

"Oh, cripes," she said.

"There some problem?" I said.

"Oh, Dad," she said, "you're tired, and I don't want to bug you and everything."

"I've had a chance to sit down and have a drink with your mother," I said. "I'm not so tired I can't listen. And I'll try to contribute anything I can."

Heather does not frown well. She has not had much practice at it, of course, but she has not benefited from what little she has had. When Heather gets upset, she mostly misses the phase of looking worried, and proceeds at once to the verge of tears, at least judging from her facial expressions. Since the change is so pronounced, and so unusual for her, it is almost enough to make me cry.

"Margie's pregnant," she said. "That was Joe you saw." She sat there in the kitchen in her maroon uniform, the little cap still in her hair, her face distorting gradually, as sad as she would have been if something awful had happened to her.

"Is she sure?" I said. I don't know why men always say that. Probably it's because the older guys warned us, when we were growing up, that girls would try to trap us into marriage by falsely claiming pregnancy. Then later we read something somewhere that a girl could miss her period because of hysteria or something, and think that she was pregnant when she wasn't. A nice hope for a worried young stud, I suppose, but in all my years on earth I have never once heard of a woman who thought she was pregnant when in fact she was not pregnant.

"The rabbit was," Heather said. "She told Joe she thought she was pregnant and asked him to drive her up to Boston, and he wouldn't. So she took the bus up . . ."

I guess I thought it was time for another stupid remark from me. "Don't they do those tests around here?"

"Dad," she said, "everybody knows Margie. Everybody knows Margie's mother. Margie can't go to a clinic here. There'd be sure to be somebody there who'd recognize her and start telling it all over town."

"There's doctors," I said. "People go to doctors when they're not pregnant."

"Yeah," Heather said, "people with thirty-five bucks. Margie hasn't got thirty-five bucks. What's she supposed to do? Ask her mother? 'Ma, I think I'm pregnant and I need thirty-five bucks so I can find out from the doctor and he charges that for an office visit'? Margie gives her mother all but eight bucks a week she makes anyway. Margie's mother probably doesn't have thirty-five bucks."

"Sorry," I said.

"It's all right," Heather said. "I'm just all upset. Margie took the bus up to Boston and went to this place that charges five bucks and then she sat there for a while until they finally told her it'd be a couple of days and they'd mail her the results, and they didn't want to let her call them up because they don't give that information over the phone, so what she did was come home and get to work late and she got chewed out for that, and then she had to spend her day off taking the bus back to Boston because that was the only way she could find out without them sending the letter to her house. And her mother found out she wasn't at the beach that day and started asking all kinds of questions, so now Margie's lying to her some more. Her mother doesn't believe her. Margie knows she doesn't. She told me, 'Heather, I stink at lying.' She's going crazy."

"Well," I said, "the way I understand it, there's only three options, and if you don't pick the first one, you're gonna get one of the other two, like it or not."

"*Get* married," Heather said, "put the baby *up for adoption* or have an *abortion*."

"She against abortion?" I said.

"No," Heather said. "She's a little worried about how the hell she could get one without her mother finding out about it, since she can't get one for free around here and if she goes away it could be a little hard to explain, but if it came to that, she would do it and just tell her mother. Or, she could have the baby and put it up for adoption, except that'd mean she'd have to drop out of school and then either forget about graduating or else forget about going to work next June in something that pays better, and she doesn't want to do that.

"As far as marrying Joe is concerned," Heather said, "Margie maybe was dumb enough to believe him when he said he loved her, and too stupid to make him use condoms or get on the pill or something herself, but she's not so dumb that she'd marry him, even if he wanted to or if he could. Which he doesn't and he can't. She was lying, Dad, when she said she was on the pill."

"Doesn't surprise me," I said, "after what you told me. But why can't he? Not that she should marry him."

"He can't," Heather said, "because he's got a couple of problems. One of which is that he says he got this other kid pregnant down in Plympton and she's only fifteen and if he doesn't marry *her,* her father's gonna get him on a rape charge and that'll mean he'll have to go back to jail."

"Parole revocation," I said. "Fertile bastard, isn't he?"

"That's it," she said. "And the other one is that . . . I don't know if I should tell you this or not."

"Why stop now?" I said. "It can't be much worse."

"The other one is that he apparently did something, and I don't know what it was, and he thinks somebody might find out about it and if they did, he would either go back to jail or else somebody would come after him, and either way he would have to run away. And he couldn't do it if he had her and the baby with him."

"She believes that?" I said.

"Dad," Heather said, "Margie is wising up, but you've seen Joe; you should believe him if he told you he was in almost any kind of trouble. He is the kind of guy that gets in trouble, that's all. He's been in trouble all of his life and he will be in trouble all his life. Besides, what difference does it make? Margie isn't crazy. She wouldn't marry him if he didn't have any of that kind of thing to worry about anyway. If he's telling her that, and he's lying, it just means he really doesn't want to marry her, and even if he's lying, she's smartened up enough to know he'd be the worst mistake she could ever make."

"So her real problem is the abortion," I said. "How to get the money for it."

"That's the easy part," Heather said. "I'm going to give it to her. The hard part is that Joe's all of a sudden decided abortion's wrong, and he says if she kills the baby, kills *his* baby, he'll do something to her."

"Heather," I said, "I'm getting old. I don't assimilate information as fast as I used to. Let's go back there about a yard or two and see if I can get it down."

"Okay," she said, "I'm going to give her my money for ski stuff that I earned this summer."

"You mean," I said, "that you are going to *loan* her the money that you earned for ski stuff. Not that I necessarily approve of that, either, but I assume that's what you mean."

"I said I was going to loan it to her," Heather said.

"I told her that. But I'm not dumb, Dad. Those operations cost about three hundred bucks. Margie hasn't got three hundred bucks. If she had three hundred bucks, she wouldn't be in this trouble. And Margie isn't going to have three hundred bucks, either. At least I don't think she will. Because if she gives her mother everything except eight bucks a week, and it costs her at least four or five bucks a week for things she's got to have, it'll be a hundred weeks before she had three hundred bucks. She'll never have it. Never. If I give her that money, I am never going to see it again, and I know it."

"And whether you give her the money or you don't give her the money," I said, "you'll probably never see her again. Do you have to adopt this kid? This woman who goes to bed with a creep when she knows very well he's a creep and hasn't got brains enough to use birth control so she gets herself pregnant—do you really think you've got the time and money to bring her up like she was some kind of goddamned stray puppy? You can't do it, Heather. This is the real world. It lands on you kids too soon, but there's nothing that can be done about it.

"You have to understand that a lot of bad things're gonna happen, right in front of you, and that you won't be able to do a goddamned thing about them. You can't feed every starving kid in India, and you can't give every ghetto kid a college education and a good job. You can't convince the muggers to stop beating up old women and snatching their purses. You can't put the Mafia out of business, and you can't save the murder victims. The old ladies are gonna get mugged and you won't be able to do a damned thing about their broken legs or their pension checks, and the ghetto kids're gonna become career soldiers in the all-volunteer army only if they're too backward to understand there's less risk and no work at all taking welfare and unemployment.

"No strangers ever bailed me out of a tight spot, Kiddo," I said, "and nobody ever came by and

handed your mother three hundred bucks because
she happened to be in a tight spot at the moment. If
I took your attitude, we wouldn't have this beach
house, let alone the other one, and you wouldn't have
one damned thing to look forward to because I made
it but I gave it all away to strangers and chance ac-
quaintances who happened to be a little worse off'n
I was at the time. That wouldn't've been fair, not fair
of me to you, and it isn't fair of you, to you, to decide you're going to sacrifice everything you've worked
for just because some lamebrain's gotten herself into
a fix because of her own actions and stupidity."

"Dad," Heather said, "she's been asking around.
She met this guy when she went up to Boston the last
time. He says she can make twelve hundred a week on
the street, and quit any time she wants, and he will
give her clothes and an apartment and two hundred
a week, plus he will pay for the operation. One of those
guys that you're always getting off in court when they
hurt somebody. Only I don't know those other kids.
Margie'll never get out. She'll be a whore the rest of
her life. Margie is a friend of mine. I know her. She's
not an old friend, but I've known her two summers
now, and I like her. And I don't think she should do
that and I don't think everything that happens to
somebody should be bad, even if they don't have any
money and they haven't got anybody in their family
or any other friends that they have got that can help
them. So I am going to give her the money." Then
Heather did cry.

I sat there like a fool for a while. I probably should
have tried to comfort her, but I did not like the
choices. I stalled for time. "Heather," I said, "I know
you like your friend. I know she's in a spot. But
she's not my daughter, and you are. If you pay for
that abortion, don't you think old Joe's going to come
after you? Isn't that why I had that little discussion
tonight? He's really not a nice guy, from what you've
told me. What're you gonna do then?"

"*I don't know,*" she said, weeping and shaking her

head. "I don't *know*. But I know from things you've said what will happen to her if she does what she says she's going to do, and I can't let that happen."

I decided between doing something that would encourage Heather to spend the rest of her life as a pushover and a sucker for every sob story that she heard—all of which, of course, would be quite true— and doing something that would diminish her total confidence in me. I decided, right there at the kitchen table, between Margie's abortion and covering my family as best I could against whatever disaster would occur as a result of Heather treating Margie to that operation. "Heather," I said, "what's Joe's last name?"

"Fields," she said, "Joe Fields." Then, sobbing, she stood up and went to bed. On the way she said, "I just wish you'd understand."

19

I WAS A LITTLE impatient with Teddy Franklin, when his call round twelve-thirty in the morning followed hard upon my conversation with Heather in the kitchen. I guess my reaction showed in my tone of voice.

"Whatsa matter, Counselor?" Teddy said. "You havin' your period or something?"

"As a matter of fact, Teddy," I said, "I was doing the Lord's work, and talking with my daughter for a change. I think I oughta be able to do that, in the middle of the night in my own house, I want to."

"Whatsa matter, Counselor?" Teddy said. "She's not havin' her period or something?"

"I take a lot of shit off you, Franklin," I said. "I think a crack like that's a little more shit'n our close professional relationship obliges me to take, at twelve-thirty in the morning."

"You take a lot of money off me too, Counselor," Teddy said, "in that professional relationship. I think all that money obliges you to talk to me in the middle of the night."

"I'm beginning to think I'm not interested in any more of your fucking money, Teddy," I said. "There're times when you're worth substantially less trouble'n you cause, and this is one of them."

"*Hey,*" Teddy said, "you're not shittin' around now, are you?"

"No," I said, "I am definitely not shittin' around."

"There anything I can do?" Teddy said.

"No," I said, "as a matter of fact, Teddy, there

probably isn't. But I appreciate you asking." Which I did. I was beginning to calm down.

"What you need, Jerry," Teddy said, "you need a good lawyer. Somebody, solve all your problems for you, you just give him the family jewels plus a second mortgage onna house. That's what you need."

"This point, Teddy," I said, "that does not sound like a bad idea. A deal I could take. You got any recommendations?"

"Yeah," Teddy said, "as a matter of fact, I have. There is this guy in Boston, which he is awful busy, but if you can find him when he's in and not going off all over the goddamned countryside chasing a buck, he will do the best he can for you. Expensive, but he's worth it."

"Anybody I know?" I said.

"And he will take calls inna middle of the night from you," Teddy said. "Except, he is not in his office right now, which I know because I just got him at home."

"Uh huh," I said.

"So," Teddy said, "he is not liable to be much help to you right now, but if you let the son of a bitch get a decent night's sleep, who knows what he'll come up with inna morning, huh?"

"I certainly don't," I said.

"Look," Teddy said, "I mean, I don't wanna press it or anything like that, but what I said, you know, I meant that. There is something I can do for you, I am willing to do it. You say the word, Jerry, is all I need."

"Teddy," I said, "I dunno what word to say. If I did, I would say it. Right now, all I know is that it's hard work, clean living and trust in the Lord. Trust in the Lord to let you starve to death, you don't give your full attention, the hard work."

"Counselor," Teddy said, "leave me get your mind off your troubles. Some of your troubles, anyway. I was in your office today."

"I was out," I said.

"I know you was out," Teddy said. "I already told

you I was in your office. Gretchen told me you wasn't in it. I even looked myself, make sure, all right? I know you wasn't there. Let *me* talk for a change, all right?"

"All right," I said.

"All right," he said. "Now, this guy Hudson, all right? The trooper there, that eats the licenses?"

"Yeah," I said.

"Interesting guy," Teddy said. "I been having some friends of mine go around, ask some questions about this guy Hudson, and he is a very interesting guy. What he is, is the kind of guy that you don't ordinarily expect to see inna blue suit, all right? He is kind of cute is what he is. He is too cute for his own good, in fact, what I hear."

"What's he do that's so cute?" I said.

"Well," Teddy said, "this guy Torbert Hudson used to have this knife, okay? It was a pretty big knife, too. It was a pretty big knife that you could carry in your pocket even though it had a blade on it you could use to stab a horse and even if you didn't pick the right spot to stick it in, you would be able to hit something that mattered before you pulled it out. Because this was a damned big long knife. And it didn't matter that it was the kind that the blade disappeared in the handle because you didn't have to take all this time to open it. See, it had this little button onna handle, and when you let the catch off and pushed the button, why that blade just come flying out there all ready to go. And lemme tell you something else: it didn't come out sideways, neither, like them chickenshit switchblades all the kids used to carry that they got through the mail from an ad they thought they was buying a stiletto. Uh uh. This was a real stiletto. This was one of them commando knives, that when you push the button that blade comes flying straight out the business end of the handle, all right? Good strong spring on the fucker, too, go right through a theater seat and the guy sittin' in the seat, you was to hold it in. Superior Coach built hearses on Cadillac bodies, didn't have springs as strong's the one in that knife, and them things gotta carry a lotta weight."

"Uh huh," I said.

"Now Trooper Hudson," Teddy said, "Trooper Hudson used to work . . . you ever meet, I ever tell you about Dottie's stepbrother?"

"I don't think so," I said.

"Not a bad guy," Teddy said. "Jake is not a bad guy. I wouldn't go out drinkin' with the son of a bitch, you know what I mean, but there's a certain number, family things, you got to see the rest of the people, make an appearance, that kind of thing, and I don't object to sittin' down with the guy and shootin' the shit, you know?

"Now," Teddy said, "what Jake does is this. Jake is a store manager, and from the looks of things he is pretty good at it. Jake is always changing jobs, but Jake is also always changing houses and he's changing cars and he dresses the wife anna kids pretty good, so he must be doing okay. He's here and he's there and then he's gone the next place, but he is always doing pretty good. The guy has got a dollar to spend.

"Guy has been all over the lot," Teddy said, "but the thing he keeps doing, he gets a better offer and he goes there, and then he gets a better offer'n that and he goes the next place, but the thing he keeps doing is this: He runs PX's. Post Exchanges, you know? He's not in the service or anything. It's just that Jake knows everything there is to know in the world about running Post Exchanges, and when he's running one of them, he's on top of the world and happier'n a pig in shit. Makes good money, gets home at night, plays with the kids, guy hasn't bought a winter coat for himself or anybody else in about three hundred years, because every time the coats start to wear out, Jake is running some other PX and he brings home about two dozen samples that he got from some guy, wants to put his line inna PX and Jake won't put it in unless he's satisfied, these're good coats the guys peddling. You got me?"

"It's Jake's bounden duty," I said.

"Right," Teddy said. "Same thing with shaving lotion, razor blades, film, cameras, portable radios, records, stereo sets, clock radios, typewriters, hair dryers, microwave ovens, ballpoint pens, overshoes, earrings, watches, slacks, all that stuff. Pullovers, huh? Sweaters? Sneakers? You need some tools or something, and you got PX privileges? Jake don't want you comin' into his PX that he's runnin', layin' out your hard-earned dollars for a fuckin' chain saw that isn't gonna work a week after you get it, you gotta go through all that shit about takin' it apart and puttin' it in your car and goin' back for the refund. 'Fore Jake lets you put that chain saw in stock, he's gonna want to test it out for himself, make sure it works all right, and if it so happens, Jake doesn't know nothin' about chain saws, he probably knows somebody who knows all there is to know about chain saws, give the damned thing a good wringing out for Jake so none of Jake's customers get stuck, they buy that particular brand of chain saw at Jake's PX."

"Conscientious man, old Jake," I said.

"Very," Teddy said. "Doesn't want no customer of his buyin' nothin', he hasn't got faith in himself."

"You're restoring my faith in human nature," I said.

"I know it," Teddy said. "Now, the thing of it is, most of Jake's customers're very seldom actually inna service."

"Retired servicemen, that sort of thing," I said.

"Retired," Teddy said, "dependents, civilian employees onna post that they let shop at the PX, and guys inna National Guard and the Reserve."

"Sure," I said.

"In which group," Teddy said, "there is a lot of cops."

"Come to think of it," I said, "I'd imagine there would be."

"Sure," Teddy said. "Every cop was inna service. There isn't a cop in the whole world, wasn't in the service. Some cops were in the Seabees, lotta cops was in the Army, there was some Navy guys that got to be cops and a whole mess of Marines that came out and became cops.

"Now," Teddy said, "every cop knows every other cop, am I right?"

"If you're wrong," I said, "you're so close to being right it doesn't matter."

"And if there is one thing a cop likes," Teddy said, "doesn't matter whether he's on a Reserve weekend or the hell else he's doing on the way to the pension, what a cop likes is a deal."

"Same as everybody else," I said.

"Now," Teddy said, "Jake knows a certain number cops."

"Probably one or two who know something about snowthrowers and power lawnmowers," I said.

"Sure," Teddy said. "They all like Jake. They'll do a guy a favor, check out a snowthrower for him, 'fore he puts it in inventory without knowing it's all right. Same thing with tape decks and blenders, you know? Jake can almost always find somebody, some customer or other of his that he can trust, give an honest opinion of things. You know?"

"Sure," I said.

"Okay," Teddy said. "Now, last weekend, we got this family get-together, and be honest with you, Jake's about the only one in the family I can stand, I sit down with Jake and we're having a little drink or two, and he asks me how things're goin', you know?"

"You told him about Trooper Hudson eating your license," I said.

"I did," Teddy said. "But first I told him about Trooper Hudson, eating Dottie's registration. Now you gotta understand this about Jake, all right? Jake *loves* Dottie. His mother, her father got married, I think he was about twelve, thirteen, Dottie was about two. She's not his stepsister—she's his baby sister. Jake don't look like he could do much to you, but I tell you something, all right? I got married to Dottie, Jake told me I better treat his baby sister all right, he was gonna do something to me that I wouldn't like. And I believed Jake, okay? So, and naturally I done pretty good by Dottie, Jake thinks I am all right. So I tell him about this guy and Dottie's registration, and Jake would believe Dottie, Dottie said the ocean was on fire. Gets all excited. Says, 'The fuck is this guy, doin' this? I dunno this guy. The fuck is he?' Then I tell Jake about my license. 'He doin' this to her, account of you?' Jake says. I tell him, 'Sure.' Jake says, 'I dunno this guy. I gotta find out who this guy is. There's gotta be somethin' wrong with him, he's doin' things like this, and if there's somethin' wrong with him, there's gotta be somebody around I know, knows about it.'

"Which," Teddy said, "is how I find out about the knife."

"I don't think I'm tracking you, Teddy," I said. "I know it's either late at night or early in the morning, but you lost me somewhere in there."

"Very simple," Teddy said. "Jake calls me back. He tells me some things. Only, of course, they can't come from Jake or from me, which I don't have to explain to you, I assume, no matter how late it is."

"Of course not," I said.

"But," Teddy said, "if you was to check around, or maybe have that guy that's half-blind do some checking around for you, and he talks to some guys the names of which I can give you right now, he will find out that Trooper Hudson used to be with the police department in a certain town on the North Shore, which is when he was carrying that fuckin' knife around with him."

"He got caught with the knife?" I said. "I don't see . . ."

"No, no," Teddy said. "He kept catching other people with the knife. See, he carried the knife around with him, and every time he saw somebody that he decided was a bad-ass guy, he would pull him over, even if the guy was walking at the time. And if the guy wasn't doing anything, Hudson would pat him down and find the knife on him, and of course it was a dangerous weapon and he would grab the guy for that. And he kept doin' it until one of the judges got smart and says to him one day, 'I think that's about the twentieth time I seen that knife, officer. You better get a new knife or a different suspect.' Counselor, this guy is no good."

"He's in the State Police, Teddy," I said.

"That I don't know how he got in there," Teddy said. "What I do know is that there is some guys in the State Police that don't know, either, and they're pretty nervous about the whole thing."

"You wouldn't have their names by any chance," I said.

"Hey," Teddy said, "if I'm gonna do all the work myself, the hell'm I payin' you for?"

"Just asking," I said.

"As a matter of fact," Teddy said, "I got one. One name. Never heard of the son of a bitch in my life, but he apparently swings more meat in the average day'n a fulltime butcher does in his whole life. Some kind of business-type honcho, law and order type, I got it here some place, Hudson got in the shit when he was local and the guy apparently backed him right down the line, and when that didn't work, got him hitched in where it counted and Hudson quits the department and gets appointed to the Staties. Yeah, I knew I had it. Richard Teller. Apparently he is a guy who can take care of a guy if he wants to."

I did not write the name down. What I did do, when I had caught my breath, was ask Teddy whether he could *do anything* about a mean kid that hadn't recently committed an act which the cops could prosecute. Teddy said he wouldn't be surprised if he could, and I told him what Heather had told me about Joe and Margie.

"I know a guy that knows that area," Teddy said, "which is what it would take, because nobody that was from some place else would know the little shit from a pisshole inna snow. But he is not around right now on account of he is taking a vacation."

"In the can," I said.

"No," Teddy said, "actually no, He is actually taking a vacation. He's down in Barbados there. Back around Labor Day. Not soon enough?"

"I hope so," I said.

20

BAD EYE MULVEY IS A MAN who is easily distressed. This is an unusual trait in a cop. Bad Eye is the only cop I know who has it, as a matter of fact. I know a great many cops who get mad and leave no doubt in anyone's mind about the state of theirs when this occurs; I have heard language from cops which clients of mine would be hard-pressed to equal. Of course I have endured this habit very well, inasmuch as the language is generally applied to my clients, and I have used as bad, or worse, on the same topics. But I do not curse, blaspheme or utter obscenities when Bad Eye is within earshot, because Bad Eye is shocked and unsettled when he hears profane language; Mike Curran's talk, when no ladies are present, would make Bad Eye uncomfortable.

It is very easy to tell when Bad Eye is distressed. It is when Bad Eye refuses to dictate his report to your secretary, demands to see you, and refuses to address the subject even then. He becomes very formal. "I do not *wish* to report what I have learned. I wish to speak to Mister Kennedy." When I heard Bad Eye saying that to Gretchen, I braced myself for the next ordeal. With that phrase, Bad Eye avoids unpleasant discussions by recitation of his principled conduct of a part-time real-estate business.

"I got principles," he says. "I got certain business principles, which I did not learn at Harvard Business School. I learned my business in the school of hard knocks, is what I did, what Al Smith used to mean when he said he was a graduate of Fulton Fish. The principal thing you got to know is this: You can only cheat a guy once. Once. So it is stupid if you decide to cheat a guy, because if he's got any cash at all, and you part him from it by, you cheated him, he will remember it, and he will do things to you all over the map, and they will come back to haunt you.

"You always give value for money. You may take a little edge sometimes, which is whenever you can get it, but you will never lie to a guy. This is not smart. He will resent it. He will let the check clear, and you will get your money, for that time. But you will never see that time again. And you will often hear after that, that he told some fellow you might have done a little business with, that you were not a good type of fellow to do business with, and that will fix you pretty good with almost everybody. You get my meaning.

"Now," Bad Eye says, "if on the other hand, you do not get too greedy, all right? If you do not get too greedy, then you can do a job of work, and the guy will be satisfied, and you will probably get yourself the chance to do another piece of work. Maybe for him, maybe for some other guy. Maybe from somebody neither one of them ever heard of before, but they heard about you and what they heard was you do not take the full skin, the first time out. You do not even take the full skin the second time out.

"You know how them sheep ranchers do it? They do not sell the mutton. What they do is cut all the hair off of the beast, and they sell that. Along with, probably, they wash all the oil out of the hair and there they got some lanolin, so they are selling lamb's wool to the people that make sweaters, and the lanolin to people that make Wildroot Cream Oil, Charlie. And in the meantime they got the poor naked beast walking around with goose bumps, shivering in the cold spring breezes, workin' like the devil, grow another fur coat before the summer's over. And next year they will sell that. Which beats the dickens out of those guys that're sellin' mutton, because who eats mutton anyways, unless they don't know anything, or somebody tells them that it's lamb, or they're Scotch and they'll eat anything that won't eat them, huh? You follow me.

"So, you see what I mean. I get a call from you, and you come down here, you think maybe I got a piece of property you might be interested in, nice water view, two and a half baths, fireplace, maybe even a stuffed moose over the fireplace, all right? I'm not gonna screw you." Bad Eye uses *screw* in its connotation of *cheat*.

"Know why? You want a place down here, you're not gonna live in it, inna winter. You're gonna use it inna summer. You're gonna use it, probably, one month, inna summer. You're gonna wanna deduct, much as you can of it, tax purposes, which means you're gonna wanta rent it for about two months, give or take two weeks, because them's the rules the IRS's got, and I know them rules. I surely do. What you pay out, in repairs and mortgage interest and local taxes, all that, you know, what you can deduct from the old income taxes is only up to and including the amount—equaling, is actually what it is—that you collect in rents. So, you spend about, say, four and one-half grand a year, on the place, you would like it pretty well, I got you four and one-half grand a year in rental income. So you're building up equity all the time, and somebody else's paying you, and you're taking off what you spend, and I wanna tell you, it beats everything out of climbing poles for the telephone company, when it comes to making money.

"Now," Bad Eye says, "you don't know about renting places for the summer. Let alone finding all them nice young single teachers that come down the Cape to teach all winter and would like a nice place to shack up with each other for not very much money, but they don't smoke in bed or do any other dangerous thing that would probably reduce the place to ashes with them in it before morning, leaving you, am I right, with a cellar hole full of debb-riss and a couple of charred corpses and an autopsy and probably a lawsuit from the bee-reaved parents, who are gonna sue you for lettin' their darlin' daughter rent a house from you that had faulty wiring.

"What you need, inna winter, as well as inna summer, is somebody that knows the terrain hereabouts, and can keep an eye on things for you. Which, if he does a good job, means that them guys that took the place for the month of Jew-lie will not probably turn out to be a bunch of queers that rolled in from New York. You see what I mean.

"Now," Bad Eye says, "I know the terrain. These here is my woods. I am not a young man. I am getting along in years, and approaching my second ree-tirement. All I got in this here world is my pension, which is what they would call *generous* but I don't call it that, not after thirty years of service. So if I want to be comfortable in my twilight years, as they call them now when they are talking about when you get old and you start peeing funny and they have to take your prostate out, and pretty soon they're coming in and punching at your stomach and showing you to interns and they're all shaking their heads and talking about chemotherapy and radiation, you see what I mean, well, then I got to work as hard as I can now, while I am still able.

"And that means, repeat business is something that I strive for. Whereas, as *my* lawyer likes to say, whereas you, being a professional man, when the kids're all grown and you are retiring from your chosen profession, it may very well occur to you, that you can sell the big house up in Wellesley, there. And then, because of that same old IRS, you are probably gonna want to sell, also, that little summer house that I sold you down here about twenty years ago, when the kids were still running around half-naked, trapping horseshoe crabs inna shallow water and getting themselves stung by bees and generally making a big nuisance of themselves by falling off of rubber rafts right where the undertow's the worst. Am I right?

"And you and the missus will want something maybe onna water, with beach rights this time, but also convenient to the golf course, and not too near Route Two-eight, on the account of the exhaust fumes and the noise and stuff, so you can combine all of the capital gains that you got on the two of them houses that you just sold and get something that is really palatial, right on a salt creek. That you will still have enough money left to get it dredged and put in a dock so you can walk down your big front lawn and get on your big yacht, and never pay a cent in taxes on the whole lash-up. Am I right? You bet I'm right.

"So," Bad Eye says, "that is what I do. What I want to do is keep you coming back. A satisfied customer is what I want. Because every time that you come back, you get sheared just like a sheep, except it is hot weather, generally, and you appreciate me getting all that hot wool off of you, so you can be comfortable for the summer. This is not Montana. We don't screw you on the house, you will give us a fair price for renting that house. Instead of one hosing that I didn't give you, which you would recognize because you are an intelligent man, I get another commission on the summer rental, another commission on the winter rental, and it just goes on, year after year, just like my pension. Which is too small.

"Except it's more money when you got a large number of intelligent men that're paying you those commissions, and who, when they have gotta good thing going, have got the good common sense to know it. Because there are a whole lot of things that're better'n working for the government, and anybody who doesn't think that he is working for the government or not, is fairly stupid and is not likely to have much money to throw around anyway. Not for long, anyway.

"And then, when you decided to sell the summer house, the value of it going up just like a rocket all the time, you are going to give it to me to sell, and you are going to have me find the new big house for you. So I am going to get two commissions from those two houses, and start the whole rigarmarole over with the guy that buys your summer house.

"You see what I mean," Bad Eye says. "I was inna Navy a while, and I learned something there that I did not forget, which is called enlightened self-interest. The best protection that you got against me clipping you is that clipping you is *not* in my best interest, and therefore I will not. You worked too hard for your money, and I work too hard for mine, that I would try and go insult you by taking it away from you when you were not getting value for it. Not because you might think I was cheating you, because you are obviously too smart to think anything else, but because you would resent the fact that I thought you were stupid enough, that I could cheat you and probably get away with it because you would not know it. That would be the kind of thing that you would resent.

"Now," Bad Eye said, "I am a working man myself. I don't think that any job's too menial. You see what I mean? In the wintertime I take it pretty easy, because what this place that I specialize in is, this place is for vacations that most people take in the summer, and the more people that come down here and live here in the winter, which are the only ones that interest me, considering the price range of the properties that I deal in, they are not what you call active in the real-estate market in the winter, or any other time as well. The summertime is when I work, and then in the winter, when I am through dealing with all the people that create my business in the summer, I relax, and I don't work too hard. But I do all right. There is very few people, my age, that're still ambitious, and willing to work, and that give an honest day's service for an honest day's pay. Or night's, for that matter. Because that is what I do. There is very few people of any age that're willing to do that.

"Now," Bad Eye said, warming up to what I had sent him out to do, "when I was down the Charlestown Navy Yard, which I was a couple years, that was always what I did, and also when I was with the department all those years, and it didn't do me no harm, either. So, that is what I am doing now. I am doing the best I can for people, and what I am doing to them is charging them a fair rate for what I do, and I think that is fair. That is the best that I can do, and that is all that I have ever tried to do.

"Now, Mister Kennedy," Bad Eye said, "you are familiar with my principles."

"I am," I said.

"May I sit down," Bad Eye said.

"You may," I said.

"This thing, Mister Kennedy, I do not actually *like,*" Bad Eye said.

"You don't like it," I said.

"I *seriously* do not like it," he said.

"*You* don't like what I asked you to do," I said, "or you don't like what you found out, doing what I asked you to do?"

"Mister Kennedy," Bad Eye said, "what I try to do is give a man who is hiring me an honest day's work for an honest day's pay, as you know, and I understand that there will be some things that you will need to find out that you will not always be able to find out for yourself."

"Yes," I said.

"I do not necessarily have to know why it is that you need to know something and are willing to pay me money in order for me to find out what it is you need to know, but I am willing to do this."

"Yes," I said.

"But there are times," Bad Eye said, "when I have to know what the information is to be used for."

This was the first time I had heard that one. "Lemme have that again, Bad Eye," I said. Bad Eye does not object to being addressed by the name that everyone uses behind his back.

"What use you plan to make of the information,"

Bad Eye said. "There are times when I need to know that, and this is one of them."

"I plan to use the information for whatever purpose it may prove useful, Bad Eye," I said. "I pay you to get facts. I don't pay you to try the cases. You do the investigating, I'll do the lawyering."

"But," Bad Eye said, "if I don't take your pay, you won't get the facts."

"Wrong, Bad Eye," I said, "if you don't give me the facts, you won't get your pay, and I will go hire someone else to get the facts and take the pay."

"No one else could get these facts," Bad Eye said.

I try at all times to be patient. I do not always succeed. "Bad Eye," I said, "let us discuss realities. Your wants are simple. You lead a quiet life. But you don't truck your butt up here to waltz around the North Shore because you love me. And I've never heard you gripe about your goddamned fucking pension before. You are a little pressed for cash right now, and you and I both know that you'll get precious little spending money out of your real-estate business to keep you afloat, if I stop hiring you. Because I'm the only one who does, and that is something else I know. I put up with your idiosyncrasies, and the fact that hiring you means I have to sign over my secretary for a couple hours while you dictate what would take anybody else no more'n twenty minutes. I do this because you're cheap and you are thorough. And because I'm nice. Unless you *are* nice, I will not do it anymore. If I hire someone else, he will get at least enough facts to suit my purposes, and I will pay him the money that I otherwise would have paid you. Furthermore, I will never pay you one thin dime again, and that will be the end of Thursday night bingo for you and the wife. Do I make myself clear?"

"Mister Kennedy," Bad Eye said, "that is not what I am talking about. When I was with the Department . . ."

"Two things, Bad Eye," I said. "You are not *with* the Department anymore, and you *are* with me. Furthermore, when Captain Roy told you to go out and get something, you went out and got it, and you came back and you gave your report, neatly typed, to Captain Roy. You did not go in and brace Captain Roy about what use he intended to make of that information. And you are not going to start coming in here, now that you are working for me, and try to do that with me."

"When I was with the Department," Bad Eye said, "that was different. That was law enforcement, and I was responsible to the senior officers. What you are doing, Mister Kennedy, is not law enforcement. You are a professional man and you, I am sure, make a great deal of money from your law practice and enjoy a good reputation in your community, but you are not an officer of law enforcement."

"Bad Eye," I said, "I am not going to sit here and explain the Anglo-American system of criminal justice to you. For one thing, I haven't got the time, and for another thing I'm not sure I could do a very good job of it anyway. Now why don't you just march out and preempt my secretary and have her write down what you found out about Torbert Hudson and Richard Teller, because I need to know those things and I needed to know them yesterday."

"Mister Kennedy," Bad Eye said, "if you decide to make improper use of this information that I have, which is confidential information and it was made available to me on a courtesy basis because I am a former law enforcement officer and enjoy the respect of law enforcement officers, and that is how I learn things that are not available to other investigators, then that will jeopardize my ability to get such information in the future, in future cases, when it would be used properly."

"Bad Eye," I said, "I am not going to use your information to damage your reputation. I am going to use your information to defend a client. The chances are that Torbert Hudson will never even know I had it, or that you went and got it. As a matter of fact, except for the people who gave it to you, no one will know you got it, and damned few more will know you gave it to me."

It took me the better part of half an hour to talk Bad Eye Mulvey into regurgitating what he had learned. To be fair to the guy, I could see why it would make a former cop squirm.

21

BAD EYE'S REPORT also made Richard Teller squirm.
When Gretchen got through a whole phalanx of secretaries who protected him in his office, she ran into a
stubborn fellow who sounded like one of those thirty-
year-olds who was making $42,000 a year, had a title
that a *Reichsminister* would envy, and a firm conviction that while his duties consisted entirely of fending
the bores off Richard Teller, he actually was serving
a purpose vital to the welfare and safety of the na-
tion, if not the free world. This concierge kept order
in an unruly universe by demanding that he be satisfied with the urgency of my call to Mr. Teller.

"Mister Healy," I said, "my secretary has told
your secretary's secretary's secretary that what I have
to say to Mister Teller is personal. I have told you
that it is personal. It has to do with his son, Emerson.
I represent his son, at his request and the request of
the company's attorney, Roger Kidd. I am not going
to tell you anything more than that."

"Mister Kennedy," Healy said, "all I have to go on
is what you say is true. Could you have Mister Kidd
call me and verify these representations?"

"I could not," I said. "Mister Kidd is on vacation,
as I was until Mister Kidd interrupted my vacation at
Mister Teller's request. All I know of Roger's where-
abouts is that he's got a house that he rented in
Chatham. I have no telephone number, for that
house, and if I did, I wouldn't use it to interrupt his
goddamned vacation the way Mister Teller got him
to interrupt mine on something as silly as this. Mister

Teller isn't paralyzed. I know. I've seen him. If he dislikes what I have to say to him, he can replace the phone carefully in the cradle and see if I have the energy to go through this foolishness again, and if you can accept my word without Roger's verification on that point, I will promise you that I do not have the energy or even the interest."

Richard Teller was deceitfully apologetic when I finally got past Healy. Teller slathered me with warmth and charm, explaining that his electronics firm received large numbers of calls from cranks who believed themselves inventors, and refused to talk with anyone but the head man. I figured he was probably jerking off or banging a file clerk, and didn't want to be disturbed, so I let that pass.

"I understand, Mister Teller," I said.

"I hope you do, Mister Kennedy," Teller said. "You see, I never expected to hear from you, after you so carefully instructed me that day in Roger's office that you were representing Emerson, not me. Otherwise I would have given instructions that your calls were to be put through."

"Careless of me," I said. "At the time I didn't think you'd be hearing from me, either. Tell me what you know about Torbert Hudson."

Teller thought that one over. "I don't believe I know anything about Torbert Hudson," he said. "As a matter of fact, I don't believe I've ever heard the name before."

"Mister Teller," I said, "some years ago you lived in Marblehead. Before you moved to Dover. Do you remember that?"

"Certainly," he said. "Actually, I moved to an apartment in Boston from Marblehead, and then to Dover. I lived in Marblehead when I was married to Emerson's mother. My second marriage."

"And when you lived in Marblehead," I said, "you became acquainted with several police officers in towns along the route that you took when you went home at night from your office, or wherever else you'd been after you left the office."

"Mister Kennedy," he said, "I don't really see what this has to do with Emerson's case."

"Patience, Mister Teller, patience," I said. "Life is a seamless web, and so is the law. Do you begin to recall Torbert Hudson now?"

"The name does have a familiar ring to it," Teller said, "but to tell you the truth, I can't place it."

"Oh, I believe you, Mister Teller," I said. "After all, Torbert Hudson was just one of many, wasn't he? Torbert Hudson was one of the local cops that you got to know quite well in the course of going home at night. Because there were quite a lot of nights when Officer Hudson was kind enough to have you move over in the passenger seat in order to allow him to drive you home in your car before you ran into something serious, such as another human being. Isn't that right?"

"Probably," Teller said. "I was drinking heavily then. My marriage . . ."

"Mister Teller," I said, "I'm not concerned with your marital woes. I'm concerned with Officer Hudson. Officer Hudson saved you a hell of a lot of trouble, and you and your friends were grateful to him."

"There were many nights," Teller said, "when any police officer would have been well within his rights to have arrested me and taken me into court. I suppose this Officer Hudson may have been one of the ones who stopped me. As you might imagine, my recollection of those trips is a little dim."

"Let me try to brighten it up for you, Mister Teller," I said. "Let's just try to focus on one night when Officer Hudson did you a small favor, shall we? That was the night you were driving a white Mercedes two-sixty-SL at a high rate of speed through a residential section at around one-thirty in the morning, when you somehow collided with a car parked in a wooded area about twenty yards off the road and absolutely creamed it."

"Yes," he said.

"In addition to some considerable property damage," I said, "there was more than a little to flesh, blood and bones, because the two high school kids making out in that car weren't prepared to meet you under quite those circumstances, and the force of the impact was so great that the boy's back was broken and the girl got a fractured skull and was in a coma for three and a half weeks before she came out of it. Remember that?"

"That case was settled," Teller said. "My insurance . . ."

"Mister Teller," I said, "I am a lawyer. I settle cases all the time." That was not true, of course, although I wish it were—that stuff pays beautifully. "I heartily approve of settling cases. It saves everybody time and pays everybody well. I'm sure those kids were generously rewarded for interposing their young bodies between your car and that big tree in front of their car. But once again, Mister Teller, that's not what we're talking about. What we are talking about is not a civil case, which is supposed to be settled, but a criminal case, which is ordinarily not supposed to be settled out of court. Plea-bargained, maybe, but not settled."

"Yes," he said.

"Is your recollection of Officer Hudson any sharper now?" I said.

"Mister Kennedy," he said, "this is ridiculous. That incident happened ten or fifteen years ago. Twenty years ago. I don't know. I was at fault. I paid handsomely for the harm I did. I was hospitalized myself after that accident."

"You were held overnight for observation," I said. "You were drunk and hit loose, and you were luckier'n Lucifer, but you weren't hurt. The only reason they held you was because nobody who saw what was left of your car could believe that anybody could clobber anything that hard and not get hurt doing it.

You've got a charmed life, Mister Teller, and if you didn't, you'd be very dead."

"Yes," he said.

"Now," I said, "the man who investigated that accident was Torbert Hudson, your old buddy."

"Oh, yes," Teller said. "I saw him when I was released from the hospital and made out the accident report. A big fellow. Young. Young then, anyway. Blond hair as I recall."

"That's the spirit, Mister Teller," I said. "Big fellow, blond hair. I knew it'd come back to you.

"Now," I said, "the procedure then, and now, was for the investigating officer to make out his report as soon as he got back to the station, and show it only to the chief or somebody like that."

"I wouldn't know about that," Teller said.

"Of course not," I said. "And he was to do it at the end of his shift."

"Or that, either," Teller said.

"But you didn't fill out your version of the accident until two days after it," I said. "During which time I presume you talked to your lawyer."

"I believe I did," Teller said. "I must have. I'm sure I did."

"Your lawyer was Barry Lee," I said.

"Barry represented me for years," Teller said, "until . . ."

". . . until Barry went to prison for certain errors of judgment having to do with giving presents of money to people who used to be in partnership with him but had been elected to the job of District Attorney and appointed to the job of Assistant District Attorney," I said. "In which capacities they decided whether to prosecute Barry Lee clients who had been in automobile accidents."

"It was very unfortunate," Teller said. "I always liked Barry."

"A fine fellow," I said, "who also happened to be the lawyer for your insurance company, which probably would've gotten whacked about a million for your little drive into the woods, if it'd turned out that you'd been convicted of driving under the influence, drunk, and driving so as to endanger."

"Never a million," Teller said. "No, I must disagree with you there, sir."

"Disagree to your heart's content," I said. "The fact is that Barry Lee had you for a client, and the company for a client, and the District Attorney for a former law partner who was later convicted with Barry and shipped off to be rehabilitated along with several of his Assistants who'd played fast and loose with the laws about bribery, extortion and larceny. And Barry Lee got you off with a speeding charge that was never even tried, but filed without a finding, and probably saved his company about three-quarters of a million bucks as a result."

"Yes," Teller said, "I suppose that's possible."

"Now the interesting thing here is," I said, "the interesting thing here is Hudson's report, especially when you compare it with your report. You say, 'I was going about forty miles an hour when I hit a patch of wet leaves and the car skidded. I did not see the car in the woods, and therefore attempted to recover from the skid without injuring anyone by steering into the woods.' "

"It was a very long time ago, Mister Kennedy," he said.

"Bear with me," I said. "Officer Hudson's report, supposedly written forty-eight hours before yours, and never shown to you, says this, 'Operator of Vehicle One was proceeding at about forty miles an hour, hit a patch of wet leaves, skidded into woods to avoid other damage or injury to others. Did not see Vehicle Two.' "

"Yes," Teller said. "Well, I suppose he may have talked to me that night, and I told him what happened. I was in shock. I really don't remember."

"Of course," I said. "So, having nothing much else to recommend, he cited you speeding, and that was the end of it."

"Yes," he said.

"The end of the accident," I said, "but not the end of Hudson. Barry Lee and his buddies pulled one too many of those little fleaflickers on an unsuspecting populace, and the populace started to get suspicious. Pretty soon there were State troopers sniffing around those towns, going over records and stuff, and after a while the Attorney General got a little grouchy himself. Which was when Barry and his henchmen turned in their briefcases and trotted off to various Houses of Correction."

"Yes," Teller said.

"But that," I said, "was long after Officer Hudson had risen considerably in the world."

"I don't know what happened to Officer Hudson," he said.

"I do," I said. "Officer Hudson was young but he was clever. He knew he was in an end game, and he got out of it before the end came. Long before Barry Lee's former partner, the DA, had his clock cleaned for him by the grand jury, back when he was still a high-ranking member of the community and people were saying how he'd be governor some day, Hudson got his powerhouse recommendation for appointment to the State Police, and that is where he is today. Hudson got his skirts clear long before the puddles got muddy. In other words, he took the money and ran. By the time people got curious, he was long gone without a spot on him. It was his successors in the police departments who got unfrocked and then fettered. Same game, different players."

"I didn't know that," Teller said.

"You knew it but you preferred not to think about it," I said. "The people who let him into the State Police didn't know about it, and they still don't, to this day. They have no idea what they've got running around out there in a uniform and a cruiser. Oh, they know he's not the cream of the crop, or he wouldn't still be just a trooper after all these years. But they literally do not know why it is that Torbert Hudson is so happy out there on the road today, and for that matter, they probably don't care."

"I still don't see . . ." Teller said.

"Mister Teller," I said, "you will. You will see it very clearly, in just a minute or two. You won't see all of it, but you will see some of it. You are going to come with me to see some people that I know. One of them is a District Attorney. The other one is a member of the State Police, and a guy with some clout in that fine organization. You are going to search your memory until you hear from me, and then you are going to come into that office with me and corroborate every single goddamned thing that I have just recollected for you."

"Oh, my God," Teller said, "I can't do that. That was years ago. I . . ."

"The Staties and the DA's don't like this kind of fellow any better'n I do," I said. "They don't know what he's doing to some other clients of mine. And they won't until somebody besides me gives them a little history on that lad."

"So I was right," Teller said. "This call had nothing to do with Emerson's case."

"No," I said, "you were wrong."

22

PAUL FINNEY ARRIVED at Mary Hartigan's in Dedham in full pack, but it's a respectable joint and besides they are used to seeing Dedham cops in there. "We've got to stop meeting like this," he said.

"Jeez, Paul," I said, "I know. It's I'm in kind of a tough spot, ya know?"

"And you didn't know who else to call," Finney said. "I hate to tell you this, pal, all right? Chose the wrong guy. I'm tapped out till payday and there's gonna be guys waitin' at the door before when I get the check. What can I do for you, Jerry?"

We had a beer. I told him what I had learned about Torbert Hudson. "This kind of thing," I said, "I could call up Marty Trainor"—the captain of the State Police in charge of internal affairs—"but I don't know Marty that well. Met him a few times, various places, never really got to know him. He's gonna look at me like I was eating loco weed. Now, I got the backup witness, which is a guy that'd really swing some weight, but old Richard Teller isn't all that keen on testifying, you know? And I would like to avoid it if I could. This Hudson guy, though, he is not much good, is what I think, and at the same time, I take him into court and prove it, I'm gonna make a lot of people mad, I didn't get the word to them first so that they could do something about the son of a bitch instead of having me embarrass every trooper on duty by makin' a fool out of one of them. You know how cops are, Paul."

"Yeah," he said.

"They'll get about one day of shit from every drunk

they stop and they ask him for his license and his registration and he asks them if they're gonna eat it. Because this one'll make the papers, Paul, and there isn't one damned thing that I can do about it."

"Yeah," he said.

"At which point," I said, "every time Teddy Franklin backs his car outta the yard, he's gonna have a posse after him, which will complicate my life."

"Yeah," he said.

"And all of this bullshit is gonna go flying through the air, my friend, because this bunghole hard-ass Hudson decided to grab a guy he doesn't like on a phony charge that don't amount to a ten-dollar fine and costs, and he won't back down," I said.

"Yeah," Paul said. "You got a point here, Counselor. Matter of fact, you got several of them."

"So I was wondering," I said, "if there was maybe somebody you would like to make those points to, being as how you can make those points a hell of a lot better'n I can."

"I dunno," he said.

"Whaddaya mean, you don't know?" I said. "Come on, Paul, this is Jerry talking. I ever give you a bum piece of information before?"

"No," he said, "no, you never did. Everything you gave me was always good. But you always wanted something for it when you gave it to me and my guess is you haven't changed. So until I know what you want for it, I dunno if I can take it. You do want something, don't you?"

"Yeah," I said.

"So," he said, "tell me what that is, and I will tell you if I think I can deliver it. They'll have to put the guy through thirty-seven different kinds of hearings and all that to get rid of him, so just what you're telling me's trouble for them, and what you want for it's liable to be more trouble for them, and if I go in there without any lead in my pencil, I'm gonna make more enemies in fifteen minutes, I made all my life."

"Paul," I said, "how do you feel about queers?"

"I got no feeling at all for them," he said. "I don't want the bastards stickin' it in my ear, but I don't care if they stick it in each other's ears."

"Think most cops feel the same way?" I said.

"Most? Yeah. All? No," he said.

"How about the Staties?" I said.

"Those guys'd come under the *most*," Paul said. "Not all of them, either. But most of them."

"All right," I said. "I got a guy that'll get 'em through the hearings on Hudson and leave the guy dead in the water. Solid citizen, respected member of the community, knows Hudson got taken care of because he took care of him. Helped to take care of him, anyway.

"The Staties," I said, "not only got that guy in their uniform, Hudson, because they don't know what he is, but they also got a guy of mine, more or less out of uniform, that they can identify precisely as being a homosexual."

"Ahh," Finney said, "and you would like to trade your fairy for their bad apple."

"Yes," I said.

"This," Finney said, "this will take some doing."

23

I DON'T KNOW what Paul Finney did, exactly, but it was effective. By the time Teddy Franklin's case came up for trial, Torbert Hudson was no longer associated with the State Police. I did not have a great deal of trouble cross-examining him. Richard Teller had been spared the ordeal of public testimony: the SP investigators were more than satisfied with what his interview and affidavit told them. And within a couple of days after that, an impersonal female voice informed me by telephone that the Middlesex County District Attorney's office had decided not to proceed with the prosecution of Emerson Teller. I asked Gretchen to call the client and deliver the happy tidings. I went to lunch with Cooper, who was in a grouchy mood and did not relish his knockwurst. He explained.

"I have a client," he said.

"Congratulations," I said.

"Condolences would be more like it," Cooper said. "I should be standing in a funeral home some place in my best blue suit and you should sign your name in the book and come into the room where I am standing and shake hands with me and tell me you are sorry for my trouble, is what you should do. I have got a client who is going to go to trial before Judge Fathead tomorrow."

"Jesus," I said. Cooper did not have to identify Judge Fathead to me, and I will not identify him to you. The guy took a vast cerebral accident about six months ago and went to a higher court. Or a lower one, if the prayers of lawyers who tried before him had been heard. His family put up with him while he was on the earth, and there is no reason to remind them of their torments by printing his name here now. Everyone who appeared before the guy hated him. While it is not unusual for prosecutors to dislike a particular judge, because they consider him too lenient on those convicted, and not unusual for the defense bar to dislike a judge because he gives out too much time, it is very uncommon when both sides of the criminal trial bar are unanimous in their hatred of one man. He was stupid, arbitrary, rude, insulting, unlettered in the rules of evidence, uncaring of the rules of procedure, disdainful of trifles such as decisions of the Supreme Court of the United States, and totally unpredictable.

Cooper delivered the customary statement of a lawyer in his circumstances: "I would rather rub shit in my hair than try before that son of a bitch."

I tried to cheer Cooper a little. "It isn't a long case, is it?"

"The trial," Cooper said, "the trial will not require more than two days of watching that crazy bastard posture and scream and jump around on the bench and laugh that laugh he's got that makes you think that any minute now he's gonna fish a cutlass out from under his black dress and run amok in the courtroom. I can stand that. I'll go home tonight and get all liquored up and then I'll go home tomorrow night and get all liquored up and then the trial'll end the next day and I'll have to appeal the goddamned thing. And I'll probably win the fuckin' appeal, too, so I have to retry the fuckin' thing, because you know how old Fathead is—the only day he didn't commit reversible error was the day he stayed home with the goddamned trots and didn't shit on anybody but himself for once."

"So what?" I said. "Guy gets convicted, whack him another fee, the appeal, whack him another fee, the new trial. You're a lawyer. You're supposed to defend the rights of the accused, and take all their money if they got any. You know that."

"I already got all his money," Cooper said, "and he had damned little of it, too, for what he's charged with. I got all his girlfriend's money and Termite Greene got all his father's money. He hasn't got any brothers and sisters, so that's the bundle. A lousy thirty-three hundred bucks, for going through hell."

"Thirty-three hundred bucks is not bad pay for a day and a half," I said, "even a day and a half in Fathead's session. Seven, eight hours of trial, pretty damned close to four hundred an hour, even counting the twenty minutes' preparation you usually think is enough. It's a hell of a lot more'n you'd have to spend if you were on the garbage truck like your aptitude tests said you should."

"Jerry," Cooper said, "I said it was a short trial. I didn't say it was a short case. This kid came into my office the first time over eight months ago."

"Then you got a speedy trial thing," I said. "How the hell'd the DA let that one slip by? Go in there tomorrow and move to dismiss. Kid's been hanging around more'n six months waiting trial. Throw it the hell out. Even Fathead's bright enough to know that one."

"Jerry," Cooper said, "I got the continuances. Me. Not the government. I've had that kid in there four times agreeing to continuances. He's waived every right to a speedy trial between here and New Zealand."

"Why?" I said.

"He doesn't wanna go to trial, of course," Cooper said. "Derry Macklin's got him absolutely stone cold and dead to rights. Three kids stuck up a liquor store in Hyde Park, all right? Guy's been held up before. Doesn't like it. Got a surveillance camera in there. Also got a nine-millimeter Walther, under the counter. Kids come in, ask for four bottles of vodka, he knows right off what they got on their mind. Puts the booze on the counter and his right hand under it.

Asks the kids for their money. Kid Number One takes
a twenty-two pistol out of his pocket, tells the proprie-
tor he'd got it backward—they want his money instead.

"Guy pulls out the Walther and lights one off at
Kid Number One and misses him. Kid Number Two
takes to his heels, obviously the only human being in
the place that night with any sense. Nobody's seen
him since. Kid Number Three, which is my kid, takes
out a knife, all right? Number Three is stupid. Here's
a guy with a Walther in front of him, defending his
property and it looks like he's got a pretty good idea
of how to go about it, too, even if he did miss with
the first one, and what does my genius think he's
gonna do? He's gonna jump the counter and stab the
guy, of course. That's good, hard common sense, you
got a knife and you go after a guy who's got a gun
that you already know's in good working condition,
don't you think?"

"I wouldn't do it," I said.

"Of course you wouldn't," Cooper said. "This is
why I am not representing you in front of Judge Fathead tomorrow and the next day. I am representing
this little scumbag, because he took on a guy with a
gun.

"Well," Cooper said, "the guy sees my kid with
the knife, and the other kid with the gun, so he makes
the right decision and he lets off another one at the
kid with the gun, and he wings him. Got him in the
belly, and you do that to somebody with a nine-
millimeter, the kind of distances you got when you're
both in a liquor store, he will not distract you very
much while you're thinking about what you should
do about this other kid, that's coming at you with
the knife. So, he did that, and my crazy kid keeps
coming, jumps the counter, slashes the guy behind it,
right across the face. Nothing serious—it wasn't a
very big knife—but I will admit his nose looks a
little funny where the scar is on the right nostril and
then across the bridge of it and down the left nostril

and his lip. The kind of thing a jury's gonna spend a
lot of time lookin' at, thinking about how this guy that
was just minding his own business and runnin' this
liquor store could've lost an eye and maybe had his
throat cut by my mean kid. And he talks funny, too,
the lip thing and all. I think they took him down the
tentmaker, get him fixed up. Worst job of sewing I
ever saw. If the Bruins used doctors like that, they'd
look like afghans.

"Now," Cooper said, "as you can maybe imagine, I
have got one or two problems with this case. Maybe
even three. I have got this guy that owned the store.
He may talk funny now, but he talks a lot, and very
little of what he has got to say is the kind of thing that
is gonna help my client with the jury, you understand
what I'm saying.

"Then," Cooper said, "I have got the surveillance
thing, the film that I got to think about also. That is
very good film. If you was to be watching 'Starsky and
Hutch' and they spliced this film in, you would not
even notice, except that it is in black and white. Usually those things look like they were shot through a pan
full of roast beef gravy, but this particular one is nice
and clear. It's fuckin' beautiful. You can see the knife
and you can see the blood gush out and everything.
And you can recognize everybody."

"None of this sounds good for your man," I said.

"It does not," he said. "It purely does not. And I
have not even gotten to the part where Kid Number
One takes the stand and tells the jury, which will be
paying close attention, of course, how they planned the
stickup because they hadda get money to buy more
guns so they could improve themselves in the world
and become bank robbers. See, while he was in the
hospital—this is Kid Number One, gettin' his belly
fixed up—he had this attack of conversation. It was
right after the cops let him know it'd be a shame, where
he was just a first offender and all, if he hadda do about
twelve years as a result of getting hooked up with my
guy."

"Who has a record," I said. "Of course."

"Not an outrageous record," Cooper said. "Not the kind of record that would qualify him for the death penalty if they put it back in. Just an ordinary, run-of-the-mill record, going back about eight years, which is not bad for a kid who's only twenty-three now. A few B and E's, couple assaults, little dangerous weapon stuff. Nothing serious. Nothing that'd make you worry if your daughter started going out with him, you know? Minor stuff."

"He might have some trouble with it, if he takes the stand, though," I said.

"This is possible," Cooper said. "Derry might just rip him up the front and down the back you think, maybe? I think so."

"Have you conferred with your client about the possibility of a guilty plea?" I said.

"Have I?" Cooper said. "I have indeed. I have conferred with my client about that repeatedly. I have conferred with my client about many subjects, and at enormous length. I have told him that my name is Cooper, not Houdini. I have explained to him that when I finish my final argument I will not have time enough to get back to counsel table and sit down before that jury finds him guilty. And do you know what he says? He says he didn't do it. Kid Two got away, so he's useless, and Kid One's testifying that my kid did do it, and besides, the victim has good eyesight still, which is no fault of my client's, and the pictures are good, and my guy sits there and tells me that he didn't do it and I got to get him off.

"Now," Cooper said, "just for my own imformation, I called up Macklin. And I said to Macklin, what would he do for me on a plea? And Macklin says, just to get rid of it, he will do the best he can to get the judge to give the kid five years indeterminate in Concord, which since he could theoretically get out any time, but he won't, means he would do, what? Three?"

"At least," I said. "With that record."

"Which is still," Cooper said, "as I pointed out to

this fine young gentleman that I represent, a far, far better thing to do than a flat twenty over in Walpole. And he says to me, 'They're not gonna send me to Concord. I'm a cripple. Not a judge inna world'd do that.' "

"How do cripples jump over counters with knives?" I said. "They must be making some great braces these days."

"He got out on bail," Cooper said. "I got him out on bail. I told him, 'Get a job, stay outta trouble.' He got a job as a helper with a roofing company and he fell off of a roof."

"Of course," I said.

"Naturally," Cooper said. "No ladder broke. Nothing. He just fell off. He was working on the roof of a four-story building up on Beacon Hill and instead of unrolling tarpaper like he was supposed to be doing, he decided to go over to the edge and see how far down it was. It was four stories, which is not a bad drop. He should've been killed, but he landed in the truck where they threw all the old tarpaper, so he just broke the shit out of his legs. Now he thinks because he's in therapy, rehabilitation, that lash-up, he's not gonna have to go to jail."

"An interesting theory," I said.

"Jerry," Cooper said, "I have had more trouble with this goddamned kid than I had with guys that're up for murder one. He's got a constitutional right to a trial by jury, and he's gonna get it, and then maybe, if Fathead doesn't fuck everything up too bad, I will be rid of him. He lies to me, he calls me up and cries to me, he tells me alibi stories that never check out. He'll miss five appointments in a row and then spend the week after the last one calling me up six times a day, complaining he can't get to see me. He is the worst kid God ever put on earth. I just pray, I just pray, that Fathead can keep his bearings long enough so I don't have to retry this thing. The sooner I see the back of that kid for the last time, the sooner I will be a happy man again. Like your fairy. How'd you do that? You mind telling me?"

"Yes," I said, "I would mind."

"Well," Cooper said, "how come I don't ever get nothin' I can win? How come you're so lucky? How come you never have no trials?"

"It has been a good day," I said. "I think what I'm gonna do is go back to the office, glance at the mail, and tell Gretchen I'm taking the rest of the day off. Just like I was on vacation or something."

When I got back to the office, Gretchen told me that Pete Riordan had called, and that it was urgent.

24

DONALD FRENCH SAT on the bad side of the steel mesh screen in the prisoners' conference room of the U.S. Marshal's office on the fifteenth floor of the federal courthouse in Boston. He looked as though he would have had trouble telling you whether he was in Boston or Bolivia. That untested face was still smooth, however he had managed to bring that off with a tour in Vietnam, but it was not going to be much longer. The wound in his arm had been dressed, but the ones he would have on his face were just being inflicted.

"Donald," I said, by way of greeting. I put my portfolio down on the steel shelf that bends when you rest your weight on it. I sat in the straight metal chair and rested my weight on the shelf.

"Mister Kennedy," he said, "thanks for coming. You gotta get me outta here so we can talk. I have to talk to you."

"You talk to me right here," I said. "We got a bail hearing coming up in about twenty minutes here, and if you're gonna be represented by competent counsel at that hearing, competent counsel has to know what the hell's going on here. And that means you talk to me. Right now."

"Mister Kennedy," Donald said, "I . . . we can't talk here. They maybe got microphones here. They'll listen to us. They'll know what I say to you. I have to talk to you. I paid you a lot of money. You're supposed to help me."

"Believe it or not, Donald," I said, "that is exactly

what I am trying to do. But my chances of bringing
it off're pretty slim unless you stop bellyaching and
start telling me just what the hell's going on here."

"They got me for shooting that cop," he said. "That
fucking guy that was talking to me, that said his name
was Gould? He tried to kill me. I'm telling you, he tried
to kill me. He was gonna kill me, Mister Kennedy.
He come up to my truck all alone and he was gonna
go in there and wait for me and he was gonna kill
me. I was, it was self-defense Mister Kennedy. I
hadda do it. If I hadn't've done it, he would've
fragged me. He was gonna wait in my truck and then
when I came home he was gonna kill me. I seen him
coming."

"Donald," I said, "that cop is dead. You have
killed a federal agent. Do you understand me? You
are charged with the murder of a federal agent who
was engaged in the performance of his official duties
at the time of the offense. Have you got any idea what
that is going to mean to you? Have you got any notion
of how the U.S. Attorney's office is about to treat this
case? You know what you got ahead of you?"

"The chair, I suppose," he said.

"No," I said, "something worse. You are destined
to spend the better part of the rest of your life in
the Atlanta Federal Penitentiary. Or the worst part of
the rest of your life. Donald, they are by way of getting around to puttin' you away forever. You're a cop
killer, and the cop you killed had a badge that said
he was a federal agent. That kind of cop's about the
worst kind of cop you could've possibly picked to kill.
That kind of cop's got more lawyers looking out for
the other cops you didn't kill'n God allowed Satan
when he was arraigned, and Satan got life in hell.
Now stop your goddamned beefing and let's start
thinking about what we have to do, all right?"

"You got to get me out of here," he said.

"First things first," I said. "What you're talking
about's the second thing, or maybe the third, and if
I were you, I'd put it about twentieth on the list. I'm

a good lawyer, Donald, but it's likely to take quite a bit of eloquence to get you sprung on bail, and probably a hell of a lot more money'n you can raise."

"I paid you seven thousand dollars," he said.

"Donald," I said, "the kind of fix you're in, seven thousand dollars won't be enough for a Coke and a hot dog. And even if it was, I couldn't pay it for you, because lawyers are prohibited from making bail for their clients, got it? I could be disbarred for doing that. I appreciate your loyalty and all, but I am not here to risk my ticket so that you can hit the street. Now, tell me what happened."

"Last night," Donald said, "I think . . . yeah, the night before last, I should start with that."

"Donald," I said, "is it important to what happened that got you in here?"

"*Yeah,*" he said. "I'm trying to tell you."

"Okay," I said, "tell me."

"The night before last," Donald said, "I was workin' onna boat all day. On *Catapult*? And I finished. It was stumbling when you got it up around four thousand RPM, and I finally figured out, there was some seawater in the capacitator. The port engine. So I took care of that, only it took me longer'n I expected because there were some parts I needed that I didn't have, and I hadda go downtown for them. I got back and I finished and then I went to have a beer down at Chris's place there. Chris Lynch. The Calumet Harbor."

"I know, I know," I said. "I've been there."

"Well, and see, that's what it was, when I started to get into, when things started going wrong, see? Because Jill was in there. She came in there while I was having my beer, and she was surprised, you know? See, she didn't expect to see me there. I usually go down the Poseidon Lounge or something when I get off, and that was where I was gonna meet her, later, when she got off work. So she was surprised to see me there."

"Yeah," I said. "Come on, get on with it."

"She was all upset," French said. "I could see that, that she was all upset, seeing me there. I couldn't understand it. She was meetin' a guy or something? So what? I knew that. I didn't like it, but I knew that when I started goin' out with her, I wasn't the only guy and she would meet guys. I knew that. So, I invite her to have a beer with me, and she doesn't want to. While she's waitin' for her date, all right?"

"It's all right with me," I said.

"Well," French said slowly, as though to indicate that the process had been burdensome, "I mean, I thought about that a little bit and I could see where maybe, she wouldn't want me where she was meetin' the guy. And if she was meetin' the guy there, said she was gonna meet him in the Calumet, she didn't, I didn't see no way, she have him meet her somewhere else, you know? Because she wouldn't know how to get in touch with him. So I left."

"Okay," I said. "Now, what time of day is this?"

"Probably about six, six-thirty," French said. "I went down the Poseidon, which is where I usually go after work, and there was this broad with tits. And I sat around and had a few beers and listened to her bullshit for a while, and then I decided I would go and get something to eat because I wasn't supposed to meet Jill until around nine and I don't like the stuff at the Poseidon. It costs too much, and I really don't like it.

"Now," French said, "this is probably a couple hours later. Probably eight-thirty, quarter of nine. And I decide, a buddy of mine told me about this place they just opened up over by the Rotary where they got drinks and they got sandwiches and it's reasonable, you know? And I hadn't been there, so I thought I would try it. And I went there. They got a jukebox."

"Good," I said. "We have seven minutes before the guards come and take you down to see the magistrate. Now whaddaya say we use those seven minutes and you leave out the jukeboxes, okay?"

"Okay," he said, frowning. "So, I was in there and I was havin' a bowl of chili and some salad and a couple beers, and Jill comes in. With the guy, all right? Same guy, I suppose, she was meeting over the Calumet, that she was waiting to meet when I left."

"That's a pretty long time for a date," I said.

"No," French said, "no, not for Jill. She will generally go, when she goes with a guy, she will almost always get something to eat, see? Which is why I was meetin' her later, at the Poseidon like I was supposed to, only I was having something to eat first before I was supposed to meet her and I went there."

"I see," I said.

"So," French said, "they didn't see me. And, I didn't know what to do. I mean, after what already happened up the Calumet, and everything, and the only back door they had had one of those signs on it that said it was a fire exit and this alarm would go off, you opened it.

"I already paid my check," he said. "So I sit there, and they sit down and they're talking, and I dunno the fuck to do, so I decide, I'll go the men's room.

"I went in there," French said, "and the guy comes in. And it's the same guy, the guy that came down the boat. Told me his name was Gould or something. Warren Gould. So I figure, he don't know me, and I say, 'Hiya, Mister Gould. Get your boat for skiing yet?' And he looks at me like he couldn't believe it. He says to me, 'What're you doing here?' I says, 'Takin' a leak.' See, I knew he knew me, and he obviously knew Jill, at least a little bit, but he don't know anything about me and Jill together, or at least I think he doesn't, so I figure it's all right if I speak to him. The hell'm I supposed to do? Pretend like I don't know him?"

"I suppose not," I said.

"So," French said, "he says something or other, I forget what it was, and takes a piss and he goes out. Now, I still think everything's all right, because I still don't know he knows Jill knows me. You follow me?"

"Yeah," I said.

"But of course," French said, "I still got the same problem which is that they are out there between me and the door and I dunno if Jill'll speak to me or get mad at me if she sees me go out right past them. But I decide something. I am not gonna spend the night in no men's room, no matter what she thinks about her dates seeing me when she's around. So I go out.

"They're gone," French said. "Their drinks're there, and the waitress was just bringing their food, but they're gone.

"Now," French said, "I couldn't figure that one out. I mean, if he don't know about me and Jill, just thinks I'm a guy he met and Jill's his early date, and Jill don't know I'm in there, which she didn't see me when I was sittin' down and she sure didn't see me when I was inna john, why'd they leave?

"I couldn't figure it out," French said. "I went back the Poseidon, hadda few more beers, broad with the tits was drunker'n a goat, she was all over me, and Jill don't show up. She don't show up and she don't show up, and I still can't figure out what happened in the restaurant or why Jill's not showing up. But I finally decide, I will go home. I have to go to bed, be up early inna morning. I got three boats to fix which I put *Catapult* ahead of on account of the guy, who-ever he is, he pays me a lot of money, put him first, and I got to get on them first thing inna morning or I'm gonna get all kindsa shit from the people that own them."

"Were you drunk?" I said.

"About half," he said. "Which is why I decide, I think I'll stop off the Calumet, have a nightcap with Chris. Only Chris isn't on duty. He's got the relief man on, and he's talkin' this guy I never saw.

"Now," French said, "Chris sees me and he sort of waves, but it wasn't nothin' like you would decide was an invitation, you know? So I sit up at the bar and I get myself some gin and tonic."

"After all that beer?" I said.

"I wanted one," French said. "I decided that was what I wanted. So I had it. And I'm sittin' there drinking it, there's this corner of the bar where you can see people but they can't see you?"

"I've been there," I said.

"I was in that," French said, "and pretty soon, in through the door comes the guy that was in the men's room at the restaurant, Jill's date. Except Jill isn't with him. He's alone. And he sits down by himself at this table and he doesn't notice me.

"Now," French said, "all I am thinking about, again, is gettin' out of that place. But then I really started thinkin' about it, because all these guys start coming in, one by one, sometimes two at a time. And, they all got open shirts and the jeans and stuff, but they might as well've been wearing uniforms for all the good it did, because those guys had *government* all over them.

"Now," French said, "now I really wanna get out. Because nobody knew that I was gonna be there, so those guys're, they didn't come in there lookin' for me because they didn't know I was gonna *be* in there. So I went around the bar into the dining room, which was closed by then, it closes at ten, I think, and I went out the dining room door and nobody saw me."

A Marshal opened the door behind French. "Sorry to interrupt," he said, "but the judge wants to see your client now."

"Any chance of ten minutes more?" I said.

"I don't think so," the Marshal said, "this is his last day before he takes off for vacation. You can come back up here and talk to him after the judge sees him."

The judge apparently liked what he saw. He ordered French held on $200,000 bail, with surety, lest he not see French again.

25

PETE RIORDAN WAS more helpful. "Jerry," he said,
"we had a routine operation down there, fairly big
but nothin' spectacular, and it turned into an abso-
lute goddamned Chinese fuckin' fire drill. You get
a chance to talk to your guy?"

"Yeah," I said. We were back in Pete's slovenly
office. We had our ties undone and our feet on his
desk, Merrill Carpenter, Pete and I, and we looked as
though we had missed the cocktail hour, as we had.
Also dinner, which we were. Missing, that is.

"Tell you anything?" Riordan said.

"Yeah," I said. "I dunno how much use it'll be to
me, and I've got to talk to him again, of course, but
he told me quite a lot. Should I believe him?"

"Probably," Riordan said. "He's probably got as
good a grip on this mess as anybody else. Which is
ranging from none to slippery right now. Jesus, I
have seen some fucked-up investigations in my time,
but this one takes the cake."

"What happened?" I said.

"Now," Carpenter said, "you understand, you're
only here because Cooper says you're all right. Are
you all right?"

"Yup," I said.

"Okay," Riordan said, "what happened was this.
At least as far as we know, what happened was this.
Harris gets a tip from Jill that thing's going down and
she's not quite sure what it is, but it is going down.
So Harris naturally goes apeshit, like he always does,

and he's runnin' around the place here scarin' up guys like he was gonna invade Bermuda or something."

"I asked him," Carpenter said, "I asked him what the hell it was, he needed this army for. And he was practically frothing at the mouth. I said, 'Warren, Warren, come on, will ya? I can't authorize this kind of thing. Shit, man, Roosevelt got in a whole mess of shit with Lend-Lease, and that was just a few old destroyers against the Nazis. You're talking about enough manpower here to lay siege to Hyannis. What the hell's goin' on? Castro marching up from Provincetown?' Guy didn't have any details."

"If I'm not butting in," I said, "or even if I am butting in—you give the guy what he wanted?"

"On that shit?" Carpenter said. "Are you kidding me?" The guy can't even tell me what he wants the troops for. Nothin' doin'. No. Of course not. I told him. I said, 'Warren, you're gonna have to do the best you can with what we got available.' Which was two men, plus some guys we sort of borrowed from SP."

"Plus me," Riordan said.

"Yeah," Carpenter said. "And I said to him, 'And Warren. I tell you what—I'll give you Riordan. He's not doin' anything anyway, and it's about time somebody took him out of that locker he's in down the basement and aired him out some.'"

"This did not please Warren," Carpenter said.

"We got down there," Riordan said. "Everybody's in the Anderson, Little pants, the golfing shirts and the fuckin' white shoes, and of course there isn't one of us, looks a bit like a fuckin' cop. 'Course not. We're just a bunch of guys down there, we're probably on the office picnic, we're gonna play a little golf and have a few drinks.

"Harris leads the guys in this place," Riordan said. "He does it real cute. One at a time. Gorgeous. We got more firepower in that restaurant'n Jesse James had on his biggest job, and enough in the parking lot to hold off Patton. 'These guys're dangerous,' Harris says.

"Right," Riordan said, "dangerous. We got—a bartender. What the hell's he gonna do to us? Throw clam-shells at our heads? We bust him. Harris's running around like he was trying to find a place, go to the bathroom. I said to him, would he calm down. He would not calm down. He's tearing around, he's telling everybody there's another one and he escaped.

"Now," Riordan said, "we have a little problem there. What we just did was arrest a guy on a John Doe warrant charging him with peddling coke. We haven't got any coke. What we've got is the affidavit that Harris got from the bimbo, what's her name?"

"Candelaria," Carpenter and I said together.

"Right," Riordan said. "The bimbo is not a federal agent, at least not on the payroll. She is an informer. I got nothing against informers. Nothing in the world. But what they are is informers. Not agents, my friend. Informers. Agents're one thing, informers're another. What we've got is an affidavit by an informant. This makes me worry. It would not make me worry if I had some coke we seized, because then we could point to where it says in the affidavit by the informer, which of course Harris signed his name to but all the stuff in it came from her, that these guys're moving coke, and then we would have a pretty good affidavit and a pretty good warrant and therefore an arrest that some fresh bastard like you couldn't throw right out of court the minute somebody let you get your goddamned hands on it.

"But we didn't," Riordan said. "What we got was an off-duty bartender who was having a drink. I have thought about that and thought about that, but I will be everlastingly goddamned if I can find a federal offense in an off-duty bartender having a drink. Shit, I don't think it's even against State law. It looked like a wash to me, and already the bartender's lawyers're drawing up lawsuits about unlawful arrest. I mean, when it came to shit, we were in it up to our ears, and that dumb bastard Harris is running around looking for another guy to arrest on a bad warrant.

"He didn't find anybody," Riordan said. "He wouldn't tell us who he was looking for, but of course I knew on account of that conversation you and I had, and I didn't say anything. Harris says he knows where the guy lives. No he doesn't. The guy is like a turtle. Carries his house around on his back, as long as there's gas around all he needs is a parking place and he's home for the night.

"Harris doesn't know this. Well, maybe he does know this, but he forgot it. So he's running around and all of sudden he's goin' out the door. 'I know where to find the son of a bitch,' he says.

"Now," Riordan said, "when he finds the son of a bitch, even assuming he does find the son of a bitch, what is he gonna do to him or with him? He has got a John Doe warrant. He's looking for some guy that's got a pocketful of coke. Hell, a fuckin' bushel basket full of coke, and he doesn't even know where the guy is.

"He has also got," Riordan said, "a full clip in the handle and one in the chamber."

"The boys couldn't stop him," Carpenter said.

"Moses and the twelve tribes couldn't stop him," Riordan said. "He was off into the night like a pack of wild horses, God only knows where the bimbo was, all by herself."

"French doesn't know where the bimbo was either," I said.

"Nobody does," Riordan said. "She'll turn up again though. They always do. She'll turn up in Utah, or Louisiana, or the Western District of New York, but she'll turn up. It's just that nobody'll know she turned up, because it'll be under a different name, and probably under a different agent.

"As near as we can make it out," Riordan said, "Harris went down to the marina and slept in his car all night with his goddamned chrome-plated forty-five loaded and cocked on the seat beside him. This is because the car, his car, was still there after the shots rang out, as the mystery writers say. And that son of a bitch always puts the gun down that way. Always did, at least.

"Apparently what happened," Riordan said, "is this: Harris wakes up in the dawn's early light and he looks around. He doesn't see anything. French's making himself scarcer'n diamonds."

"I didn't think he was that smart," I said.

"He's a veteran," Riordan said. "Combat veteran. Those guys know an ambush set-up when they see it.

"Harris is also a veteran," Riordan said. "He is a veteran asshole. Dim as he is, he figures out that French ain't gonna show, boats or no boats to fix. Harris gets cute, which is a good time to go down into the cellar and hide out in the coalbin.

"What he did," Riordan said, "was go into town and have breakfast. He must've walked because he left his car at the marina. Probably figuring French'd recognize it."

"This I doubt," I said. "He's not bright enough."

"I can believe that," Riordan said. "The problem here is that you got two stupid guys, one of them chasing the other and the two of them both got guns. We know Harris had breakfast at the stand on Main Street. We know he went from there and rented an Avis car at the office at the bus terminal."

"So far, so good," I said. French told me that he had driven to the marina around eight in the morning, saw the government car, and left immediately. There was no need to breach the attorney-client privilege by telling Riordan and Carpenter that. I was there to learn, not teach.

"We lose him after that for the whole day," Riordan said.

French had told me that he got lost himself that day. He drove down to Nauset and watched the surf for a while. Then he went into the back of the camper and slept. When he awoke, it was evening.

"Some time that night," Riordan said, "last night,

Harris went back to the woods where your client had been parking the camper and the camper was there."

French had bacon and eggs at a diner catering to surf fishermen who eat breakfast at odd hours and chase bluefish and stripers up and down the Cape, sleeping in their Jeeps. Then he drove back to the clearing and parked the truck. He did not sleep. He did not use his portable radio. He did not use his battery-powered lights. He sat there in the dark with his plastic-stocked bolt-action Savage 12-gauge shotgun in his lap, the chamber loaded with Remington Express chilled number-four pellets, the magazine with the plug out and four more shells in there.

"Look, Donald," I said to him, after he had been held in more bail than Benedict Arnold would've gotten, "why'd you go back at all?"

"Jill," he said.

"Jill," I said. "Jill, Donald, is a hooker."

"I know that," he said, as though it did not matter. It probably didn't.

"Did you know she was an informer?" I said.

He did not say anything.

"She was, Donald," I said. "She was, and she is. That's why she didn't come back to the clearing, and that is why she is gone. She is a government agent. A Mata Hari. She was setting you up." That was the first time I ever saw a man charged with murder react as though the news he had just received was worse than the charge against him.

"Harris got out of his rental," Riordan said. "He went up to the camper, but he didn't reach it. We know this because when he started walking, our other people were just coming through the woods to stake out that goddamned clearing. Harris had that goddamned gun in his hand. He went up to the camper. He tried the back door and it opened. He brought the cannon up and your client fired through the doorway. He's not a bad shot, Mister Kennedy, your client. Not at that range, with a couple ounces of heavy-duty lead."

"No," I said. "I won't argue with you there."

"Any questions?" Carpenter said.

"Yeah," I said. "The hell do we do now?"

"You," Riordan said, "you do nothing. Not until you hear from us."

"We," Carpenter said, "we have got to talk some with the U.S. Attorney."

"Okay," I said. "But one thing: Cooper says you guys're all right. Is that true?"

"That is true," Riordan said.

"You can depend on it," Carpenter said.

When I got back to Green Harbor that night, it was after eleven. I stunk. I was hungry. The butt of that thirty-eight was chafing my left kidney. I had had a damned good day go straight to hell. I was glad to see the lights on in the house, on the last night of my vacation. It meant that I would have some company. I was thoroughly annoyed when I saw Mr. Kelly's shadowy form beckoning me to the fence at the edge of his vegetable patch. I like Mr. Kelly. He is a good man and a fine neighbor. But I did not wish to chat with him about his goddamned lettuce after the day that I had had. I wanted a vodka martini, a steak, a beer, some tender loving care and no more shit.

There are times when I am grateful that my mother raised me to be polite, and respectful of my elders. When I got to the fence, Mr. Kelly played the hose across the lawn to his right and said, "My friend, there is something going on in there that I do not like the sound of. Now that you are home, I believe I will call the police."

26

By Sunday we had all more or less recovered. We got up in shifts, me first. I cooked sausages and eggs and sent the smell of coffee through the house. That roused Heather, who came into the kitchen planning to wake up almost any minute. She hugged me and we did not say anything—the kid had taken the Valium that the doctor prescribed early Saturday morning, and she was still a little woozy from it. I took her orange juice away from her and laced it with a good jolt of cognac. She said she hated it, but I made her drink it.

Mack wandered out of the bedroom about half an hour later. She was hungover. So, as a matter of fact, was I. She kissed me and made bloody marys without asking me. We all sat at the kitchen table and ate like wolves. You get hungry when you spend most of Saturday, or any other day, in bed, and do not wake up until Sunday.

"Anybody want to go to the beach?" Heather said. It was then that we began laughing. Again, of course, but also at last. It seemed like years since we had laughed, and it was only hours.

It was a gorgeous day on the Irish Riviera. The little kids played ball. The larger kids threw Frisbees into the water, for their Labrador retrievers to pursue and return. Several Sunfish sailboats tacked back and forth, and the beer in the cooler was medicinal and wholesome. Heather went off to play volleyball with the young studs, and I saved the batteries in the portable radio until the Red Sox game came on.

Mayor Curran came on first. "Senator," he said, "and I hear you had a bit of excitement at your house the night before last."

"We did, Your Honor," I said, "we did. It was not as though we invited it, but it did seem to seek us out, in a manner of speaking."

"And is everything all right?" he said. Mike Curran is a good man. I have always enjoyed him.

"It is," I said, "also probably through no fault of our own. But it is. We were able to cope with the emergency, thanks to the assistance of Mister Kelly."

"A fine man, Martin," Mike said. "I've said so many times myself. A man who knows how to take care of his own, he does, and he does it well."

"His own," I said, "and others as well."

"Well, Senator," Mike said, "after all, you've been here a long time. We consider you one of our own."

"As I am," I said. "I should expect no less."

"Could you tell me," he said, "understandin' that I am an old man, with very little on my mind, and therefore inclined to poke around in other people's business, but could you tell me, perhaps, what exactly it was that happened?"

Ah, Mike, if I only knew, I thought. It seemed very simple. Mr. Kelly told me there was something going on. It was then that I recalled wondering idly who had left the purple dune buggy parked three doors down, and where I had seen it before. I went into the house through the screen door on the porch, my suit coat over my right arm, the gun under it. The kid was behind the kitchen door. When I opened it, and went in, he slammed it behind me and told me to keep going until I reached the stove. I did not move. I saw Heather tied up on the floor, wearing her panties and nothing else. She was gagged. I saw Mack tied to the wooden chair at the kitchen table. I turned slightly and saw Joe's hand snaking around the left side of my head. There was a knife in that hand. I did not drop my suit coat on the floor; I brought that thirty-eight up under it and lighted it off with the muzzle next to his left ear. I shot a hole in the woodwork over the door. I didn't do his eardrum any good, either—that snubnose has got a muzzle blast on her like an atom bomb. He reeled away and I thought seriously of blowing his head off. I settled for using that gun like a club, and I beat the shit out of Margie's boyfriend with that club. Time passed very slowly, and when I had reduced his worthless little head to pulp, kicked him in the ribs and in the balls as hard as I could, and stomped on his ankle, I cocked that gun and tucked it right up under what remained of his left ear. That was when at last I heard Mack asking me please not to shoot him. The police took him away.

"Well," I said to Mike Curran, "we had ourselves an intruder, is what we had. But I was able to subdue him, and no harm was done."

"And I understand," Mike said, "that you did yourself proud in subduing him. Indeed what I hear is the fellow may lose the sight of one eye, and there is some problem with his hearing. Plus the broken leg, of course."

"This is possible," I said. "I haven't heard. You take care of your own, Mike."

"And I heard also," Mike said, "that he was holding hostage your women." Mack was faking sleep again.

"More or less," I said.

"And why would he be doin' a thing like that, do you suppose?" Mike said.

"Mike," I said, "my daughter loaned his girlfriend some money, so she could get away from him. And I guess he got angry about it, and decided to do what he did."

"But to do a bad thing like that," Mike said, "over a loan of money? Why would anyone do a thing like that?"

"Mike," I said, "I really don't know. After all, Your Honor, I'm just a trial lawyer."

"And," said Mike, "when was the last time you had to try a case, Senator?"

"A very long time indeed, Mike. I'm happy to say," I said. "I'm a very good trial lawyer, which means I try but damned few cases. But I have my trials, Your Honor, I have my trials."

"Well," Mike said paternally, "so does everyone. Isn't that so?" I nodded. "Now," he said, "there was Kitty Tobin there. Is Mack asleep?" I nodded again. "Well," he said. "I will tell you what I did." Mack stirred a little. "I went down there after Frank died and I saw Monsignor Cahill. And I said to him, I said . . ."

Mack reared up suddenly. Mike recoiled. Mack said, "Mike, what did you do to Kitty Tobin?"

I thought poor Mike was going to have another heart attack. "Why," he said, "why, I tried to get her knickers off, is what I did. The same as every other buck."

"And did you?" Mack said.

"No," Mike said, "I didn't. But I tried, Mack, I tried. She would have none of it."

"Well," Mack said, lying down again, "that's what we all do, Mike—we try." She closed her eyes and slept. Three weeks later, Donald French pleaded guilty to a reduced charge of assault on a federal officer, and was sentenced to five years in prison. He was very pleased, and so was I. That night Mack and I celebrated by taking Heather to the ski sale at the South Shore Plaza.

A NOTE ABOUT THE AUTHOR

George V. Higgins practices law in Boston, Massachusetts and writes a column for the Boston *Globe*. He is the author of several novels, including *The Friends of Eddie Coyle*, *The Digger's Game*, and *Cogan's Trade*, and a book about Watergate, *The Friends of Richard Nixon*.